Daughter
of
Sherwood

by

Laura Strickland

The Guardians of Sherwood Trilogy
Book One

Daughter of Sherwood

Cover Art by *Tina Lynn Stout*

The Wild Rose Press, Inc.
PO Box 708
Adams Basin, NY 14410-0708
Visit us at www.thewildrosepress.com

Publishing History
First English Tea Rose Edition, 2013
Print ISBN 978-1-61217-917-9
Digital ISBN 978-1-61217-918-6

The Guardians of Sherwood Trilogy, Book One
Published in the United States of America

In the gathering gloom, the man looked tall and slender, a shadow seen only indistinctly. But she knew him, had seen him numerous times in both dream and imagination.

A sob burst from her throat. "You are dead."

"But I live on, here in Sherwood. That to which we give our love in life is never lost."

Rennie continued to examine him through narrowed eyes. This must be how he had looked at the time of his death, strong and handsome, vital as the forest itself.

"Long have I tried to reach you, Daughter, to tell you the importance of your place here."

There, he had said it: daughter. A chill chased its way through Rennie's limbs.

"Wren, life is a series of cycles. The flesh rises and falls as do the stars in the sky; the spirit endures. The three of you—Sparrow, Martin, and yourself—must prepare to take your places on the wheel."

"The wheel?"

"Of life."

"It is not fair," Rennie cried, suddenly aware of how much she would have liked knowing this man.

"It is not fair," he agreed, "when a child is born into serfdom, an old woman bled to death for the king's taxes, or the father of a family deprived of his hand, so those he loves must starve. There is but one thing fair about our world."

"And what is that?"

"That love does not die, but rides the wheel and goes around until it meets again with those who love. You must do as you must do. Keep the magic strong."

Also by Laura Strickland

DEVIL BLACK

Disgraced in her father's eyes, Isobel Maitland travels to Scotland to purchase her sister's happiness at the cost of her own. But when she is abducted by a dangerous highwayman, she faces an unexpected choice: suffer the loveless union to which she has resigned herself, or marry this ruthless, Scottish outlaw who can ignite her desire with a single touch.

~available from The Wild Rose Press, Inc.

...

"A fascinating historical world, and engaging characters,…some brilliant lines of dialogue and a few laugh-out-loud moments, to ease the tension from the underlying violence. …genuine characters…all very vivid and real, each fully realized with distinct personalities. …A violent, harsh, racy, and utterly compelling and gripping tale. I defy anyone to put the book down before they finish reading it."

~Helen, Love Romances and More (4.5 Hearts)

"I'm a sucker for historical romances. The hero was exactly as he should be. …The long hair and the kilts, oh my! …This was a good read and I'd recommend it to my friends who enjoy historicals chalk [sic] full of adventure, intrigue and set in the Scottish Highlands. I'll be keeping an eye out to see more from this author as well!"

~Hydrangea, Long and Short Reviews (4 Stars)

Dedication

For my daughter, Alix, with many thanks
for all the hours spent together with Robin.

Chapter One

Nottingham Castle—April 1216

"The Sheriff of Nottingham is dying, and Geofrey of Oakham is dead."

The stark words penetrated Rennie's sleep the way hunger might, or a bad ache. Uttered in a deep, smoky voice, they wove through her senses and drew her irresistibly to wakefulness.

She opened her eyes and stared into the soft dimness of the flagged scullery. A virtual womb, this place was—a hard womb paved with stone and furnished with the great, granite sink to which Rennie spent her days spiritually shackled. A comfortless place, but the only home she had ever known.

She did not recognize the man's voice that whispered from beyond the scullery doorway, yet something about it pulled her. She sat up in her nest of blankets, tangled brown hair swinging behind her like a mane.

Who was Geofrey of Oakham? The Sheriff of Nottingham, she knew—God take his rotting hide! He was master of this place and, she supposed, of Nottingham proper, answerable only to King John, and also a cruel, soulless hulk, dispossessed of even one part mercy.

"Geofrey?" A second voice, and one Rennie knew

right well. Aye, and she should—had not old Lil raised Rennie from a pup and provided the only love she had ever known? Now Lil sounded shaken and grieved over the passing of this stranger. But who brought her the news, and why come in the dead of night while Nottingham's vast kitchen slept? "What befell him?"

"A sudden turn," answered the first voice that so affected Rennie's mind. "He arose this morning, spoke his prayers, and then fell as if touched by the hand of the god. I came to you as soon as I could."

"Ah." The weight of grief carried in Lil's voice increased. "I should have known! How could I fail to tell? My powers must have betrayed me."

Her visitor snorted. "As if that could ever happen!"

"It can, and it will. You know that as well as I. Is it not why you have come to me?"

The male voice became tentative. "I only brought you the news that affects you so deeply. But, Lil, do you see what this means?"

Lil ignored the question. "I would that I might have seen him one last time. A good man, Geofrey. A man I loved."

"I know. It is, after all, love that kept the circle strong. I am sorry for your grief. But we cannot let the warding of Sherwood waver or, worse, fail. I have come for the girl."

"Rennie?" Lil's tone sharpened. "It is far too soon!'

Rennie stiffened at the sound of her name, and kicked her blankets aside.

"Hush!" The man must have ears like a stag. "What was that?"

"Naught, Sparrow. Everyone sleeps."

Sparrow? Rennie frowned and her body tensed. She had never before heard the name.

The man's voice lowered to a whisper Rennie barely caught. "For these last three years you have told us it is too soon for the girl to come to us. Now there is no choice. With the circle sundered, the spell shattered, we are all in danger. We need her, Lil—you know that."

Rennie scrambled up. Her bare feet made no sound as she left her corner of the scullery for the maw of the great, shadowed kitchen, where Lil always slept.

Lil was undisputed queen of this place and had run it as long as Rennie could remember. She ruled her kingdom with firm kindness, but when Rennie's eyes found her now, she looked, for the first time, old.

And the man beside her—

The desire, the need to see him had prodded Rennie from her bed, but now there was very little to see. For he came swathed in a cloak and hood that covered his hair and obscured his face. But he had striking hands, broad in the palms, long-fingered and graceful, those of a young man.

His head lifted when Rennie appeared in the doorway; he came to his feet swiftly, as if drawn by strings. For a moment suspended in time they stood so, regarding one another. Then Lil swore softly.

"By the Green Man's horns, lass—you should be asleep."

"Who is this?" Rennie could feel his gaze all over her—the length of her hair, her hands, face and bosom—personal as a touch. His regard made her tingle disconcertingly. She turned to Lil in challenge. "Why is he here?"

Lil clacked her tongue. Rennie, who had been with Lil since birth, could discern the old woman's moods as well as her own and knew Lil to now be much overset. The news brought by the hooded man had disturbed her deeply.

"Sit, child. Do not wake anyone else."

Disobedient, as she so often was, Rennie remained standing. "Tell me first who he is."

Lil got to her feet. A small woman, she still moved like a girl despite her advanced years. Rennie had often wondered if Lil did not carry some fairy blood. Her tiny stature, her strength in spite of it, her ability to command others, persuade them to do her bidding, and the very magic that swirled around her, all argued it. She must have been beautiful in her youth. Now her hair had turned dove gray, and the green of her eyes had faded except when angered, as now.

"Sit, for pity's sake, and be quiet. Do you want him discovered?"

"I do not know. Do I?" But Rennie sat, folding her long legs under her and tossing her hair over her shoulder.

The man still had not taken his eyes from her, and his regard made her feel naked. Aye, and the only male who had ever made her feel more uncomfortable that way was Lambert, the captain of the Sheriff's guard.

"This is she?" the hooded man breathed. "Not what I expected."

"No? And what did you expect?" Rennie threw the words at him like knives. She did not like men. Despite the awareness washing over her in waves, she did not like him.

In an unexpected move, he pushed the hood back

onto his shoulders, and Rennie found herself blinking in surprise.

Ah, and he was not what she expected, either. For the face thus revealed did not, somehow, match the deep, smoky voice or the awareness streaming off him.

He looked ordinary. It might be the face of any peasant: a broad forehead, narrow chin, unexceptional nose. Rennie saw strength in the weight of bone—aye, he was not a small man—but that was all, save for straight brown hair, now messed by the hood, and brilliant, dark eyes set beneath strongly marked brows.

Then he smiled, and Rennie caught her breath.

The smile held a singular sweetness, somehow at odds with his rough appearance. Not ordinary, then—no, not he.

He said softly, "I suppose I imagined you would be cowed and broken, raised here in the den of the devil himself."

"And why should you imagine me at all?"

He gave Lil a sharp look. "She does not know—?"

Lil scowled. "Of course not. 'Tis no burden to lay upon a child."

His gaze brushed Rennie again. "This is no child."

Lil regarded Rennie also, her expression grave. "You are right. The years slipped away from me, and keeping her safe seemed more important than anything else."

"What—?" Rennie began again.

The visitor interrupted. "But we need her, Lil. We need her now. Martin went at once after Geofrey's death and consulted with Alric. With the triad broken, she must be ready to take her place."

"Who is Alric? What is this 'triad'?" Impatiently,

Rennie leaned toward the man. "What do I need to know?"

"Hush, child!" Lil told her again.

Rennie bristled. The restlessness she had felt so often lately translated easily to irritation. She had never taken the word "no" well—now she clashed eyes and wills with Lil, who sighed.

"Perhaps you are right, Sparrow. It becomes increasingly difficult to hide her light."

"Aye." The man's gaze touched Rennie yet again. "It fair shines from her."

"I needs must tell her all."

"Tell me!" Rennie demanded.

"But not here. And, lad, it is far too dangerous for you to linger. I will bring her later this morning."

"Where?"

"The hollow near Oakham. Best to have Martin there."

"As if I could keep him away!"

"And Alric also, if you can manage it."

"That may prove more difficult."

"It is all difficult."

Sparrow shifted his weight lightly. "You will tell her?"

"Aye, but such things cannot be spoken here where the walls have ears. Now, lad, go—we shall see you anon."

He moved off and disappeared into the shadows that cloaked the kitchen, gone as completely as if he had never been. Rennie blinked.

"Lil—"

"Quiet!" Lil jerked her head toward the scullery.

Rennie moved back into the dank room she

considered both sanctuary and prison. For as long as she could remember she had inhabited this place, and she loathed it—lightless, airless, the very atmosphere heavy as chains, an endless stream of hand-chafing, back-breaking labor from first light to last. She detested the damp and the smell of the salt-scrub and rotten food. She resented that her only refuge was a nest of blankets worthy of the rats that came to steal crumbs.

This place represented her life, and she loathed that also.

Yet she sat on the tangle of blankets in the corner, and Lil came to join her.

"I know you are full of questions," Lil began.

"Who is he? Who are Geofrey and Alric?"

"I shall tell you everything later." Unexpectedly, Lil reached out and stroked Rennie's hair. Lil was rarely demonstrative, yet Rennie felt love emanating from her now, along with a mix of other emotions.

Lil whispered, "I do not suppose I could have kept you here much longer. There is too much inside you, and what is within must eventually come out—'tis the way of life."

"I hate when you speak in riddles."

"You seem to hate everything, of late. I do not like this harshness about you."

"What is not to hate? My life here, as a virtual slave? The attentions of that vile monster, Lambert?" Lately the captain of the Sheriff's guard had come sniffing around, making it clear he wanted favors and, moreover, suggesting what Rennie did not offer willingly could be taken by force.

Lil shook her head. "I can no longer hide you. And with the death of Geofrey—"

7

"Who is Geofrey?" Rennie asked again. "What is the 'triad'? And that man—"

"Sparrow?" Lil smiled briefly. "He lives in Sherwood. He and his companions—outlaws all—keep alive the tradition of the Green Man, and of Robin Hood."

"That old legend?" Rennie tossed her head. "A story for children."

"Is it?"

"Aye. A tale meant to give hope to the hopeless."

Lil gazed at Rennie and said nothing.

"Not that there is hope anywhere," Rennie concluded bitterly.

"We live under the heels of the Normans, aye," Lil conceded. "But that does not mean hope is dead—it lies beneath the soil like yarrow in winter. And it lives in Sherwood with Sparrow and his crew."

Lil leaned closer and lowered her voice until it made a thin whisper. Even the silence of the sleeping kitchen seemed to bend in and listen.

"I assure you, child, Robin Hood was a real man, and flesh and blood. He must have been, mustn't he? Because you are his daughter."

Chapter Two

"Did you see her? What is she like?"

The questions assaulted Sparrow as he slipped through the trees, silent as a shadow, and entered the outlaws' camp. Night always meant life to Sparrow, in Sherwood. At home here since birth, he knew the animals who stirred only under cover of darkness—and the men.

Now one of those appeared before him as if by magic, and blocked his way. Sparrow sensed others beyond, but the bulk of emotion came from Martin, who hovered threateningly, demand in his every line.

"Peace," Sparrow said, though Martin never seemed to find much of that.

What a curse it was to be able to feel others' emotions the way Sparrow felt the warmth of the air or the breeze on his cheek! He did not want to be assailed by Martin's unstable brew, especially now when his own head still spun. He pushed at Martin in order to pass, but, stubborn as always, Martin stood firm.

"You can give me an answer," he growled. "That is simple enough."

"Aye." Sparrow's anger, a rare commodity, flared. "You always think everything simple, do you not?"

Martin scowled; even in the soft, dim light Sparrow could see his expression. Or maybe he did not need to see it.

9

"I still say I should have been the one to go to Nottingham. I would have brought her back with me. We need her here. How dare the old woman contrive to keep her from us?"

"Would you drag her away from her home, and she not knowing who—and what—she is?"

Martin nodded his shaggy, fair head. Whipcord strong and but a few inches shorter than Sparrow, Martin displayed the old Saxon blood, run true. With an often-murderous expression in his iron-blue eyes, he always looked like he should have a sharp axe in his hands.

"It is time, and past time," he grumbled.

Someone moved behind Martin, a far more soothing presence: Alric.

"Come, sit down," he told both men. "We have much to discuss."

"Words!" Martin tossed his head in rampant frustration. But he listened to Alric as to no one else.

A small fire burned, releasing the sweet smell of ashwood into the air. With a hand on each man's forearm, Alric led them there, nodding to Martin's mother, Madlyn, in passing.

Madlyn—the only resident woman in camp—had played nursemaid and mother to them all over the years. Other females came and went; members of the outlaw band brought their lovers and wives from time to time. But few stayed long. Life in Sherwood always proved too risky, too difficult, and too dark. Madlyn, like Martin, was made of sterner stuff.

She nodded at Sparrow now, looking serious. They all knew how much rode upon the lass at Nottingham—the protection of Sherwood, their very lives.

The trouble was, Sparrow thought as he sat within reach of Alric's hand, he and Martin had differing opinions about how to move forward now that everything needed to change. And Martin rarely backed down.

Aye, well, Sparrow determined, neither would he, this time.

"Someone needs to be in charge here." Martin spoke almost before his rump hit the ground.

"I think it should be me, do you not?" Alric might be ancient, but there was no weakness in him. Though the old hermit appeared humble, power simmered in his blood, and he could split rock—or a man's will—with one glance from his pale eyes. He wore his white hair long, half-braided, and it shone now in the graying light.

To Martin, he said, "What we must do here is too important to allow for argument. You must stand together as never before."

Martin, predictably, scowled. He drew his short knife from his belt and began to play with it.

Alric turned his compelling gaze on Sparrow. "How did you find the lass?"

Martin also raised his eyes to Sparrow's face, awaiting his answer.

Sparrow smiled slightly and shrugged. "She is a wild thing, trapped. I do not know how Lil has held her so long."

"The power stirs. It calls to her. No doubt she can feel the coming change." Alric spoke softly.

"She is no weakling, then?" Martin asked. "No shrinking miss?"

Sparrow shook his head. "She has been raised in a

scullery. I doubt she is troubled by fine manners."

"Lil will have coaxed some manners into her," Alric said. "And there is good blood behind her." He stared into the fire for a moment.

Martin leaned forward. "She is Robin, to all purposes. 'Tis well she has some iron in her."

"She carries a third of the magic. Sparrow, how did you find Lil?"

"Same as ever, save grieved at Geofrey's passing. Why do you ask?"

"Because, aye, Geofrey is dead, and I grow weary. My own time is not far off."

Both young men stared at him in dawning horror.

"Do not say that," Sparrow breathed.

"Why not, lad, if it is true? The Sheriff, my old enemy, dies also, by inches. It shall be a contest to see which of us passes first." His bright gaze defied his words. "Then shall two parts of the circle fail. Before that happens, you three must be prepared. Matters grow urgent."

Martin waved his knife at Sparrow. "I keep telling him that. But Sparrow would not stir himself if his toes were on fire." He leaned toward Alric. "Sherwood must be protected, and our fight must continue. The magic must be kept whole. You agree?"

The old man nodded.

"Then," Martin continued, "put me in charge. Give me leadership, if you would see anything done."

Alric gave Martin a long look. "No one is in command, lad. It is a balance. If you cannot see that, we have strayed farther afield than I thought."

"I do see," Martin retorted. "But there must be a leader, else folk will mill about like sheep. We are no sheep, but wolfsheads."

Sparrow spoke. "What makes you think she is not meant to lead us? Her father did."

"Her father was Robin-fecking-Hood! She is a scullery maid who has scarcely been away from Nottingham. Who carried the fight all these years in Robin's name, letting folk believe Robin was still alive? Our fathers, that is who—yours and mine—and ourselves, after them. Nay, Alric, if you would have us stand strong, leave it in my hands."

Alric shook his head and got to his feet with a grunt. "The two of you are not meant to compete but to work in harmony. I have failed to teach you that, as did Geofrey before me. If you cannot learn that lesson, we are doomed."

He stalked off, and Sparrow eyed Martin doubtfully. For as long as he could remember, all during their years spent growing in the forest, they had vied with one another for position: who was taller, who cleverer, who the better shot. Aye, raised together they might have been, but they thought very differently. Sparrow favored consideration; Martin was all fire and purpose.

Now Martin asked, in Alric's wake, "When does she come, the wolfshead's daughter?"

Sparrow shrugged. "That is up to Lil."

Martin leaned toward Sparrow and his eyes glowed cold as the blade of the knife in his hands. "She will have to choose one of us, you know—me, or you. That is how it works. Just so you know, pup, it will not be you."

Sparrow felt his own rage gather and simmer. "Only let her come, and we shall see about that!"

Chapter Three

"It cannot be true." Rennie spoke the words to herself as she stumbled out into the new light of morning. At this early hour the air felt sharp and chill, and the kitchen yard remained sparsely populated. Rennie, come to fetch water for the day's endless rounds of scrubbing and wiping, spared little thought for her purpose.

She and Lil had continued to speak in the gloom of the scullery until morning dragged itself over the kitchen windowsills. Well, Lil had spoken. Rennie had struggled with pure disbelief and voiced an occasional objection, a bleat like the lamb she most definitely was not.

"Robin Hood was my father? But you told me you found me whilst out gathering herbs and knew my parents not!"

"I lied," Lil admitted, with no apparent remorse. "I did it to protect you." A small smile crooked one corner of her mouth. "What better than to hide our greatest treasure beneath the Sheriff's nose and feed you from his table? He would have done much to get his hands on you, had he known you existed."

"He is dead, Robin Hood?" Rennie had always sneered, secretly, at the legend of the man, as she dismissed all childhood stories meant to provide false comfort. There existed very little comfort in this

14

world—just subjugation, weariness, and pain, and the Norman fist raised always above it all. It was like the tales of God, distant and requiring the Latin tongue, of no real value.

"He died nearly twenty years ago," Lil whispered, "not three weeks before you were born. But those left behind in Sherwood—his band and their supporters—wished to carry on the fight. So was created the legend that Robin had not died but lived yet, protected by magic. Over the years, much good has been accomplished in his name. Folk have even claimed to see him."

"Aye." Fools. Rennie's lip curled in disparagement. "Who is my mother, then? And how came I into your hands, if not gathered along with your herbs?"

For the first time, Lil hesitated. "You have heard the tales," she said, "of how Robin loved a baron's daughter called Marian, and she forsook her father's house to follow him."

"You would have me believe that true, as well? No one would leave the comforts of a Norman dwelling for the forest."

"You did not know Marian, a woman of considerable passion. But she was not Norman; equal parts Saxon and Celt fired her blood, just as that of Robin himself."

"She lives still? Where is she?"

Lil's expression turned grave. "She crumbled when Robin died, all her considerable spirit torn to shreds. To be sure, we feared for her sanity. She gave birth to you in Sherwood but decided she could not bear to stay and raise you."

"She abandoned me?" Pain squeezed Rennie's heart, a familiar ache that seemed to have accompanied her all her life.

"Child, she had no choice. Her love for your father was a desperate thing, fierce, unending. Well, we all loved him." Abruptly, Lil's voice wavered. "That was how Robin inspired his followers, through love and belief. He wove a kind of spell—it is that we refused to let die."

"But my mother, Marian—what happened to her?"

"She entered the convent near Lincoln, three days after your birth."

Rennie's anger acquired a thread of hope. "I might go there and see her, then?"

Lil shook her head. "She died three years ago. Child"—she grasped Rennie's arm—"I wanted to tell you then. By Herne's horns, I wanted to tell you a score of times. But I knew your ignorance protected you. And you are far too important."

"Important? Me?" Rennie scoffed. "Now I know you lie." And that hurt unbearably; Lil never lied to her. At least, never that she had known. Suddenly the beloved old woman seemed a stranger.

"Everything rests upon you—on you and Sparrow, and Martin."

"Two fellows named after birds? What—"

"Not two named after birds—three." Lil spoke with emphasis. "Three is a magical number. You were birthed three weeks after Robin's death, your mother nursed you three days that you might live, she died three years ago. Three of you." Lil's voice dropped so Rennie had to lean forward to hear. "Three birds."

"Three?"

"Martin, born first, so very much the son of his father, Will, with that fierceness bred into him: Martin Scarlet. Sparrow Little, with his father John's strength and gentleness. And you, child—Wren."

"Eh? But my name is Re—" She stopped abruptly, unable to go on.

"Wren, lass, not Rennie, though 'tis what I always called you. Three birds, all birthed in Sherwood. And now the time has come. You must go back."

What was time? Rennie wondered now, standing in the cold air of the yard with her bare toes biting into the damp cobbles. It ground to a halt in the scullery when she scrubbed endless piles of crockery, while her back ached and the salt stung her raw hands. Time meant nothing. It held no more significance than she.

Rennie hated the scullery; she hated the castle and time itself. Yet they made up her world, and her place was with Lil. Even though she longed to leave, such a prospect, like time itself, surpassed understanding.

A shadow stirred at the corner of her vision as she stood, witless, with the bucket in her hands. Only those as unfortunate as she tended to move about so early, so she failed to take heed in time. She missed her chance to duck back into the kitchen before he approached, moving like one of Lil's roosters, and with the same purpose.

Lambert. Rennie did not know his given name, though surely he must have one. He was just Sir Lambert, captain of the Sheriff's guard, newly come since Sir Guy, who had served the Sheriff long, had been killed last winter. A young man, this, and dangerous. Stories had soon circulated about how he liked to spread his seed among the castle's serving women. Four were rumored, even now, to carry his child.

Lately he had come into the kitchen yard more and more often at times like this, when it was quiet. He had approached Rennie more than once, with increasing persistence.

He displayed his Norman breeding clearly, but she found him ugly for all that, or maybe because of it. Tall and fair-haired, with a touch of ginger in his beard, he had the eyes of an adder, sly and cruel. Thin lips curled downward beneath a nose that must once have been broken, and his face bore marks of the pox.

The very sight of him now made Rennie recoil. She clutched her bucket and, even though it was only half full, turned back for the door of the kitchen.

"Stay where you are." The voice of command shivered round the yard and froze everyone there— Rennie and two lads hauling a sack of cabbages. Lambert moved quickly for a man his size. Before Rennie could blink, he was at her side. "I want to speak to you."

Even Rennie, unversed in the ways of men, knew he did not truly wish to speak. He stood far too close, and the cruel eyes were all over her. Much like the young visitor's eyes, last night, they touched her hair, her throat, her bosom. But Lambert avoided her eyes.

"You are the lass from the scullery. What is your name?"

"Rennie, sir." *Wren.*

"You will perform for me a service."

"Sir, I am needed in the kitchen."

"It will not take long. Besides, my needs supersede those of that witch who runs the place. You are a pretty enough thing, in your odd way."

Rennie, frozen like a rabbit before the fox, said nothing, but her anger turned her stomach.

"On your knees."

"I am needed—"

"Silence! I can put those lips of yours to better use." He reached for the front of his breeches and Rennie's stomach heaved still more violently. She had heard stories of this, when the maids whispered in the kitchen. But if this beast put any part of his vile body near her mouth, she would vomit.

"On your knees, wench!" He seized her hair, which hung loose down her back, and wrenched hard, causing Rennie to fall. The pain was astounding and her landing on the cobbles less than gentle.

He let go her hair and thrust his hand down her bodice until he encountered a breast and squeezed hard. Rennie's anger flared into something blinding.

Any good servant, as she knew—any who wanted to survive—would meekly comply with a Norman overlord's demands. Rennie, hidden so long in the scullery, had not encountered her masters often, and now discovered herself not suited to obedience.

Even as Lambert reached again for the front of his breeches, she surged to her feet with a cry of rage. She had one glimpse of the two lads' shocked faces before she swung the wooden bucket with both hands, scribing a wide circle that ended with a crash at the side of Lambert's head.

Whatever the burdens of scullery life—heavy pots and platters, endless tubs of water—they lent a woman strength. Rennie heard Lambert's skull crack before he fell, soundless, onto the cobbles.

"Gaw!" one of the lads cried. "Get out of here before he wakes up!"

Rennie ran back into the kitchen, instinctively seeking Lil, whom she found engaged in discussion with one of the many undercooks. Both women and half those around them turned to stare.

Lil's eyes widened. "What is it, child? You are pale as death."

Rennie whooped; the rage had stolen her breath. "I—"

The lads ran in from the yard. "She has just killed the Sheriff's captain. Lambert—is that his name?"

Lil straightened and her eyes flashed green. "Is this true?" she asked Rennie.

"He wanted me to—to—" Rennie pointed to the floor, and then to her own crotch. Not a woman there needed further explanation. "I hit him with the bucket. I doubt he is dead."

Lil gave her a look such as she had never seen and went out to the yard, accompanied by half the kitchen staff. Rennie stayed where she was, trembling yet defiant. Those left in the kitchen shrank from her as if she carried plague.

Lil returned in an instant, her eyes blazing green fire. "He is not dead, but when he awakens his temper will be far from sweet. Come, Rennie."

"Where?"

Lil seized her arm in a bruising grip. "This decides things, I fear. You can stay here no longer." She lowered her voice to a whisper. "You must away to Sherwood."

Chapter Four

"I do not wish to go to Sherwood." Rennie repeated the words for the third or fourth time. In truth, she had lost count. Her litany had begun in the kitchen, continued as she and Lil stepped from the castle proper and again when they entered the gloom that was the eternal forest.

Sherwood—long had it haunted Rennie's dreams and the imaginations of everyone who dwelt in Nottingham. Was there a tale told these many years that did not concern it somehow, peopled by wolfsheads—their head price the same as that of a slain wolf—Sheriff's men, and the ever-elusive Robin Hood?

Strange to say, for all that, Rennie had never before set foot here, had never gone much of anywhere, despite how her heart yearned for freedom. She had lived her life by the instinctive knowing that came to her, by her connection to a nameless "something" that lurked just beyond her ken, a clearer, purer feeling than the anger that always simmered.

Now she and Lil actually trod the magical soil of the wood, the great boles of trees soaring above their heads into a green roof of leaves. Morning grew stronger around them as they went, and the light sifted down, green and golden, secretive and sublime.

Lil, who led the way puffing and hurrying, sounded impatient when she said, "By the god's blood, girl, you have never stopped complaining about your life in the scullery. I should think you would be glad to escape it."

"Aye." Lil had a point. The scullery made a prison that rendered Rennie a slave, but this—

Ahead of her, Lil stopped abruptly and bent over, struggling to catch her breath. Alarm flared in Rennie's heart.

"Lil, are you all right?"

"I am not as young as I once was. Give me but a moment."

Rennie stepped up and placed her hand on Lil's back. The contact let her feel what Lil felt, that acuity Rennie intermittently possessed. Sometimes she could hear what others thought, as well, were the thoughts strong enough.

Now she felt the rush of Lil's emotions—urgency, distress, determination...and pain.

"What hurts you, Mother?"

Lil straightened slowly and looked into Rennie's face, her eyes as green as that mysterious radiance streaming through the trees.

"Naught, child."

Rennie knew Lil lied, and that made her frown. "Are you ill?"

"'Tis but the need to hurry. Come."

They had not gone much farther before someone stepped out to bar their way. Rennie started violently, but Lil behaved as if she had expected this.

At first Rennie thought it the young man who had come to the kitchen; he wore the same kind of hood, made of dun-colored deer hide, and he moved just as silently. But a different feel came off him, and Rennie could see this man was more lightly built, and not so tall.

"Mother Lil?" His voice revealed his youth. "What has happened?"

"The tide has turned on us, Simon. I must see Martin and Sparrow. And Alric, if possible."

"Alric is here already. Come."

They went on still more swiftly, and Rennie feared for the breath rasping in Lil's lungs. They were deep in the forest when a second man appeared.

This one had no secrecy about him, and his aura preceded him the way a wind precedes a storm. Indeed, his impact reared Rennie back on her heels and made her stare.

Broad in the shoulders and tall, he scorned the hood cast back from his face to reveal a straw-colored mane and a tracery of beard. Iron-blue eyes raked Rennie the way Lil sometimes raked the kitchen fire, and stirred her the way the embers always stirred in response to the raking. She sensed in this man great energy and an anger almost as intense as her own.

"You have brought her!" he crowed. "It is well."

"It is anything but well, Martin. We need to speak."

"But this is the answer to prayers."

Did he pray? He did not look a man willing to rely on anyone but himself.

"I have come to confer with you and Sparrow and Alric."

"Fine, then. Alric is here."

He stepped to Rennie's side as they moved off once more, the younger man in the lead. His presence assaulted Rennie's senses and contained a thread of what she always felt from Lambert. Lust? But why should this stranger desire her?

"So, you are Wren."

She glared at him. "I know not who I am." All too true, at the moment. "Leave me be."

To her astonishment, he grinned. It changed him as had the smile Sparrow gave her in the kitchen, but in a far different way. Rennie felt something flare, within.

"No meek miss, this," he murmured, but he did not move from her side.

Rennie's nose caught the faint scent of wood smoke before they reached the camp. A small fire breathed a trickle of gray into the leaf-green enclosure, and a quick eye might catch signs of habitation—a wooden cup here, a pack tossed there, an ashwood bow leaned against a tree. Rennie's group halted and people began to appear as if by magic. One of them, a very old man with white hair, came forward leaning on a staff and clasped Lil's hand.

"How are you, Lillith? It has been far too long."

She leaned forward and embraced him. For an instant, light seemed to shimmer around their joined forms. Overhead, the leaves whispered.

Martin stepped forward from Rennie's side. "Alric, it is Wren—she is come!"

Alric released Lil and enfolded Rennie with his gaze. She had never seen the like of his eyes, serene as a bottomless pool and warm as pease pudding. A sense of peace poured off him, underlain by a current of worry. "Wren, my child." He reached for her hands. "Long have I imagined seeing you again."

"You have seen me before?"

"Aye, soon after you were born—here, in Sherwood." He shot Lil a look. "You have told her?"

Lil nodded. "Events have moved beyond us, and made it necessary."

Alric nodded also and gazed again into Rennie's eyes, so deep she felt he might see her soul. Rennie flinched, for she knew her soul contained dire imperfections.

"Ah, well," he said. "Let us sit and decide what is to be done."

****

The man called Martin stuck to Rennie's side the way treacle pudding sticks to the bottom of a pot, and Rennie continued to feel the eagerness flowing off him—eagerness and confidence. Martin did not lack for confidence! So strong was his aura Rennie scarcely noticed Sparrow had also joined them until she caught sight of him sitting on the far side of the fire.

Other folk came and went, moving about like spirits. Curious faces swam just beyond the reach of Rennie's acuity—men mostly, and young rather than old, and one woman with a kind expression. Mostly Rennie was taken with those who made up their circle—Lil and Alric who sat side by side, the lad who had brought them in, Sparrow, Martin, and Rennie herself.

Rennie's senses, overwhelmed, struggled to keep up. The place itself sang to her; her heart beat fast, and the emotions coming off everyone pulled at her.

In a soft voice, Lil informed them what had happened at Nottingham Castle, which prompted still more emotions. Anger flared in Martin, along with fierce protectiveness. Alric felt mild distress. Sparrow had his emotions wrapped tight, but he watched Rennie steadily with those eyes so dark and wild.

"So," Lil concluded, "she will need take refuge here, else her life will not be worth the crook of Lambert's finger."

"Just as well," Martin voiced before Alric could speak. "She needs to be here with us anyway, given what's passed."

"'Tis terrible sudden," Lil objected. "I would have had her better prepared."

"Why not ask the woman herself what she thinks?" Sparrow suggested.

Everyone looked at Rennie. She shrugged uncomfortably and lifted her hands. "I scarcely know. All this—it is far too fanciful. Lil would have me believe my father—" She could not speak the words.

Alric's expression softened. "I assure you, lass, all Lil has told you is true. Your mother was great with child when your father died. She near went mad with the loss of him. We feared for her mind. 'Twas a difficult time for all. You see, when your father lay sore wounded, we realized we could not let the outside world learn of his death. His presence in Sherwood meant too much to those of our world, lit their hope and salved their hearts. So long as Robin lived, their will to fight their oppressors lived also."

Lil took up the tale. "After Robin's death, we put out word that he had recovered, and those close to him took up the fight—Sparrow's father, John Little, Martin's father, Will Scarlet, the bard Adale, the rogue friar Tuck—all those who came to Sherwood with missing limbs or stripes on their backs, who had fled Norman tyranny. The three of us—Alric, Geofrey of Oakham, and myself—wove a threefold spell to keep Sherwood protected and preserve your father's magic."

"Magic?" Rennie could not help but repeat the word.

"Oh, aye, he had magic," Alric said softly. "How could a mere serf's son accomplish all he did, without? Some say his forefathers carried the blood of the Green Man himself, that one of the maids of Loxley, from whence he hailed, had once lain with the horned god. Who knows if 'tis true?"

Rennie's head spun in slow, sickening circles. "So you pretended he had not died, but he had?"

"Aye," Lil assented, "and your mother's will to live was buried with him. When you were born, I had to beg her to nurse you. After three days, she refused. I had no choice but to take you myself. I found a wet nurse at the castle."

Lil smiled ruefully. "Rumors swept the district that Marian had borne a child and so Robin had a son. We let them fly as they might."

"Why a son?" Rennie asked.

Sparrow spoke. "It makes a better tale than a daughter."

"Eh?" Rennie questioned.

"Those who followed Robin did so with their hearts. What better than him having a son to walk in his footsteps?"

"It suited my purpose," Lil said, "when I 'found' a girl babe in an abandoned dwelling. I meant to keep you with me at Nottingham only until I could secure a better place for you. Then I thought what cleverer hiding place than right under the Sheriff's nose? He and Sir Guy did search for you, you know. No one suspected the sickly scrap of life in my kitchen was the treasure they sought."

"Scrap?"

"You were a pallid, squalling thing and near did not survive."

"But," Alric said softly, "you were too important to die."

"So we kept the legend alive, and you hidden, all these years, the three of us," Lil concluded.

A brief silence fell while the fire seethed heat and the trees swayed overhead, like breath.

"Now you will have to stay," Martin said then, "and take your place with us."

Rennie turned to stare into his gray-blue eyes. "And if I choose not to?"

It was Sparrow who answered. "I am afraid, Wren, you have no such choice."

Chapter Five

"She will choose me, you know." Martin dropped the words into Sparrow's ear in passing and accompanied them with a taunting grin. "Just see if she does not."

A familiar feeling of mingled frustration and irritated impatience flared in Sparrow's heart. Martin never could resist sinking a barb into his flesh. The gloom of the evening now gathered over the forest. Wren's first day in Sherwood was nearly done. And Sparrow felt no nearer to her than he had in Nottingham's kitchen.

He stole another look at her now, even though it seemed to be all he had done that day. As out of place as she should have looked, with her shabby apron and pallid skin, she did not. She carried a kind of wildness that suited the place. Her brown hair, far darker than his own, hung down her back in a tangle, and her eyes were everywhere; they carried an uncanny light.

He shrugged for Martin's benefit, feigning indifference. "We shall see."

"Aye, that we shall, for she needs must choose one of us. Just as Lil chose Geofrey."

"Perhaps not."

"Do not be a fool! Once she chooses me, I will lead just as Geofrey did. I am tired of talk and contemplation. We have become like an arrow with no head. I will change all that."

"Are you saying Geofrey did not lead us well, and him not yet in his grave?"

"I do not say that."

"Good, because I will not hear you speak a word against him. He kept us strong all these years, since the death of your father, and mine. He kept the legend of Robin alive."

"As we continue to keep it alive now. It was not Geofrey stopping lords and barons on the roadways, nor helping folk pay their taxes." Before Sparrow could speak, Martin held up a hand. "Peace! I pay Geofrey the respect he is due. I say only, the next headman of Oakham better have some fire about him."

"And you think that will be you?"

Martin raked Sparrow with a barbed glare. "You will surely make a better hermit, following in Alric's footsteps, than I."

"Damned if I will!" Sparrow muttered, even as Martin walked away. Martin was an arrogant braggart, just like his father before him. Sparrow well remembered Will Scarlet—sharp and dangerous as a honed sword, grizzled and soured by the time he died. Sparrow still recalled how Scarlet had railed over falling victim to a winter ague—no warrior's death, that. Martin and Sparrow had both been about fifteen, and Scarlet had taken Martin's face between his hands like that of a child and shouted, "Be fierce! Be all I was, and more. Give those Norman bastards hell!"

Sparrow's own father, John Little, had perished by then, dead of an infected sword wound. Men did not live long in Sherwood. Sparrow barely remembered his own mother, a lass from the hamlet of Great Barrow, who had coupled with John Little and lived with him until Sparrow was six or seven. But Martin's mother, Madlyn, lived here in Sherwood yet, a surprisingly gentle influence who more or less, like Lil, played mother to them all.

At the thought of Lil, Sparrow looked for her. She stood taking her leave from Wren before returning to Nottingham. He wondered how badly she grieved for Geofrey; she displayed no outward signs of it, had not lived with him as a wife nor even seen him very often. Yet, according to all Sparrow had ever been told, they had been closely bonded.

Three held the spell—two bonded to each other, the third to the spirit of the greenwood. That kept Sherwood safe and enfolded in magic.

Aye, and Martin had already spoken for his place in that triad. He always went at everything with his sword flashing. Sparrow smiled quietly; it was he, though, whose arrow always found its mark.

Moving softly, he joined the two women. "Mother, can I see you home?" he asked Lil.

"No, lad. Alric means to accompany me. We have things to discuss. You make my girl feel welcome." She stroked Wren's hair. "I fear she will find her first night in Sherwood strange."

Wren shivered. Her eyes were large in her face, and her hands clung to Lil's.

"Let me come with you," she begged.

"Nay, child. You have burnt that bridge. Anyway, this day had to come. I only regret I could not have told you more gently."

Wren cast a look into the darkening forest. "I cannot imagine sleeping here. Everything is alive and moving, and there are so many sensations."

"I will look after you." The voice came from Sparrow's shoulder as Martin stepped to Wren's side. "You need not fear."

She glared at him, her eyes those of a trapped fox, wary and golden. "I fear nothing," she declared, and Sparrow knew she lied.

He felt Martin's surge of emotion as he responded to her courageous defiance. Martin was in danger of overstepping himself; this woman would not appreciate bullying or blatant persuasion. Martin, though, had great confidence in his charm, which had seduced many a lass in Oakham and beyond. Did not poor, bonny Sally virtually haunt their camp for the love of him?

"I will come back soon," Lil promised Wren. "Meanwhile, Rennie, do not return to Nottingham for any reason. Understand?"

Wren frowned. "Not until the furor over Lambert dies down, you mean? Then I will be able to come home?"

"This is your home now," Lil caressed the girl's cheek. "Best grow accustomed to it."

"Lil—"

"Hush, Rennie. Look after her, lads—both of you." Lil walked away quickly and did not look back. She joined Alric at the edge of the clearing, where they linked hands before disappearing into the trees.

"Here," Martin said to Wren, "will you have some supper?"

"I wish I could say no, but I am ravenous. I do not know why."

"Come, then." Martin offered her his arm, but she put both hands behind her back and shied from him.

Summoning manners from some unknown source, Martin bowed slightly and led her away to the fire.

So it begins, Sparrow thought. He refused to fight over the lass like a hart contesting another for a hind. Wren was much more—a woman of spirit, with her own mind and her own lessons to learn. He smiled to himself again. Let Martin toss himself for a while against the stone wall of her resistance. When he grew spent, he, Sparrow, would still be here.

****

"You watch her the way a priest watches the holy Lady, but you do not approach, Sparrow. Will you let my son do all the courting?"

Madlyn spoke softly as she bent to fill Sparrow's cup with ale. Night lay like a soft shawl over Sherwood, and Sparrow waited for his turn at watch. Across the clearing, Martin and Wren sat with their heads together, even though Wren should have been abed long since.

Sparrow looked up into Madlyn's face. Her hair, as fair as her son's, was covered by a rough wimple, and her face looked serene. A hint of a smile pulled at her lips.

"'Tis no mere matter of courting," he replied.

"Is it not? Martin seems to feel otherwise."

"This is far more important than any needs of the heart. And she, I am thinking, will not be easy to win."

"You are right. I myself tried to speak with her, words of comfort and reassurance, but she held me off most fiercely." Madlyn sighed. "Well, my Martin ever did love a challenge."

"She must make the choice freely, if one is to be made. Do you remember how it was between Lil, Geofrey, and Alric?"

"Oh, aye." Madlyn eased herself down at Sparrow's side. "Lil was a healer then. She had not yet taken her place in the castle kitchen. We all thought she would choose Alric. In the end, she surprised everyone."

"Geoffrey was a good man."

"There was justice in him. All his strength was wrapped up in doing what was right, no matter the cost." Again Madlyn glanced at the couple beside the fire. "My Martin is not like that. He carries his father's rage, I am not sure why. I think this Wren harbors anger also. I do not know how they would suit."

Sparrow's heart clenched at the thought, but he said, "She has barely arrived. Let her find her feet. Most women I have known have no trouble making up their own minds."

Madlyn smiled. "True. Yet you know how persuasive Martin can be." For an instant, she frowned. "Sally will not be happy with all this, I am thinking."

"And does Martin care for Sally's happiness?" It did not seem so. Martin dallied with Sal because she was available and willing. Aye, this would set the poor lass on her heels.

"I think he does, in his way. Ah—" Madlyn nudged Sparrow as Martin got to his feet. "Here is your chance."

"What makes you think I desire a chance?"

Madlyn gazed into Sparrow's eyes. "Get you over there, lad. You have not been able to fool me since you were six years old."

Chapter Six

"You must be weary. Will you not take your rest?"

Rennie tipped her head up and up to take in the man standing over her, the one called Sparrow. Her emotions stirred within, making her feel restless. Already she felt bruised and bombarded, barely able to think. Too many sensations assaulted her. She was tense enough to break.

Yet Sparrow had a kind face, and she could feel waves of reassurance rolling off him, the opposite of the man who had just left her—Martin.

"I shall not be able to sleep," she told Sparrow, and waved her hand. "Not with all this."

"It must seem strange, indeed."

"I am used to being in my scullery, alone. I do not know when I have talked with so many different people."

"And some of us no doubt seem daunting." He smiled, and Rennie felt the warmth of it, clear through.

"If you refer to Martin, he is like a flock of crows, pecking. He shreds my composure." She frowned. "He should have been called 'Crow' instead of 'Martin.'" She shot Sparrow a considering look. "Perhaps you can tell me something: why are we three named after birds?"

"Mind if I sit?"

She shook her head. Sparrow folded his legs under

him and dropped down by her side. Rennie had the immediate and powerful impulse to reach out and touch his hand but fought it back hastily. Sitting so near, she could catch his scent—wood smoke, leather, and a tang of male underlying it all. He wore his hood back on his shoulders, and she could see his hair, long, glossy brown, not so shaggy as Martin's. He wore no beard.

"We were named in honor of Robin, of course, as were many born in Sherwood, back then." He grinned. "To be sure, there can be only one 'Robin,' so other birds had to be selected."

"Aye?" Rennie studied him closely. "Why 'Sparrow'? Would not Hawk have suited you better?"

"My father, so the story goes, wanted me to become a fine archer, one to rival Robin himself."

"How does the name lend that?"

"It carries the word 'arrow,' does it not? 'Tis said the rogue friar himself—Tuck—named and blessed us before he died."

"Did your name do its work? Are you a fine archer?"

"If I answer that honestly, I fear I will sound as full of myself as does our friend Martin."

"Oh, him! Who would believe a word he says?"

"I do not know what he has been saying to you, but he is very good with a sword and with his fists, for all that."

Rennie continued to study him in the flickering firelight, fascinated by his eyes, which held that hint of the wild and were shadowed by lashes surely longer than her own. And she found herself hoping Martin would not return. The emotions she gleaned from Martin were tumultuous and disturbing. This man, however, emitted a measure of calm.

"Do you remember him, Robin Hood?" she asked.

"Your father? Aye."

"Can you tell me something about him? I cannot quite believe he is my father. It is oversetting, finding oneself the daughter of a legend."

"I remember them both, your father and your mother. I was about six when you were born. But I do not know to what extent my memories are colored by what I was later told."

"What was he like?"

Sparrow closed his eyes and considered his words before speaking. "Strong and kind. I remember that about him. When he looked at you, you could feel his kindness. I never saw him angered with anyone, not like Martin's father. But when Robin took up a cause, the magic in him flared and he became unstoppable."

"Magic." That word again. Rennie sighed.

"It abounds, here in Sherwood. And your father had it in full."

"Is that what I feel?" Rennie glanced round at the trees.

"You look like him."

"What? How is that?"

Sparrow smiled again, almost ruefully. "You have his strength about you, and the cast of your face is the same, but I think you have your mother's eyes."

"Can you describe him to me?"

"Well, he seemed very tall to me then, but I was small. He was not big like my own Da, who was a veritable giant. He had hair just the color of yours— dark brown—and I remember his eyes glowed blue, like jewels."

Rennie's breath caught in her throat. "I think I have dreamed of him, over and over again, for years, not knowing who he was. He used to speak to me while I slept." A shiver made her tremble. "His eyes shone with blue light, just as you describe."

Sparrow leaned closer. "What did he say to you, in these dreams?"

"Many things, most of which I did not understand." Rennie pressed her lips together. The strange man had visited her dreams at times when she felt at her most desperate and vulnerable, when she wept. She would not admit that to Sparrow, whom she barely knew.

"And your mother," Sparrow began.

"What is all this, then?" Martin loomed over them, his shadow leaping ahead of him, cast by the flames.

"We are just talking," Sparrow said mildly. "Wren has questions."

"Time for you to take watch," Martin told him, and dropped to Rennie's side. Immediately she could feel his emotions resume beating at her, and she surged to her feet.

"I need to rest." Suddenly, her longing for her nest in the scullery was so intense she could have wept.

"Here, child." The woman who had been introduced as Martin's mother, Madlyn, held out a hand. "Come with me. I shall see you settled."

Rennie put her fingers in the woman's hand. They left the two young men sitting together in silence.

****

A strange sound woke Rennie from deep, dreamless sleep. She had lain long before finding oblivion last night and had half expected the man—her father—to visit her dreams, but he had not. Now, eyes still closed, she registered a hollow *thunk, thunk*, almost like someone chopping wood, or like Master Eddoes cutting meat on his block. And she could hear voices, calm and quiet.

"Ah, you cannot do that again."

"I can. Set the target farther off."

"Braggart!"

"No bragging about it. Stand there just in front of the target, if you like. I will hit a hand's breadth above it."

"Do you take me for a fool?"

"Always!"

Rennie opened her eyes and sat up, her loose hair swinging round her like a brown blanket. Green light shone everywhere, and sensation rushed upon her. The forest, alive and in movement, whispered far overhead, and birds flicked by like shards of brightness. By God, she was still in Sherwood. Yesterday had not been an ugly dream.

Not far off a fire smoldered. Rennie saw Madlyn there, stirring a pot of something that smelled so good Rennie's stomach rumbled.

The lad called Simon sat beneath a tree, stringing a bow, his attention all directed farther off where—

Ah, there they were, the two men who had vied for her attention last night. They competed again now, with bows in their hands. The sound Rennie had heard was that of arrows finding their marks.

She got to her feet slowly. Neither young man noticed her, but Simon did, and the old fellow who lazed in the corner of the clearing, both of whom gave her sharp looks.

Rennie stumbled to Madlyn's side and spoke but

one word. "Privy?"

Madlyn's kind face turned sympathetic. "There is none. You must just go off by yourself. For the god's sake, be careful. Shall I come with you?"

Rennie shook her head, able to think of few things she wanted less, and slunk off.

When she returned, both men stood beside the fire, having abandoned their archery practice. Rennie could feel their emotions, all stirred up and tangled. She fought the impulse to turn round again and just run and run, into the trees.

Martin held a bowl in his hands, which he offered Rennie. "Hungry?"

She was, yet she shied from him instinctively. A spark of impatience lit his blue eyes. "You must eat. Mother, pray get her a portion."

"I would rather have a place to wash, and some time on my own."

"One of those we can offer you," Sparrow said. "But you must remain under someone's protection."

Martin's gaze inspected Rennie as if stripping her naked. "You will need some decent clothing. Everyone will be coming, you understand."

"Everyone?"

"They will have heard about you and be feeling curious." He tipped the bowl to his lips. "You will need to look as they expect."

Rennie's anger flared. "And what do they expect?"

He waved a hand. "Something grand, as befits Robin's daughter."

Rennie drew herself up and declared, "I do not play at 'grand'!"

Both men grinned, as did Simon and Madlyn.

Martin's teeth flashed white, and Rennie found herself assaulted by his all-too-potent charm. "I think you just did. You cannot blame folk for being anxious to lay eyes on you. All these years they have kept the faith alive. Now something is going to happen."

But what? Rennie wondered. These outlaws here in Sherwood, and the folk in the surrounding hamlets who supported them, could not possibly expect her to step out of the scullery and lead them...could they?

Madlyn placed a bowl in her hands. Half dizzy with hunger, she reconsidered and raised it to her lips.

"Not so fine as what you had in Nottingham Castle, I will be bound," Madlyn remarked. "I am sure Lil's kitchen has more than a little magic in it."

"This tastes wonderful." Rennie pushed her hair out of her face, all too aware of how closely both men watched her. "Some grand dishes get prepared at the castle, aye, but I never tasted them. A full two score people work in the kitchens, and the Sheriff is not about to let them sup his gravies and sauces."

Madlyn clicked her tongue. "Imagine seeing and smelling of all that food, and having none of it."

Rennie shrugged. "'Tis hardest for the youngsters who stir pots and turn the spits."

"So," Martin asked suddenly, "just what did you do to the bastard, Lambert, that you are banished from Nottingham?"

The rich stew caught in Rennie's throat and she nearly choked. She raised her eyes to Martin's on a flare of anger. "He demanded what I was not willing to give."

Martin nodded. "That Norman get seems to think he can take whatever he wants. Needs to be put in his place, like Sir Guy before him. At least he got what he deserved."

Rennie nodded uncertainly. She had laid eyes only a few times on Sir Guy, the Sheriff's longstanding captain of the guard, killed last winter. A fierce, cruel man, at least he had never come hunting his pleasure in the kitchens.

Sparrow spoke with an edge of irony. "I may as well inform you before Martin, here, decides to brag on himself—'twas he who struck Sir Guy's death blow."

"Death blow?" Rennie echoed.

"Aye." Martin took it up. "'Twas just before Solstice, and the Sheriff's guards, led by Sir Guy, were transporting the last quarter taxes over icy roads. We halted them on the far side of Oakham, where Sir Guy fancied he could best my sword." Martin's grin flashed again. "There were folk had meat for their Christmas table, thanks to us."

"And Sir Guy?"

"Went home and died—slowly," Martin said with satisfaction. "Word is, it took him ten days and cost much in pain." He leaned toward Rennie and widened his blue eyes. "Stay with us, Wren, and I promise I will serve Lambert the same."

Chapter Seven

"Mother, I wish to go home." To Rennie's consternation, her voice broke on the words. "I know you say Sherwood must be my home now, but it feels not! The trees whisper at me, and I can find no rest."

Lil said nothing. The two of them walked together in the forest, not far from camp. Birds came fluttering from the surrounding trees to follow in Lil's wake, but Rennie barely noticed, so intent was she on persuasion.

Hurriedly, she went on, "Surely Lambert has forgotten all about me by now. I am naught but an insignificant peasant, to him."

"Forgotten? You broke his cheekbone with that bucket. I doubt he is likely to forget," Lil said wryly. "He has been to the kitchen looking for you no less than three times, and the Sheriff has issued a decree that, if caught, you are to be whipped."

"What said you to Lambert, when he came looking?"

"That you had run off, and I knew not how to find you."

"Oh." Rennie could not imagine so much furor over her instinctive act of self-defense. Then again, neither could she imagine being the daughter of Robin Hood. The last thing she wanted was to cause more trouble for Lil, even though her own unhappiness cried aloud.

Ruefully, she said, "I never imagined I might be homesick for the scullery, dank place that it was."

Lil stopped walking and faced her. "You must learn to take your place here—for it is your place, child, though you believe it not. You were conceived and born beneath these trees, and the waters of Sherwood run through your blood."

"I hear them speaking to one another—the trees, I mean." Rennie lowered her voice, as if fearing the overweening branches might listen. "What does it mean? And how is it I can sense what those two are feeling so clearly, Sparrow and Martin?"

Lil's green eyes searched Rennie's closely. She sighed. "Perhaps I should have prepared you for this long ago. But, the god help me, I thought it safer if you did not know and so could not let slip some truth that might endanger you. Lately, though, it has been like trying to keep a young falcon in a cage. My heart told me. I should have listened."

"Your heart told you what, Lil?"

"I had no right to keep you so long. I should have educated you long since, then set you free into Sherwood."

"But you did educate me, Mother, in so many things. You taught me the histories of England, all about healing herbs, and how to set a bone. You even taught me to read a few words."

"And I neglected much, as well, perhaps those lessons you needed most. I should have taught you the truth about magic. It shall be a great part of your life."

Rennie caught her breath. "Everyone at Nottingham knows magic is dangerous. Women have been killed for using it."

"Old biddies, thinking they can speak curses! I am talking of real magic, Rennie, the kind that turns the seasons and makes the stag run."

"That is life."

Lil nodded. "Magic is life, quickened. 'Tis what the old word means, is it not? Wicca—the quickening of life. You feel it all around you, here in Sherwood. You feel it streaming off the trees, and it is what you are sensing from those two young men."

"How do you know what I am sensing?"

"I have felt it myself, all my life. Listen to me, Rennie. All folk are of the earth, and connected to her. But in some, the sensing is very bright. They can read the life force the way a scholar reads a book. 'Tis a gift and a burden, one you and those two men share."

Rennie struggled for comprehension. "Why? How?"

Lil smiled gently. "The 'how' is easy: your fathers all gave themselves to Sherwood, heart and soul. Sherwood gives back. Those who have met the god possess a magic that flows through them and manifests in many ways."

"I have never met the god."

"Can you be so certain? He comes to us in many guises. 'Tis he guards the spirit of Sherwood, keeps the folk who are connected to the land safe, and the flame of hope burning in their hearts. Do you think the Green Man cares for lords and barons? He rewards those who see—and hear and feel—him best."

"Where is he, then, this green god?"

"Beneath your feet, dancing through the air, in Sparrow's eyes, and in Martin's smile. The longer you stay here, the more strongly will your powers come to you. And when they ripen, you will need to make a choice."

"What kind of choice?"

"Eventually, child, you will bond with both of them."

"Sparrow and Martin?"

"Aye, but you will need to bestow on one of them the fullness of your heart." Lil gazed into the far distance. "As I did, before you."

Rennie's mind leaped ahead. "Geofrey? Did you love him, then, full well?"

"Not love as you imagine it. 'Tis the love of the Lord for his Lady, and all men for all women—a holy, as well as a carnal, thing."

"I do not understand."

Lil reached out to smooth Rennie's hair. "Nay, but you will." She smiled sadly. "I half pity and half envy you. Promise me one thing: you will stay here and learn all those here have to teach you, even as in the past you learned from me."

"I will try." Rennie frowned. "But you know how I hate being told what to do."

"Oh, that I do know!" Lil laughed with affection.

"Very well, I do so promise, if you will promise me something in return: you will be here when I need you."

"I will try, love. But you need to be able to rely on yourself."

"Say that I will see you tomorrow."

"That is when Geofrey will be laid to rest. Alric and I must be there."

"Where?"

"Beneath the great tree at Oakham."

"Let me come."

Lil gave Rennie a hard look. "Well, then, yes. Sparrow may bring you. But you must heed all he tells you. I will speak with him now."

Why Sparrow, Rennie wondered, and not Martin? She seized Lil's arm and immediately felt Lil's serenity, her grief—and strength. "Promise me a second thing, Mother—that you will not abandon me."

****

"Here." A bundle landed in Rennie's lap, soft deerskin and well-worn cloth.

She looked up into Martin's blue eyes. "What is this?"

"Clothing. If you wish to go to Geofrey's burial, it must be as a lad. Anyway, those rags you are wearing are fit only for the fire."

Rennie narrowed her eyes at him. Was he not a fine one to talk, an outlaw by birth, who had lived his whole life rough, in the forest? He wore leather leggings, overwrapped with deer-hide thongs, and a leather jerkin so soft it molded to his broad shoulders, loosened in front to show a strong, tanned throat. No denying Martin Scarlet was a comely man and a challenging one, given the way he stared back at her, tit for tat. Rennie did not want him to get the idea he could give her orders of any kind, and she did not like the implication that her own clothes might be manky. Yet there was some appeal in the prospect of wearing men's clothing, and disappearing into a disguise.

She scrambled to her feet, hampered by the bundle, and Martin reached out a hand to assist her. The instant their hands met, palm to palm, sensation came rushing, so strong she almost fell down again.

Darkness, light, courage, intensity, and searing anger, burning up a great bitterness the way flame consumes dry tinder. She could feel his spirit, and it knocked the breath out of her, swayed her right back on her heels. She stared into Martin's face and saw his eyes widen, the irises clear gray-blue, and knew he also felt the blazing connection.

And what did he sense in her, then? Her overwhelming frustration? Her bone-deep loneliness and yearning for light? Her ever-present fear of abandonment?

He gasped and, as soon as Rennie stood on her feet, extracted his fingers from hers. Wordless, they stared at one another while Rennie's heart began to pound.

Then Martin swore, soft and deep. "By our Lady!" Something kindled in his eyes, and he stepped toward her.

Just as quickly, Rennie slipped away.

"Wren." He spoke her name like claiming.

Instinctively, she shook her head. No. Too intense. Too terrifying.

"Martin?"

The spell, fast-woven, broke when someone spoke his name. Rennie looked round to see a young woman approaching with a smile in her eyes.

A lovely, slender thing she looked, with rosy cheeks and fair hair all tucked up into her cap, save a few strands. Dimples flashed when she smiled at Martin. "I am to attend Geofrey's burial with you. Father says I might."

Martin nodded woodenly. "'Tis well, Sally. This is Lil's girl—Wren—come to join us, from Nottingham."

"Welcome, Wren! 'Twill be a fine thing having another lass about to help me deal as fit with these lads."

"Aye." So, this was the young woman said to have given Martin her heart. But how did he feel for her? Impossible to tell now; his expression had closed like an oaken door.

"You live in Oakham?" she asked, striving for politeness.

"Aye, just my Da and myself, since Mother died." For an instant her expression, transparent as clear water, clouded.

Martin spoke. "Sal's mother was cut down by Sir Guy's men last winter." His anger surged once more. Rennie felt it clearly, even though they no longer touched.

"I am sorry," Rennie murmured.

Martin shrugged stiffly. "The flaming Sheriff thinks it his right to destroy the homes—and the lives—of those who sympathize with us." He gazed at Sally for a moment. "Take comfort, Sal, in the fact that Sir Guy met his just end, as will Lambert, after him. So have I promised Wren."

Sally's gaze clung to his worshipfully.

Martin strove for a lighter tone. "Now, Sally, perhaps you can help Wren into her lad's disguise."

He went off quickly, and Sally turned her eyes on Wren. "Why has he promised to kill Sir Lambert, do you know?"

"Aye, you will hear it soon enough. I faced off with Lambert in the kitchen yard, and am now banished to Sherwood, in hiding."

"Faced off with him? How is that?"

49

"He thought he could take what I was not willing to give."

"Oh!" Compassion filled Sally's eyes. She stole a look after Martin, making it more than clear where her desire lay. "It is an evil thing, indeed, when a woman's most prized possession is not hers to bestow as she will."

Chapter Eight

"As light always follows darkness, as the new leaf replaces the sere, as summer always comes to us when the wheel of the year turns again, so will our brother one day return to gladden this world we know."

Alric's quiet words seemed to float upon the glittering afternoon air, the way the sunlight danced in ladders through the branches of the giant oak for which Oakham was named. Sparrow tipped back his head, his eyes following that light, and felt sorrow tangle inside him with a sense of renewed purpose. Aye, Alric was right—all things that died came again. Yet some bonds reached beyond the grave, and some spirits remained ever-present.

Like Robin's, and that of Sparrow's father and, no doubt, Geofrey himself.

All Sparrow's life, Geoffrey had been there, a force of wisdom and strength, someone upon whom Sparrow's world relied. Even though they had now laid Geoffrey, with all due dignity, beneath the loam of Sherwood and the sheltering branches of the tree, Sparrow could not conceive of his absence. Surely his spirit rode those motes of light; his wise eyes yet watched the folk for whom he had cared so long.

Seldom had Oakham seemed so quiet, its inhabitants gathered with those come from the forest to remember, and grieve. All around Sparrow, folks wept openly. And at his side—

He stole a look at the woman who stood so silent beside him. Not a sound had escaped her this long while, not a hint of reaction. She held herself tight, the leather hood she wore raised to shield her face. Her borrowed clothing suited her well. Tall for a woman, she was slender enough to play a lad, indeed, and the boots laced about her calves fit as if molded to them.

Sparrow turned his eyes on Lil, who stood at the grave's edge with Alric and Martin. Grief ravaged the woman's face and added years to her appearance; no need to ask what she felt. Sparrow wondered at the love she and Geofrey had shared. He had rarely seen them do more than touch hands, yet she looked, now, like a woman whose heart had been torn from her.

Magic shivered in the air; if Sparrow narrowed his eyes he could virtually see it, a shimmer of pure green that surrounded Lil, a haze of violet-silver around Alric, even radiant crimson dusting Martin's outline. He could see the grief also, gray as smoke, linking soul to soul.

And those others, the many who had lived and died in Sherwood—did they come as well, to take their leave of the honored dead? Robin, with his fierce kindness and vision, Scarlet, with his heedless courage and headstrong anger...Sparrow's own Da, with his great laugh and even greater heart? All the others who had chosen freedom over safety and been willing to pay the required price for it, for an England they could call their own, this blessed ground—did they hover here also, like the light?

"Know," Alric said, "he is not gone from us, nor can ever be."

Suddenly, Lil's head came up. Her nostrils flared

even as Sparrow's own senses unfurled.

"Danger! Children!"

Sparrow never knew who spoke the words. It might have been Lil, or Alric, or Sparrow himself. The warning came mere moments before horses crashed into the gathered crowd, and the peace shattered into chaos.

Sparrow thought first of the woman at his side. Even as his eyes noted the dull glint of armor and the blazons that declared these were the Sheriff's men, he realized her particular danger. She could not be caught. As screams and hollering erupted all around them, he seized her and thrust her to his back. It was the first time he had touched her, and his fingers tingled. A horde of sensations rushed upon him: terror, distress, and overwhelming anger. He could not think about that now. Her safety must be his one purpose.

"Down!"

The oak, standing more than a hundred feet high and with a spread of branches nearly as wide, created its own clearing. Now the Sheriff's mounted guard seemed to fill it, swords flashing, hooves crushing everything in their path. Sparrow caught one glimpse of Lambert, on his coal-black steed, at their head. The man's eyes were everywhere, and Sparrow hurried to move Wren to the edge of the open space.

A stream ran just here, cloaked with sedges and bullrushes. He shoved Wren down its bank. Still she had not said a word nor cried out. He knew cover meant safety, and they must reach the trees at any cost.

With a great splash, a horse came through the stream, and its rider filled Sparrow's vision. His fingers reached for the bow on his shoulder without conscious thought. An arrow came to his hand just as swiftly.

"Behind me," he told Wren again.

Sparrow wore a sword, but the bow would always be his first choice. He saw horseflesh, sword and shield all coming at him in a surge of power. He whispered a prayer and let his arrow fly.

The soldier fell with a grunt nearly at Wren's feet, and the horse shied away. Sparrow heard Wren gasp even as he seized her wrist, intent on pulling her on, but past the stream their way was blocked once more. Soldiers seemed to materialize out of the forest—how had they approached so quietly?—to surround the gathered mourners. Sparrow notched his second arrow.

Behind him he heard screaming—high squeals of women and children, bellows from the throats of villagers and soldiers alike, someone shrieking in pain. Where was Martin? Could he defend Lil and Alric on his own? What was Lambert after? What did he know?

Three horsemen converged upon him and Wren. An arrow to the throat felled the first, but the second came at Sparrow with a sweeping sword blow that nearly took off his head. The third tried to separate him from Wren, the way a sheepdog peels away a ewe, and terror touched him, raw and pure.

You must protect her. She belongs to you.

He drew his sword. A man on foot had no advantage facing one on horseback, but he could not choose. From the corner of his eye he saw that Wren, bless her, stood firm; refusing to be chased, she ducked back and forward, keeping out of the third man's reach. Sparrow shook the hair from his eyes and lunged with his blade, getting in a blow to his opponent's leg.

He would never be the swordsman Martin was.

Martin's father, a rogue soldier himself, had taught his son well. Sparrow's own father was a shepherd and woodsman before turning wolfshead, but desperation now made up for any lack of skill. Sparrow parried two crushing blows before using his strength to good advantage, seizing the soldier's bleeding leg and pulling him from his mount to the ground, where Sparrow's sword took him in a welter of blood.

He spun toward Wren. She had doubled back through the stream, her hood fallen loose upon her shoulders, and her eyes burned toward the man chasing her. Never had she looked more the wild thing, trapped. Sparrow heard a loud cry and cast a look at the thick of the fighting, where he saw Lambert, eyes fixed on Wren's face, trying to force his mount through the intervening combatants.

Terror stung him, and he leaped to haul the third soldier from his horse. Escaping his grasp, the man immediately engaged Sparrow's sword.

"Wren!" Sparrow barked over his shoulder. "Run!"

Her eyes, held fast by Lambert's approach, did not waver—neither did she obey.

"Curse it—Wren!"

Brought to his senses by a blow from his opponent that laid open his sleeve, and the flesh beneath, Sparrow experienced a surge of rage worthy of Martin himself. He thrust with his blade, following the impetus of his emotion, and ducked the soldier's shield. He felt his blade scrape bone as the man fell.

"Come!" He caught Wren's hand, and they ran until the breath seared his lungs and Wren at last stumbled. He tried to catch her as she fell, and they both went down and landed in the soft loam, Sparrow's heart pounding so loud in his ears he could not listen for sounds of pursuit.

"Be still."

Bless her, she did not move. She lay on her side with her back to him, as if they spooned in a bed. Her breath came in big, deep gulps she fought to quiet. His lips were at her ear.

Silence now made their best cover. Trees arched above them, restless in a breeze that stilled even as he held his breath. The very forest listened.

Time crept by. Sparrow's hand lay on Wren's breast, and he felt it when her heartbeat began to calm. His own limbs eased, and he raised his head.

Far off he still heard faint sounds of the continuing battle. How far were he and Wren from Oakham? He heard no sound of pursuit, but under his hands and pressed to the front of his body he could feel Wren, both her body and her spirit. He sensed the life moving in her, the rampant curiosity, the simmering terror, all overlying courage like bedrock. His heart rose in response, and in wonder that he could feel her this way.

"Are you hurt?" he breathed, stirring her dark hair.

"I am all right. But your arm—"

He sat up, and she came with him as if they were attached to one another, as perhaps they were. She turned her head and they looked into one another's eyes. He saw—

Wild places, rushing water, the rising and setting of the sun. He saw every peril of the future and all the beauty he could ever hope to know.

He could do nothing, then, but capture her lips with his. The desire came to him like the need for water after a long run, or winter's-end hunger. Her mouth felt unexpectedly soft beneath his, and she tasted like the sweetest honey wine. He could not tell where his lips ended and hers began.

Her spirit rose to meet his, rushing. All that she was bounded upon him, mingled delectably with what he was, tangled, and came apart again. In that instant he knew her every fear, every weakness, and every strength, and saw she knew him as well.

As a child he had once stuck his hand in the fire on a dare—from Martin, of course. It felt like that, and like the sunlight after a storm, and the longing he experienced when he gazed at the stars at night. It pulled at the roots of his soul.

She raised her hand, and he thought she might strike him, as she would any man who dared take such liberty. Instead she caressed his cheek, touching him as if she feared he might disappear under her fingers.

A raging desire arose in him. Ah, but he could not take her here on the floor of the forest. He wanted to. Yet they fled pursuit, and his first duty was to protect her, always.

The breath left him as he eased away from her, and she sighed in response. Her fingers fell from his cheek.

"Come," he told her, "we must away."

"But your wound—" She groped for the torn fabric of his sleeve, revealing an injury which bled copiously.

"'Tis naught."

"Let me tie it up, or you will leave a trail."

Sparrow nodded. Without hesitation she tore what was left of his sleeve, folded it deftly, and pressed it to the long wound.

"You have skill in those hands."

"Lil taught me." She glanced into his eyes and

stole his breath again. "Just as well I can make myself useful, eh?"

Now it was he who lifted his hand and touched her hair. "Aye, and you will learn the ways of Sherwood," he heard himself say. "Because you are meant to stay here always, with me."

Chapter Nine

"It will be dark soon. How much farther must we go?" Rennie had no idea where they were. The forest seemed endless, and they had tramped what felt like a circuitous route. She knew herself to be utterly dependent on Sparrow's sense of direction.

At least her terrible trembling had ceased. Maybe Sparrow had charmed it from her, for they walked with their hands linked and emotions flowed easily between them. She could feel how badly his injured arm pained him, how he craved water and rest. She knew how he craved her.

Ever since that kiss—but, it had been no mere kiss. A power lurked in it, and a terrifying current of desire, maybe even belonging. But Rennie could not be sure about that. She had never belonged anywhere, save the scullery, and to no one but Lil.

She stole another look at Sparrow. In the soft light of encroaching evening he appeared mysterious, a mere shadow moving at her side, with the brown hair lying sleek against his shoulders and his eyes veiled. He had a fine profile, a strong nose, and those lips... Remembering the feel of them, desire stirred deep in her belly, and he turned his head to look at her again.

His gaze was that of a hart, dark and secretive, holding wisdom deep enough to inspire awe in her heart. Mating with him, she thought, would be like mating with the forest itself.

She spoke, in an effort to deny what she felt. "I would not like to stay out here all night."

"Here, or back at camp, it is all the same. The forest looks out for us. But we are not far from camp. What I am wondering is whether camp will still be safe, or if soldiers have already discovered it."

"How many of our folk died, do you think?"

"Ours? Villagers and forest folk, all? I saw at least four go down."

Her fingers spasmed in his. "Lil—"

"I did not see what befell her, but I thought I saw Sally's father, Edgar, fall."

"No."

"And old John. Two others of the villagers—"

"Why would Lambert's men attack at a burial? You do not suppose they were looking for me?"

Sparrow shook his head. "I much doubt it. Lambert had no way of knowing you were there."

"I think he saw me, though." Remembering, Rennie shivered. "He looked right at me. What if he saw Lil, also? Will she be able to return to Nottingham?"

"Lil can look after herself."

"By using magic, you mean?" Rennie stopped walking and dragged at Sparrow's hand.

He looked at her. "If need be. Now come and let us see if camp is where we left it."

It was. Night just kissed the tops of the trees as Sparrow and Rennie entered the clearing to find a cold fire, and folk gathered in grim silence.

The first to catch sight of them was Martin. He leaped up and rushed over, anger and relief both in his eyes.

"About time you showed yourself, Sparrow. We thought her dead!" His gaze dropped to their hands, still linked, and his jaw grew tight. "What do you think you are about?"

"We were followed and had to take the long way round. I waited for things to grow quiet."

"I will just wager you did." Martin's eyes turned wild. He planted the flat of his hand on Sparrow's chest and pushed. "Get away from her."

Sparrow stumbled back and then stood his ground. It would take more muscle than that, Rennie knew, to shift him.

She released his fingers and glared into Martin's face. "Why are you so angry?"

"He is a fool, worrying us, when he should know how dear you are to us all!"

"This is no time for your mad accusations." The authority in Rennie's voice surprised her. "Where is Lil? Is she all right?"

"Bruised from being knocked about a bit. She and Alric made off; she means to return to Nottingham." Martin tossed the words at Rennie and then, still aggressive, stepped up to Sparrow. "I do not know why Lil gave you leave to guard Wren, anyway. She should have been left in my charge."

Sparrow's head came up. "So you could protect her as you did Sally's father?"

Martin flared like a torch igniting. Before Rennie could draw breath he flew at Sparrow, and all at once the two of them grappled together, muscle against muscle, straining mightily before they went down, thrashing.

Everyone else in the clearing came to his or her feet as the two men rolled, grunting wordless snarls, a flurry of blows landing so fast and hard Rennie could not tell who got the worst of it.

She ran to Madlyn, who stood with her arm around Sally. "Stop them!"

Madlyn shook her head. "No stopping it now."

"But he is your son. He will listen to you."

"If that is what you think, you do not know him."

"But Sparrow is sore injured—"

"As is Martin. Do you think he faced those soldiers and came out of it unscathed?"

"Then I say to you again, stop him. Sally—" Rennie looked into the girl's eyes. They were red and swollen from weeping, and she did not react to what Rennie said.

"Then I shall stop them myself." Rennie started forward, but Madlyn caught her arm.

"Nay, let them work it out. This has been days coming. I am only surprised it took so long."

But Rennie could not stand and watch blow after blow given and received, much less endure the onslaught of anger and ugliness she could feel flying off the pair. She turned and fled.

The two men came off the ground as if hauled by ropes.

"Wren!" Sparrow hollered, and started after her. Martin pushed him aside, and it was he who caught Rennie before she had taken ten steps into the shadowed forest.

"Little fool!" As soon as he touched her, she felt his anger and raw panic. They broke over her like a sea.

She turned on him. "Get away from me."

"What?"

"Leave me alone. It is too much. Can you not see that?"

He stared at her. Blood trickled from one corner of his mouth, and already one eye had begun to swell. "I only wish to protect you."

"Oh, and is this truly about what you want? What he wants? What I want, for all that?" Rennie sensed that the vortex in which she found herself might be bigger than any mere desire or intention. Her eyes stabbed the dark behind Martin; Sparrow did not appear.

Why did he not come?

"Listen to me, Wren. You and I together could make a difference for the folk of Sherwood, of Nottingham, and beyond. 'Tis time we threw off the yoke laid on us by our Norman overlords. We have been stagnant and compliant far too long, ever since your father's dream fractured with his death. But I can feel what is inside you—the fire and the magic. We can turn the tide."

"And, what?" Rennie challenged. "Overthrow Lambert? The Sheriff? The King?"

"Why not?" His voice flicked like a whip. "Do we not have right on our side? Your father believed in the power of right. My father taught me so! He told me justice is won a battle at a time—one man at a time."

"Very admirable. But as one raised in the scullery on the Sheriff's crumbs and leavings, I can tell you there is much injustice, and great distance between us and the King."

"You think I do not know it?" He leaned toward her and widened his eyes. "There is a long score to settle. You and I together, though—" His fingers tightened on her arm. "Can you not feel what lies between us?"

Rennie could. She also knew the potential of what lay between her and Sparrow. She stole another look past Martin's shoulder.

Martin stepped closer. "Stop looking for him—he is not coming. Do you know why? He is weak. He speaks of peace and compromise, the promise in this document the barons forced King John to sign."

"The Magna Carta?"

"That is it. But I will tell you something, Wren. That grand document assures the rights of those very barons and lords, most of them Norman. It does nothing for the likes of you and me, serfs with no more liberty than a hound. They will live, still, off the efforts of our hands and the strain of our backs, if we let them. They must be made to reckon with us."

Rennie challenged him back. "How?"

"Wage war on them from Sherwood. Since your father—and mine—died, we have done no more than exist and protect ourselves. That must change. Let the King himself come here and deal with us, and our success will spread. There are more serfs in this land than lords—let us all rise at once!"

"You are mad."

"Am I? All it will take is the right leaders. Once I declare myself Lord of Sherwood and you my lady—"

He bent his head and kissed her. All his fire and enthusiasm flooded into her from the place his lips met hers.

Rennie promptly caught light in response, the wild streak in her responding to that in him. His spirit called to her, and the power of the call both thrilled and daunted her.

No sweet inquiry, this. Martin drew her close against him and explored the interior of her mouth in a manner that left no question as to his intent. His body, pressed hard to hers, kept no secrets.

Both his spirit and his body inflamed and battered Rennie with equal impact.

A wind came up and stirred the trees overhead, and in the distance thunder rumbled, its promised lightning matching the heat of Martin's embrace.

He broke the kiss suddenly to say, "Give yourself to me, Wren, and nothing will stop us."

"I need time." Her fingers had anchored themselves in the soft leather of his jerkin. She discovered she wanted his mouth on hers again—the taste of him might well be addictive, like strong wine.

"Nay, Wren, come with me now. I will ask Alric to join us."

"Join?"

"Handfast. Wed."

"I scarcely know you."

"You do—you can feel me, Wren, even as I feel you."

She could certainly feel something, a hot power surging at her from between his thighs. Rennie remembered the girls in the kitchens talking about one suitor or another, comparing their endowments. *My lad Cedric is a regular bull in the hay, he gored me right well last night—twice!* She recalled how Lambert had reached for his fly.

Rennie struggled to draw breath, fighting the force of Martin's desire which, somehow, seemed to have become her own.

"I am ready to wed with no one," she declared, and freed herself from the hot grasp of his hands. "And one thing I will tell you, Master Scarlet—you shall never bully me."

Chapter Ten

"I cannot believe my father is dead, gone." Sally repeated the words for the third or fourth time, brokenly.

They wrenched at Sparrow's heart. He had no comfort for the lass, who had wept most of the night. Now the chill of morning had come creeping, and the forest camp felt as barren and sere as Sparrow's own emotions.

A thin spire of smoke curled up from the fire, and all the trees drooped. Last night's storm had passed, but the clouds hung low, and it felt more like winter than spring.

Sally clung to Madlyn, who possessed far more patience than her son. Martin, to whom Sally had first looked for a shoulder on which to weep, remained distracted by Wren.

That knowledge was a knife in Sparrow's gut. The curse of feeling what Wren felt, even in part, told him she had been inflamed when she and Martin returned last night from the dark under the trees—angered, but stirred, as well.

Now Sparrow's arm ached with a raw, biting pain, the damp seemed to seep into his bones, and the future looked hopelessly bleak. If Wren chose Martin...

Even now the two of them spoke together, huddled on one side of the clearing, their heads far too close for

67

Sparrow's liking. He did not know of what they could be speaking, but he caught spikes of emotion from both of them, uncertainty and then enthusiasm from Wren, and from Martin, jubilation.

Sparrow forced his fingers through his hair. Yesterday, when he kissed Wren, he had been so sure he had won. Not that Wren's love was a contest, like the countless others between himself and Martin all these years past. But he had been able to feel Wren respond to him even as his heart came alive at her touch.

"Come, lamb, lie down a while. You have had no rest." Dimly he saw Madlyn lead Sally off to one of the sheltered bowers. When Madlyn returned, she sat beside Sparrow and elbowed him.

"If you want her, fight for her, lad."

"Eh?"

Madlyn nodded at the couple across the way. "Will you sit with your head in your hands while Martin works his wiles? Oh, do not look so surprised. Do you suppose, just because he is my son, I do not know what he is like?"

Sparrow said nothing.

"I love both of you," Madlyn went on. "You have been a second son to me, since your mother died."

The pain inside Sparrow eased a little. "I know, and I am grateful."

"Martin is like his father, whom I loved despite knowing better. Will was heedless, hotheaded, and started more fights than he had pots of ale, and that is saying something. Martin—well, he bred true."

"He thinks me weak."

Madlyn snorted. "He thinks everyone weak. It is

one of his greatest faults. Ruthlessness and wisdom seldom travel together. She will not think you weak, lad, if you show her otherwise."

"Easy to say, when he has already won all her attention."

"There is naught easy about love, or life, for all that. But, you know, we would not be here if not to learn hard lessons."

Sparrow shot her a sidelong glance. Her blue eyes looked thoughtful.

"Here, Madlyn?"

"In the world. I once heard Alric say 'tis all life is, a place to learn and shape our spirits. I believe that. Otherwise, I do not think I could go on, for there is too much loss, and far too much pain."

Impulsively, Sparrow touched the woman's hand. "You are very wise, Madlyn."

Madlyn shrugged. "I have made mistakes in plenty, and I have lived with them. Benefit from my knowledge, lad, and do not let something go by, if you want it very badly. Failing, and even feeling the fool, is better than sharp regret."

Ruefully, Sparrow asked, "Do you not want your son to become headman of Oakham rather than a humble hermit, wed to the forest?"

"Well, that is just it, Sparrow. I am not sure but it is the place he wants, rather than the lass. And I am not about to claim I know what he needs."

Later that morning, a young lad brought news from Oakham. No less than five of their own had perished in yesterday's encounter, including Sally's father and John, the senior member of their band. Alric sent word urging the outlaws to stay away from the hamlet for a time.

"He also asked that you keep Sal here for now," the lad reported. "'Tis not safe, with her father gone."

Sally, exhausted, still slept, but those gathered in a ring around the lad nodded gravely.

"What news from Nottingham?" Martin asked.

"None. Alric says if Sir Lambert or his men saw Mistress Lil beneath the oak, they gave no sign."

Martin sneered, "And how many of the Sheriff's men did we successfully cull?"

"Some say five, some more. 'Tis hard to tell, for they took their dead away with them." The lad looked round at the circle of faces. "May I tell Alric and Adam you will keep Sally safe? And, Alric says, the wolfshead's daughter, as well."

Sparrow felt Wren stiffen, but it was Martin who answered. "You may rely on it."

So, Sparrow thought bitterly, once the lad had gone, Martin thought to assign himself the role of Wren's protector, did he? Had something significant happened between them last night, beneath the trees? Madlyn was right; Sparrow needed to talk to Wren and let her know it was her choice, and not Martin's, that mattered.

He saw his opportunity not long after, when Martin once more took Wren aside and presented her with something. Nothing could have kept Sparrow from walking over to see what.

He caught but the end of Martin's words, "—and I will instruct you in the use of it."

Sparrow narrowed his eyes on the object lying across Wren's extended hands: Martin's best knife, it was, the one stolen from Sir Guy himself, a treasure.

Wren shot a look at Sparrow before she said to Martin, "I think I know how to use a knife. I lived in a kitchen."

"Not properly, you do not. Yesterday, you saw how quickly things can happen. You may need to defend yourself at any time."

Sparrow felt Wren's impatience and frustration flare. "If anyone comes too near, I will stab him." She stared at Martin meaningfully. "Anyone."

Martin, curse him, missed the message. "Look you, a blade is a fine weapon because 'tis silent and can be kept well concealed until it bites like an adder. The best places to strike are here, in the soft flesh under the jaw, or here, at the side of the throat." Lightly, he touched Wren in both places; she shivered.

Enough, Sparrow's heart cried. He stepped forward. "A blade can also be turned against its user quite easily. That is dangerous. I can teach you how to throw—"

Martin snapped, immediately, "I will teach her."

"—and how to shoot. You need a bow of your own."

"Everyone seems to know what I need!"

"I can fashion a bow for her," Martin declared, "and teach her—"

Sparrow strove to clamp down on his own ire, and failed. "Should she not be taught by the best shot among us?"

"For the sweet Lord's sake," Wren said, "do not begin with arguing again."

Martin ignored her. "She is Robin's daughter. Do you not suppose she will be an excellent shot?"

"No one is an excellent shot at the beginning."

71

"I will fetch my bow, and show you."

"You two will drive me mad!" The cry turned heads throughout the camp and at last served to silence Martin. "Leave me be," Wren requested, and pushed past both of them.

Martin immediately made to follow her and Sparrow put out a hand. "Did you hear her not?"

"Aye, but she needs—"

"Why not let her decide what she needs?"

"You would like that, aye, so you can move in and sway her your way," Martin sneered.

"*She* would like that—she demands it." Sparrow stared into Martin's wild eyes and tried to swallow his aggravation. "If you keep at her like a fox worrying after a hen, you will do naught but chase her off."

"Fool. There is no time to waste. Should something happen to Lil or Alric, we need to be ready to step into their places. Already the circle is weakened."

"And if Wren runs, we will all be doomed."

"Where would she run? She has nothing, save us."

"A creature escaping a trap cares not for that. Why do you not spend some of your time on Sally, who needs your comfort?"

Martin shook himself like a wet hound. "You know I am no good at holding hands and speaking soft words. That is more your ilk."

"Yet you had time for Sal when you wanted a warm bed, this winter past, a few hours' comfort. The lass loves you right well, and she needs you now, as you needed her then."

"She will just have to get over her feelings, then, will she not? For what we must do here in Sherwood is far more important than the feelings of one foolish lass."

"So Sally must weather her hurt and her father's death as well?"

"As must we all. Because, you mark my words, Sparrow, there will be far more deaths in Oakham, and beyond, if we do not keep Sherwood strong."

Chapter Eleven

"Does that man ever listen to any words besides his own?"

Sparrow could feel Wren's anger even before he approached her. She had fled deep into the trees beyond the far side of the clearing and now sat on a fallen tree, looking distracted.

With some hesitation, Sparrow seated himself beside her. Right now her feelings were those of a startled hawk, wild and primed for flight, and he knew he needed to go carefully.

"No," he replied. "Martin's head is made of pure rock."

"I told him last night I will not be bullied. This situation is intolerable. I feel like I have been torn up by the roots and am being battered from every side."

"I know."

She turned her head and looked at him. "How could you know?"

Sparrow drew a breath. "Because I feel what you feel, at least in part. 'Tis as if I pick up the echo of your emotions, just as you surely must mine, and Martin's. We are all three linked."

She continued to stare at him with those wild eyes. "How is it that we are linked? You and I do not even know each other."

"I believe we are connected through Sherwood

itself, by ties both of blood and devotion. Martin and I were dedicated by our fathers, soon after our births."

"But my father was already dead when I was born, and my mother abandoned me."

"And Lil dedicated you before she took you with her to Nottingham."

"Well, I do not want to hear your thoughts, or Martin's. And I do not want you to hear mine. Such intrusion is more than I can bear. I am used to the solitude of the scullery and the bustle of the kitchen beyond. No one ever cared if I lived or died, and my greatest worry was the salt biting my hands."

"Salt?"

She made a face. "We scrub the Sheriff's kettles with a mixture of salt, sand, and lye." She held out her hands. "They are only now starting to heal."

Sparrow fought the tendency to catch her fingers in his; he remembered again the taste of her, during their flight, and had to wrestle his desire. She did not need that from him, now. "It sounds like a hard and joyless existence."

"No, this is hard! Pray, how can I get Martin to leave me alone? As it is, I want nothing so much as to stab him with his own knife."

Sparrow's mind groped hurriedly for the right thing to say. Wren balanced on the very edge of control. "Perhaps a wee prick might be the best solution—just here, under his jaw, you understand."

Unexpectedly, she smiled. It transformed her face and made Sparrow think suddenly of her father. Surely Robin himself had such a smile.

"He is a wee prick," she declared, and they laughed together.

More easily, she said, "I still cannot believe any of this is true—the forest, and the two of you, and the fact that my father was the legendary Robin of Sherwood. I went from knowing nothing of my parents to having two of the most well-known of all."

"Aye, it must seem strange."

"Tell me more about this triad everyone keeps talking about, the three of us and the magic."

"'Tis four of us, verily, as it was for Alric, Geofrey, and Lil before us—three of us and Sherwood. The wards were set up at the time of Robin's death."

"Lil told me that, but it makes no sense. How can Sherwood play a part?"

"Sherwood is alive." Sparrow glanced up into the trees that arched above them. "Its soul is a living thing, sacred to the Lord and Lady themselves."

"The god and goddess, you mean. The old religion."

"It never grew old, here. How could it? Its very roots are here, deep in the soil, carried in the light and the water, and the life that burns in the heart of the hare and the hart. The protective wards Lil, Alric, and Geofrey set in place call on that life force, that magic, but the magic itself is far older. Sometimes you can hear it whisper, in the leaves."

"I have heard that. I find it terrifying."

"But it is not! It must seem strange to you, aye, but you should not be afraid, because it is part of what is in you."

"And what are we meant to do—you, me, and Martin? Please tell me, as you understand it."

"With Geofrey's death, the wards that keep us safe and hidden here in Sherwood—and that keep your father's memory alive—are weakened. If the Sheriff dies before we can renew the wards, a new, vital force will be brought in to oppose us. Lil fears Sherwood's magic could fail, then. We will all be in danger."

"And these wards, what are they, exactly?"

"Old magic, raised and woven. They come of belief, and joining."

"So, how do we strengthen them?"

Sparrow hesitated. "Did Lil not tell you?"

"I wish to hear it from you."

"You must choose between us, Martin and me, where to gift your heart. The one you choose will devote himself to you and become the new headman of Oakham. The other will take Alric's place and bond with Sherwood itself."

"With Sherwood?"

"As a priest bonds himself to the church."

"Oh." Wren's golden eyes widened.

Wryly, Sparrow told her, "Martin does not fancy the life of a hermit. Headman is far more to his taste. He will sway you any way he can."

"And you? How do you fancy the place in the forest?"

Not sure how to answer, Sparrow danced around it. A bit roughly, he replied, "Sometimes sacrifices must be made. In Sherwood, they are demanded often. Your own father sacrificed himself, and Lil spent many years away from Geofrey, in Nottingham."

"I see." She gazed away from him, through the trees, and he thought she might leave it there. But she did not.

"How am I supposed to make this vital choice, then? By love? By desire? For the good of all?"

Sparrow did not reply.

"What if I feel no love or desire for either of you?" *Or for both.* Those words remained present but unspoken.

"Only you can make the choice, by the knowing within you. Do not let Martin persuade you, nor I."

"I have no 'knowing' within. I have spent my life in a small stone room, given very few choices. But as for Martin, I do wish he would leave me alone until I can catch my breath."

"Let me defend you from him."

Her eyes narrowed. "How?"

"I will make you a bow, and instruct you in its use. He may keep away, if he sees you occupied. Anyway, archery is my one strength."

She widened her eyes at him again. "Oh, Master Sparrow, I do think you underestimate yourself."

****

"Hold it this way. No, with the fletchings just at your chin, a bit higher."

As Wren raised her elbow, it brushed Sparrow's chest, and he had to close his eyes against the sensation. Since early morn they had worked together using a light bow meant for one of the lads and, with the sun now high in the sky, his resistance wore thin. Wren stood within the curve of his arms, holding the bow in her hands. Occasionally her hair brushed his cheek and he could smell her fragrance, light and beguiling.

Across the clearing, Martin brooded, his eyes constantly upon them, but he had not yet interfered. Madlyn had sent him early to bring the last of Sally's belongings from Oakham and help her settle, but with that done he kicked his heels and grew steadily more restive. Sparrow could feel his tension and judged they were mere moments from a fine explosion. But meanwhile...

He placed his hand beneath Wren's wrist and let his lips brush her ear. "There now. Try again."

He stepped back, and she let her arrow fly. It clove the air cleanly and flew true to the target, perhaps sixty paces off.

"Better!" She turned and flashed him a smile, judging herself. "But not yet good enough."

"You come easy to this," Sparrow said, and meant it. Her stance with the bow was elegant, her form that of someone who had worked for years before the target. Her eyes, as might be expected, were those of a hawk.

"Move the target farther off," she requested. "I would see, can I hit it still."

Without a word, Sparrow complied, while keeping an eye on Martin. Wren followed him into the trees and waited while he hung the target—a ragged sack daubed with markings—on a tall ash tree.

"I did not expect to enjoy this, Sparrow. Thank you for urging me to it."

She looked happy, and he smiled.

In a murmur, she went on, "I can scarcely recall the last time I enjoyed anything so much. Lil's lessons, no doubt. She taught me much, late in the evenings when most of the kitchen slept."

"'Tis a fine thing, discovering a talent. In time, you may come to appreciate other things about Sherwood, as well—the sense of freedom not known in any village or, indeed, any scullery, and even the sense of connection that so worries you now."

"You need not stand whispering! What are you

doing back here among the trees? She is not yours alone, Sparrow, to keep out of sight."

Outrage flashed in Wren's eyes even as she turned on Martin, who stood just behind them with fists planted on his hips, primed for the promised uproar.

"I am not anyone's," Wren told him before Sparrow could draw a breath, "save my own."

Mildly, Sparrow put in, "We were but moving the target."

"And that takes the both of you, does it, off alone?"

"Not alone," Sparrow returned. "Obviously you could still see us."

Martin elbowed Sparrow aside and presented himself to Wren. "I will instruct you with the bow, and the sword as well, if you like. Only put yourself in my hands."

Wren's head came up and her eyes glittered. Sparrow suddenly remembered once seeing a look just like that on Robin's face, before an encounter with the king's guard. He had been a small boy, but it was not a look easily forgotten.

"Get away from me," Wren told Martin.

"Eh?"

"Did you not hear? Are you deaf as well as stupid?"

Martin's anger flamed. "Now, you listen—"

"I will not! I am weary of your voice, Martin Scarlet, and I can no longer bear you watching me endlessly. You are nearly as bad as Lambert."

"Do not say that." Martin reached out to touch her, but her emotions boiled over; she stepped away and raised the bow, arrow well notched.

Something flared in Martin's eyes—passion,

mingled with admiration. "Hey, now—you will not shoot me."

"Are you willing to wager your life on that?"

"Aye. Give me the bow, Wren, and do not behave like a child. There is too much at stake."

"I, behave like a child? It is you, brooding and sulking like an infant denied a sweet."

"You do not understand, Wren, how I feel."

"And you do not care how I feel! Now clear off before I force you to." Golden eyes locked with blue and dared Martin to step wrong. Sparrow, caught and bombarded with the feelings of both, felt scorched. "Go back to Sally," Wren seethed, "where you are wanted. For I do not wish for your company!"

"You do not mean that." Martin, frustrated at last, waved a hand at Sparrow wildly. "You cannot say you prefer him?"

"I renounce the both of you!" And Wren cast down bow and arrows, spun on her heel, and pelted away into the forest.

Martin and Sparrow were left staring at one another.

"Aye, fine work, that!" Sparrow said scathingly.

Chapter Twelve

"The good God preserve me from arrogant men!" The words rumbled in Rennie's throat as she ran blindly, heading nowhere but away. Roots caught at the toes of her soft skin boots, and branches whipped her face. Tears filled her eyes, but she ran on, deeper and deeper into the trees, trying to leave her confusion and frustration behind.

What a relief to be away from the people in camp, with their assumptions and expectations. Her heart bounded and rose in her chest. And how free it felt to run in a lad's clothing, no tangled or ragged skirts to hold her down, no false modesty to hamper her stride.

She ran until the breath seared her lungs and then paused to listen for sounds of pursuit. She could not imagine Martin failing to come after her. But she heard nothing save the soughing of the wind in the branches overhead. Suddenly the stillness penetrated, and filled her with awe.

Where was she? And how would she ever find her way back? She quieted her breathing and took stock of her position. A wild place, indeed. The ground before her sloped downward slightly, clothed in moss as green as velvet, the trees so close together they cast deep wells of shadow. The oaks, just leafing out, looked like the boles of a great cathedral, but the ash, elder, and beech trembled like live things.

Rennie blinked. Aye, and they were live things, and though she had fled in order to be alone, she found herself far from solitary.

Something flashed far overhead—a bird?—and a shadow moved at the corner of her vision. The trees seemed to gather still nearer, to bend and whisper her name. She could feel life moving in them, and they watched her. Surely something did.

Solitude, amid a rush of confusion, was familiar to her. Just so had she spent all her life, alone yet not alone, in the scullery. Was anyone less visible than the slave who scrubbed and toted endless mounds of pots and platters until her hands bled? Folk thought no more of her than of the wood that warmed them. Yet this felt different. Sherwood seemed aware of her, and she remembered what Sparrow had said—the forest itself had sentience, and a spirit.

Ah, but what nonsense. They were mad, all of them, these wolfsheads. How did they expect her to accept either Sparrow or Martin into her life—and, presumably, her bed—while the other supposedly wed himself to the essence of this place? She wanted no man. She wanted no one to have a say in her life, ever again.

"Wren?"

She turned her head sharply, thinking one of them had followed her after all, and saw no one. A shiver traced its way up her spine. She could not stay here, yet she needed a chance to catch her breath before returning to face them again.

If she could even find her way back...

She narrowed her eyes at the light sifting down through the branches and forming bars like golden ladders. How far had she fled? Days grew longer with the coming Spring, but she knew once night fell here it would fall hard and completely. She dared not let it catch her so close to Sherwood's heart.

Wren.

The whisper came from behind her this time, and spun her around. A spike of terror widened her eyes.

Wren, Wren, Wren—

No human voice, this, nor from any mortal throat. A sudden shudder gripped her, shook her as if she had the ague. She needed to run, but which way?

Listen.

Her ears must be playing tricks on her. What she heard was but the rustling of the leaves. Her mind had unhinged itself and now flew off like a bird. Aye, it must be the birds she felt, watching, or a deer or a wolf. She could not allow herself to be trapped here tonight, or she would likely become prey for that last—the wolfshead's daughter, brought to her end by wolves...

Carefully she turned back the way she had come, trying not to hear the voices around her, expecting at any moment to hear the cries of the two young men—Martin and Sparrow, both skilled in the wood, could surely find her.

She raised her fingers to one stinging cheek. They came away wet with blood. Would that be enough to draw whatever watched her? Fear speared her suddenly, and she ran once more.

****

Distance passed in a blur of green and brown, bark and leaves, that swallowed time. Rennie suspected it swallowed her soul, as well, for when she paused again her senses tingled, so linked with the forest she could not tell where the trees ended and she began. Deer kept pace with her, and hares, foxes, other creatures unseen but felt, and birds by the score trailed in her wake.

And the dark came down. Utterly lost, Rennie wrapped her arms about herself and began to pray.

She had never felt much need for religion. All the castle servants were required to attend chapel, but that made a cold, colorless exercise in no way connected to worship. Now, however, awe and terror filled Rennie's heart, and something akin to belief bloomed in her mind.

Lil spoke often of the Green Man—her personal god—the Lord who predated Christ by countless centuries and dwelled in the earth itself, the trees, the fire. With his companion, the Lady, they begat all life. Here and now, for the first time, Rennie could sense him.

Exhausted, she fell to her knees on the bank of a stream, cupped her hands, and drank. The water, cold and flavored with the taste of leaves, peat, and the earth itself, filled her. Above the restless trees, the sky was the color of the robes the Sheriff wore to high mass, deep blue, almost purple.

"Wren." The voice, just behind her, sounded almost conversational. Rennie spun around so fast she nearly fell into the stream. Breath clenched in her lungs.

In the gathering gloom, the man looked tall and slender, a shadow seen only indistinctly. But she knew him, had seen him numerous times in both dream and imagination.

He smiled at her, a kind smile that lit grave, intent eyes—not the color of Rennie's, no, she must have those from the mother she never knew either. But his hair was hers, thick and rich brown, tumbling to his shoulders. And something in the structure of his face echoed Rennie's, the slant of the cheekbones and jut of the nose.

A sob burst from her throat. "You are dead."

"Aye. But I live on, here in Sherwood. That to which we give our love in life is never lost."

Rennie continued to examine him through narrowed eyes. This must be how he had looked at the time of his death, strong and handsome, vital as the forest itself.

"May I sit?" he asked, gesturing to the bank beside her.

Rennie made a futile gesture. Could she deny him?

He wore clothing almost identical to her own and, once he sat, she might have reached out and touched him, though she was careful not to.

"I have seen you before, in dreams."

"Long have I tried to reach you, Daughter, to tell you the importance of your place here."

There, he had said it: daughter. A chill chased its way through Rennie's limbs.

"Never was I successful. Lil has guided you well, but Lil's season is nearly done."

"What does that mean?"

"Wren, life is a series of cycles. The flesh rises and falls, as do the stars in the sky; the spirit endures."

"Are you saying Lil is going to die?" Fear gripped Rennie's heart. No, not that. Anything else.

Her father did not answer directly. "The three of you—Sparrow, Martin, and yourself—must prepare to take your places on the wheel."

"The wheel?"

"Of life."

"But I do not want—"

"Daughter, do you think I wanted what I became? I had a talent for hitting a target true, and a stubborn dislike for bending my back to those who called themselves my betters, no more than that. I could have been happy tilling a plot of garden and living in obscurity. Do you think I wished to become wolfshead and legend?" His voice softened. "Do you think I wanted to die before I could see you born, or watch you grow?"

"It is not fair," Rennie cried, suddenly aware of how much she would have liked knowing this man.

"It is not fair," he agreed, "when a child is born into serfdom, an old woman bled to death for the king's taxes, or the father of a family deprived of his hand, so those he loves must starve. There is but one thing fair about our world."

"And, what is that?"

He smiled at her again. "That love does not die but rides the wheel and goes round until it meets again with those who love. Wren, I loved you before you were born, and I regret the place you must inhabit is so hard, but there is no help for it. You must do as you must do."

Rennie swallowed a lump in her throat. "And, what is that?"

"Keep the magic strong. You three are the only ones who can."

"Me, Martin, and Sparrow." Rennie linked her fingers desperately. "I am not sure I can stand it."

"Neither was I, when first I felt the hope of a people, like the weight of the world, on my shoulders.

But, Wren, there is joy in the magic of it."

"They keep talking of this magic. Where is it? I see only the wishes of others, and obligation."

"Then you are not looking." He gestured to the trees around them. "It is in the wild places, in the water, the wind, the soil the roots hold, deep, and the fire of the stars. The fire, here, as well." He pressed his fist to his chest.

Ruefully, Rennie said, "Martin has the fire, enough to scorch us all."

"As did his father before him. Scarlet burned very bright. Martin is right to harbor the flame and guard it well—it is sore needed. Should we let anger at injustice die? Are we not, then, dead ourselves?"

"So you say I am to choose him? For it seems I must choose, though I desire not, or," she added all too truthfully, "desire both."

Her father smiled yet again. "You must choose, aye, but only as your heart directs."

Stubbornly, Rennie said, "Love cannot be forced, and that is what Martin would do—force me."

"It is his way, to take life into his hands and grapple with it. Do not underestimate the valiant nature of his heart."

"What of Sparrow?"

"A quiet heart, but no less devoted, and no less deep."

"I am to decide, through my choice, which of them will be headman and which holy man?"

"Aye."

"On the face of it, Sparrow would make the better hermit, with the quiet in him. I cannot imagine Martin wed to Sherwood."

"No? Yet opposite forces do call to one another, and fit just because they are two halves of the whole." Robin held out his hand, and a hare pushed forward from the underbrush and came to him, almost lost in the gloom. "I never could have imagined your mother would wed with me."

Rennie asked, with sudden hunger, "What was she like? Lil made a fine mother to me, but I have always wondered."

"Aye. Marian was a ward of the Sheriff when I met her, he having stolen her father's lands. She was strong and rebellious, and fled to Sherwood, where she encountered our band. You have her eyes."

"Lil says my mother died for love of you."

Robin remained silent.

"I want that kind of love," Rennie admitted, "the kind that knows no bounds, would give anything—but perhaps I do not deserve it."

"Each spirit, Daughter, deserves its fill of love, as love is its remembered home. There is love in Sherwood, and you are of the forest, lass, conceived and born here. Ask for Sherwood's help in making your decision."

"Ask—the trees?"

"Why not? There is help to be found."

Rennie looked up and around the small clearing. Scores of eyes watched them, faces but vaguely seen in the gathering dusk—not only Robin's hare but deer, owls, mice, a fox. For the first time, she found their presence comforting.

"Thank you. I—" she began to say to her father. But when she returned her gaze to him, he had faded from sight.

Chapter Thirteen

"Wren? Wren, where are you?"

The call, soft yet persistent, cut through Rennie's restless slumber and brought her awake. Morning light drifted through the trees, and birds sang and fluttered above her head. With difficulty, she sought to remember how she had come here, to the deep forest.

Was it her father who called to her? She had dreamed of him—Robin—dreamed they sat and spoke together while the wild things listened all around them. But no, this sounded not like her father's voice.

"Wren? I know you are nearby. I can feel you."

She scrambled up from the place where she lay, on a bed of moss beside a fallen tree, and her hair swung around her. It was full of twigs and leaves, and the very scent of Sherwood pervaded her clothing. She felt as much a part of the forest as those creatures to which Robin had beckoned, last night. But for all the wildness that surrounded her, something in her heart had settled.

"Sparrow?"

He slipped between two trees and materialized beside her. In his garb of green and brown, with his brown hair and secretive eyes, he seemed to embody the forest the same way her father had, when she sat and spoke with him. But surely that had been a dream.

"Thanks be to Herne," Sparrow breathed. "Are you all right?"

Rennie nodded. Moving softly still, Sparrow stepped forward and took her into his arms.

Rennie's heart expanded; she felt it rise, and then soar. She allowed herself to shelter against Sparrow's shoulder for one moment, then drew away and looked into his face.

He spoke before she could. "We have been half frantic with worry. We searched everywhere."

"'We'?"

"Myself, Martin, Simon—everyone who could be spared. What made you run off that way? You do not yet know enough about the forest to spend a night here alone."

But I was not alone. Rennie did not voice the thought. Instead she gazed into Sparrow's dark eyes, sampling his unspoken emotions. "What is it? What has happened?"

Sorrowfully, he answered, "Lil."

****

"What has befallen her? Please tell me she is not dead." The words, breathless, came raggedly from Rennie's throat as she and Sparrow ran, hand in hand. He knew where he was going, and she put her trust in that.

"We do not know much. Word was brought from Nottingham last night, not long after you left. She has been arrested and accused of witchcraft. I came looking for you then, and learned nothing more."

The ache in Rennie's chest increased. "It is a grave charge."

"Indeed. Wilfred, who brought word—he is a guard at the castle, and in with us—said she is to appear before the Sheriff as soon as he is well enough."

"Where is she now?"

"The dungeon."

"No!" Rennie stumbled and slowed to a halt, dragging Sparrow with her. The dungeons at Nottingham were legendary, stinking holes where torture and pestilence reigned. Few people ever came out alive. "She cannot be there! I cannot bear it." No, not Lil with all her wisdom and generous spirit. "She has been everything to me, all my life."

Sparrow grimaced in sympathy. "I know."

"What says Alric? He will never leave her there?" If the dungeons did not kill her, trial for witchcraft could.

"I have not heard him say anything, yet. Come!"

They ran again, and kept at it until the breath rasped in Rennie's lungs. A crowd awaited them at the wolfsheads' camp. Martin saw them first and broke away to seize hold of Rennie, what looked like bright anger vivid in his eyes.

"Where have you been? What is the matter with you, haring off like that?"

She pulled away from him and ignored the questions. "What goes on?"

"I barely know—I just returned from searching for you. Wren, do not do that again."

She glared at him defiantly. "I shall do what I wish, especially if you two insist on growling over me like two dogs with a bone. Now, let us go listen."

Alric stood at the center of the crowd, his white hair streaming across his shoulders, his face troubled. He shot one look at the three of them when they joined the group, which included a large number of villagers and what must be outlaws from farther afield in

Sherwood.

"An accusation of witchcraft cannot be brought without certain claims of evidence. And it must be answered by trial, over which the Sheriff, himself, must preside. He is said to be near death."

"Who has brought the accusation?" someone called out—Adam, of Oakham.

"Wilfred, will you speak?"

Another man stepped forward. He wore the garb of a castle guard. He it must be who had brought the word of Lil's arrest. "No one seems to know, but I suspect it was Sir Udolf Lambert. From what we have been able to learn, he complained his food, gotten from the Nottingham kitchens, was hexed. It made a furor in the dining hall, people falling about and thinking themselves harmed. No one was seriously hurt, but after that the accusation against Lil was made."

"Just because she is in charge of the kitchens?" asked Simon.

Rennie shook her head. "No, he wants revenge against me. He does not believe Lil's claims that she knows not where I have gone. He is punishing her the worst way possible." Grief flooded her, sorrow that Lil, who had never been aught but loving and kind, should suffer for her sake.

Alric inclined his head. "A harsh punishment, indeed. We know not what the trial itself may involve. But few have ever survived, in any case." He looked at Rennie sadly. "Lil is a strong woman. But she is no longer young."

A murmur rose among the onlookers, fear and incipient grief.

"An added difficulty," Alric went on, "is that Lil

represents the second part of Sherwood's protective triad, now in danger of being lost. Should she fall, Sherwood and all who depend on her will be open to the worst kind of danger."

Rennie felt someone take her hand. At first she thought it was Sparrow. The feelings and sensations bombarding her made it impossible to tell. But Martin stepped forward, bringing her with him by their linked fingers.

"Father, we will not leave Lil there, in the hands of the dark-minded. Surely we will rescue her?"

Rennie's heart lifted with sudden hope. Yes, surely love alone would mount the effort.

But Alric looked at Martin sorrowfully. "A rescue from Nottingham's dungeons? It is a steep task."

"My father accomplished it, in the past," Martin declared, "along with Robin and other members of his band. Did they not once rescue Alan Adale and John Little himself?"

"Indeed," Alric conceded. "But that was Robin Hood."

"And we have Robin's daughter!" Martin lifted Rennie's hand high, and his voice rang with confidence. "Was she not born to be invincible?"

"No one is invincible," said Alric, almost kindly. "Robin was."

"My son, Robin fell to a hail of arrows and with a score of wounds."

"Aye," Martin met the words swiftly, "but that did not overturn his legend, or his spirit! He has remained alive, we have kept him so, each one of us who believes. You, Master, and Lil and Geofrey—ask anyone in Nottingham if they believe Robin Hood still lives and fights for justice, and they will answer, 'Aye.' Now it is time for Wren, Sparrow, and me to take it up. Robin would not leave Lil there, and by the blood of the Green Man himself, we are Robin!"

The bold words stirred Rennie's blood and heightened the hope in her own heart. She thought of her conversation with her father last night. How true it was that he lived still in Sherwood, part of its magic. Perhaps, truly, he could never die. For the first time, a sense of what these folk strove to accomplish, and what the triad actually meant, touched her. She wanted to be part of that.

She could feel Martin's strength, his power, flowing to her through their linked hands. His confidence might have been a magical spell for the way it lifted the spirits of those gathered.

"Very well." Alric inclined his head. "I bow to you, Martin Scarlet. But you will need a careful and canny plan."

"Aye. Who is with me, for Lil's sake?"

Nearly everyone there clamored. Rennie turned her head, and her eyes met Sparrow's, dark and guarded. He remained silent.

Martin's fingers squeezed Rennie's hard. "Wren?"

"I will do aught I can to help Lil."

"There. You hear courage, Robin's courage!" Martin declared. "With Robin's daughter on our side, can we fail?"

Excitement rose; a number of people stepped forward with suggestions, from the daring to the fanciful.

"Go under cover of night."

"Have Robin's girl cast a spell to stun the Sheriff's

95

guards."

"Use magic to spirit our Lil from that dungeon."

At last, Wilfred stepped forward. "I may be able to get you into the castle, but I do not see a way to get in or out of the dungeons themselves. The best chance would be to wait for the trial and snatch Lil on her way."

"But that may not happen for days, weeks." Rennie surprised herself by speaking. "Can Lil survive so long?" She fixed Wilfred with a stare. "You will know the truth. Just how bad are these dungeons?"

He shrugged and looked uncomfortable. "They are, my lady, vile holes full of filth and suffering. If she be left there until that villain, the Sheriff, makes up his mind to die—"

"Then we cannot leave her there," Rennie decided. "Surely so many minds can think of a means of rescue."

"Aye, that is my lass," said Martin softly, and squeezed her fingers again. "You will plan a rescue."

She cast him a look. "It is, I think, just what my father would have done."

Chapter Fourteen

"You look precisely how I feel." The soft voice, just at Sparrow's shoulder, caused him to start and pull his gaze away from the couple sitting on the other side of the clearing. Sally stood beside him, her pretty face clouded by grief and another emotion, locked down tight. "Yet I can promise you, staring at them will change nothing."

"Was I staring?" Sparrow asked, dismayed.

"Endlessly, ever since he promised her they would rescue Lil."

Ruefully, Sparrow met Sally's eyes, green as leaves and full of wisdom. "They have been inseparable since then." Three days, and Wren had virtually lived and slept by Martin's side. Intense huddles, endless meetings with Wilfred and others from inside Nottingham, planning sessions with Alric. Sparrow had barely spoken to her in all that time.

Had she chosen already?

"Why not?" Sally's voice oozed pain. "Can love not come so swiftly as that? And was she not born to love one of you?"

"Aye, but why him?"

Sally's smile was hard and rueful. "Look at him. Is he not everything any sane woman might desire? Handsome, bold, courageous, and the very essence of Sherwood. I, myself, loved him from the moment I saw him."

"You were but a child then."

"Aye, and all that time I have never looked at another. Did you know he slept with me all last winter?"

Sparrow knew. He had half envied Martin—to whom things came so easily—but not half as fiercely as now.

"I thought I had won his heart, back when the snow fell. But now he turns away from me as lightly as if I never mattered to him."

"I am sorry," Sparrow told her awkwardly. "You have lost much." Her father, her home, and now Martin, who poured his attention and charm over Wren with a persistence that bordered on the maniacal.

"I have lost everything," Sally corrected. "You probably think I should have some pride. But what I feel overweighs that."

Sparrow understood. Oh, how he understood.

"One thing I do know." Sally gave Sparrow another, bitter smile. "Watching them changes nothing. It only deepens the pain."

"You are right. Yet I cannot seem to help myself." Already Sparrow had memorized everything about Wren—the precise color of her hair, the length of her limbs, the grace with which she moved, and the flash of intelligence in her eyes. He liked to keep watch for her smile, rare and fleeting, loved the way she handled a bow or stood, sometimes, gazing up into the trees as if listening for something, or someone.

"Can you keep a secret?" Sally asked, lowering her voice.

"Aye." Sparrow bent his head closer to hers.

"I am carrying his child. Martin's."

Sparrow's stomach plummeted. "Are you sure?"

She gazed away and nodded. "I show all the signs."

"By God, Sally! How far—?"

"I would say three months, maybe a bit more. Not so he can tell."

"He needs to know, Sal."

Her expression grew mutinous. "No. You promised me, Sparrow."

"But that is not a thing to be kept from a man."

"He wants her, now. He wants the place at her side, as headman of Oakham. Deny that is so."

Sparrow could not deny it.

"But he deserves to know."

"Do not be a fool, Sparrow. He has but one thing in his mind, and 'tis not me, nor any child of mine."

"Of his, you mean."

"I mean to take care of it, Sparrow."

"How is that?"

"There are ways to lose a babe—drenchings and potions. I meant to go to Lil."

Sparrow's heart dropped still further. "Lil would never help you do such a thing."

"No? Well, there are other women who will. Gert, over in West Riding—"

"She is no better than a butcher. Sally, listen to me. Children born in Sherwood are rare and special, often important, often blessed."

"This one will not be born here, nor at all."

"Have you spoken to Madlyn of this?" Her first grandchild—surely Madlyn would fight for its preservation.

"Not a word." Sally tossed at him before walking

off. She did not look back.

Sparrow clenched his fists against a sudden urge to hit someone—Martin, preferably, to knock some sense into him. Why could the man not see what lay before him? Sally went round with her heart in her eyes. Was Martin truly such a prize?

You are jealous, lad, Sparrow told himself, and knew it for truth. Why could Wren not look at him the way she looked at Martin, with trust and admiration? That one shared kiss had made him believe she felt something for him, yet in the three days since they received word about Lil, she had stuck to Martin like a burdock. Seldom did Sparrow see her chestnut head without Martin's shaggy, fair one beside it.

Except now.

Sparrow watched as Martin walked away, his sword in his hand, and left Wren standing on her own beneath the tall beech at the northeast corner of camp.

Sparrow wasted no time in approaching her. She looked up at him with a guarded expression, strained and grim.

"Where has Martin gone?" he asked before he could stop himself.

"Something is amiss with the pommel of his sword. He means to take it to the smith at Oakham."

A miracle! Sparrow drew a breath. "Come walk with me."

"No."

"Eh?" Her abrupt refusal made Sparrow cock his head.

Wren sighed. "I am not in the mood for a stroll in the forest."

"You seem to have plenty of time for Martin." As

soon as he spoke the words, Sparrow wanted to thump himself.

The look in her eyes cooled; now he could see lines of weariness in her face. "Listen to me, Sparrow. I care nothing for any rivalry between the two of you. I care for nothing at all save Lil, and I have not slept since the news about her came. Whatever you wish to say to me, you can say here."

Sparrow's spine stiffened. "I understand you are distraught. We all care about Lil. But this scheme of entering the castle is ill-conceived."

"Is it?"

"Aye. You may as well put Martin's sword to your own throat as take yourself into Nottingham." Why did he hurl these hard words at her when he wanted so badly to take her in his arms? She wore an air of toughness and showed, always, such a desire to fight. But he could sense the vulnerability underneath it all, and he longed to kiss those lips she barely kept from trembling.

"You chide me, Sparrow, for spending my time with Martin. Yet he has offered me a plan, a means to the one thing I desire—winning Lil free. She has been a mother to me." Wren blinked against tears. "The only one I have known. I would follow Martin anywhere in order to save her."

"What is this grand scheme of Martin's, then?" Sparrow asked, not without an edge.

"Of his and Wilfred's, for we shall have help inside—Wilf, plus others within the castle who are sympathetic to our cause. Many there love Lil and are unhappy about her imprisonment. In the evening at the close of market day, when folk are still coming and going, we will gain entry to the castle proper. Martin says that has already been done successfully, many times."

"So it has."

"Wilfred will meet us there, he and another guard named Cedric, who is in with us and who means to wrangle for himself duty at the dungeons."

"How?"

"Eh?"

"Lambert does not seem a man whose plans are easily manipulated."

"Martin says Wilfred is confident."

"Does he? What then?"

"Wilf leads us in, and we take Lil away with us."

"As easy as that, eh?"

"Do not patronize me, Sparrow. I do not hear you offering anything better. In fact, I do not hear you offering at all. At least Martin has the courage to try."

"Oh, aye, Martin has courage in buckets, some of it the foolhardy variety. Why must you go, and endanger yourself?"

"Shall I ask anyone else to take a risk greater than I am willing to take myself?"

Sparrow blinked; it might be Robin Hood himself speaking. Not that Sparrow remembered him well, but his parents had told him scores of stories about Robin taking the lead in perilous situations, because he would ask no one else to undertake what he refused.

"No," he said softly. "Yet I do believe it wiser to wait until Lil is brought forth for trial."

Wren challenged him with her eyes. "And if she does not survive that long? If the Sheriff dies and she is left where she is, to rot?"

Sparrow, unable to help himself, reached out and smoothed her wild hair. He knew his touch would allow her to feel his concern and anxiety. "And should Lambert catch sight of you? What then?"

"Surely he has forgotten all about one lowly peasant who spurned him, among the many he has forced?"

"One who broke his cheekbone."

"I shall go in disguise. Look, Sparrow, I appreciate your desire to protect me, a mere woman."

"It is not that."

"But if you truly wish to do something useful, teach me to shoot well enough to pick a guard off the wall above the foregate."

Sparrow sighed deeply. Had he any choice? "Very well. Come along with you, then."

Chapter Fifteen

"She watches you still. I vow, Martin, Sally scarcely takes her eyes from you."

Martin glanced across the clearing to where Sally sat with Madlyn, supposedly sorting herbs yet keeping him and Rennie under a careful eye instead. He said carelessly, "Let her stare, if she will."

Rennie shot him a cool look. This last seven-night she and Martin had been virtually inseparable, doing everything but sleeping together—and to be honest, Rennie had considered even that. Martin possessed potent, if wild and dangerous, charm. Perhaps the wildness made part of the attraction, Rennie admitted. And the more time they spent together, the closer the bond she could feel between them. The fact was, he had stolen more than one kiss while they were alone, and she had felt the fire in him. And she found the idea of losing herself in that heat beguiling.

And, if she did, might she not then belong somewhere, to someone?

"It makes me uneasy," she confessed, "being constantly under her eye."

Martin paused and a wicked smile came to his face. "Let us give her something to see, then." He drew Rennie up hard against him. Instantly his warmth and strength enfolded her, both thrilling and disturbing. She could feel not only his body but his emotions, hard and confident, a heady combination. Not for the first time, she wondered how it would feel to lie with a man she could sense so intensely.

He placed his lips close to her ear. "Kiss me, Lady Wren."

Rennie's pulse began to drum, yet she drew away slightly. "Here? Now?"

"Here. Now."

"You possess an evil streak, Martin Scarlet."

"Look into my eyes, and you will see it is more than a paltry streak."

Rennie almost feared gazing into his eyes. She had heard there were creatures that could mesmerize their prey with a stare. She suspected she might fall into that sea of blue-gray and never resurface.

"Nay," she told him. "We have important work to do." Tomorrow, it being market day, they would journey to Nottingham and attempt a bold rescue. Word from the castle had proved scant and unsatisfying, but the Sheriff still lay far too ill to conduct Lil's trial. And so Lil languished yet in her cell, Lambert conducted castle business, and rumor had it he planned to execute a number of prisoners on May Day, now but a few days off.

"All our allies are in place, and will keep their word?" she asked Martin, not for the first time. "You are certain?"

"Aye, it is as I told you. A few days hence we will be celebrating, and you will be so grateful to me you will deny me nothing." Rennie knew him well enough, now, to recognize this as teasing, which Martin enjoyed full well. Of course, his badgering conveyed much intent. Now he lowered his voice to a purr. "Then again, you might reward me beforehand, so to stoke my courage."

Rennie could not deny she enjoyed the banter, and his kisses. "What had you in mind?"

"Come, and I will show you." Suddenly her hand was in his and they were moving off through the trees. Madness, Rennie thought, her practical side rearing its head even as something inside her responded to this spontaneity. The encounter had been days in coming, so she felt little surprise when, once out of sight, he paused and backed her against a tree.

"Now then, Wren—you know full well what I want. Being so close to you all this while has driven me half desperate with need. Say you will not make me wait. Let us plight ourselves to one another before we go to Nottingham."

Rennie struggled to catch her breath. The heat of his body—so hard and intense—trapped her and ignited her own desire. But was that what giving herself to him would mean: a plight, a vow, a choice made?

She found it so hard to think with his emotions beating at her, along with her own. "Martin, I do not know that I am ready."

"I am ready enough for both of us."

Aye, and she could feel that right through his leather breeches. The man must be a right bull.

She managed to meet his eyes. "I have never yet lain with any man."

"Aye, well, Wren, I want to be the first. The only." Suddenly his hand plunged into her hair. Hot as his touch felt, still it made Rennie shiver. "Give yourself to me now." The words were demand, and temptation.

"Here? Out among the trees?"

"What better than to couple in Sherwood?" His gaze held her as surely as his hands. And suddenly Rennie found herself more than half convinced. What could be more right?

A sound she did not recognize came from the back of her throat. Taking it for assent, Martin kissed her.

So far, every kiss he had given her blazed with heat and masterful possession; this one surpassed them all. His lips drove hers apart and his tongue touched hers. Fire poured through her from that point of contact, stealing all resistance. The force of his will bore her over, and her good sense flew away.

Oh, but he tasted of nut-brown ale and danger and irresistible desire. His beard scraped her chin and his hands seemed to be everywhere, roaming her body as freely as if he owned it. The laces of her tunic proved no barrier to him. She felt the cool air caress her skin but an instant before his hand covered her breast.

This felt nothing like when Lambert had touched her, nothing like. Martin's rough, callused palm abraded skin made suddenly alive with sensation and brought a hard rush of pleasure.

By the holy Lady, she had never imagined anything like this.

And still his hands moved; one cupped the weight of her breast and the other wandered downward even as his body bore hers back against the tree. How had his clever fingers got past the barrier of her leggings? She wore nothing beneath, and his knee nudged her legs apart; his fingers went where she barely dared touch herself.

Rennie gasped, but his mouth was there and swallowed the sound. His fingers mimicked the movement of his tongue, spearing, stroking, and an entirely wicked thought invaded Rennie's mind: what if that tongue replaced those fingers?

Now he groaned and broke the kiss to gaze into her eyes and whisper, just as if he had heard the thought in her mind, "Wren, let me show you."

He slid down her body, to his knees. Rennie seized his golden mane, digging her fingers deep, and he laughed softly. The sound further ignited Rennie's blood.

But oh, she could not let him. Surely such a thing might steal her very soul.

"Martin, nay!"

"Oh, aye." Gently, he parted her thighs. She felt his lips—or was it his tongue?—brush her private heat and stiffened in alarm.

"You cannot. Martin, by God!"

"God, or the devil?" He gazed up at her, his eyes dancing with naughty light.

Unable to face that look, she dropped to the ground and hid her face against him.

His voice wrapped around her like the purr of a cat. "Wren, do you know how lovely you are, how much I want you? Give yourself to me now, before we face the danger ahead, so I go knowing you are mine."

He did not await her answer but laid her down beneath him, there on the moss below the trees, just as if he had done so a hundred times. His desire—and Rennie's—made a powerful spell, and she lay gazing up at him wonderingly. The sun made a nimbus of his hair, and she could no longer see what lay in his eyes.

"Give yourself to me," he urged again, "and let it be settled between us. I swear, you shall never be disappointed in me."

His hand went to the laces on his leggings, now straining against the weight of him. Rennie's own pulse pounded in her ears; she knew if she let him he would play her body the way a minstrel played a lute. And there would be no going back from it. She did not just choose her own pleasure, but the very cast of the future and, perhaps, the fate of Sherwood.

But he did not wait for an answer. Her tunic had fallen open, and he bent his head and took the tip of one breast into his mouth.

Ah, sweet holy heaven, she had never felt such a sensation. Warm, daring, it made her desire dance— clever tongue and clever fingers also, that once more entered her and made her entire body begin to thrum. Rennie closed her eyes against the unbearable pleasure, the tickle of his beard on her skin, the soft tug of his lips, that soon became so demanding she arched herself into him.

She could feel his strength, his muscles bulging, his desire raging like a fire in dry tinder, and knew, despite the overweening pleasure, she must stop him now, if at all.

And she must stop him, for she was not ready, she was not sure.

"No." Somehow she forced the word through a throat gone suddenly dry, and against a desire that cried out just the opposite. For an instant she thought he did not hear. Then he took his lips from her breast and gazed into her eyes, all demand.

"Choose me, Wren—choose me now. Let me fill you, and forge our bond."

Rennie fought for breath. It would be so easy to

open her legs to him, open her soul to him, and let this happen. Yet among all the impulses screaming inside her, one thought held her back. "Do you want me, or the place?"

"Eh?" The bright eyes narrowed quizzically. "I want you, Wren. You are like drink in my blood. If you doubt it, let me show you." He had freed himself from his leggings and now pressed his hot, scorching heft against her. Rennie's eyes widened; he possessed a mighty weapon.

Yet she had begun to know him, what dwelled inside him. These many days, she had felt his emotions. Martin Scarlet was a man driven, and not merely by desire.

What of love? Neither the word, nor any hint of it, had crossed those clever lips of his. Was she to be denied love in the cause of duty, in the service of this triad, set to rule her life?

She planted both palms on his chest, where she felt his heart thumping. "No."

"Wren, you know not what you are saying." He snuggled himself more firmly between her thighs. "Together we can achieve anything. Have you not felt that?"

"I do not know what I feel."

"Then place yourself in my hands and I will tell you—"

"I just wager you will." She shoved him harder and in response her emotions fell into place. "You wish to beguile me, Martin Scarlet. But you will not. Get off!"

The expression in his eyes changed, and anger licked through him. Rennie warranted he did not often hear refusals. He did not budge. "This is how it must be, Wren."

Her anger rose, a reflection of his, even as had her desire. "What makes you think I would choose you?"

He sharpened like a blade. "So, that is it. Sparrow." He spat the name. "Do you mean to let him have you instead? To claim you?"

"Is that what it means to you—claiming?"

"Has he touched you here? And here?" The light in his eyes turned cruel and his fingers, at her breast and between her legs, pinched. "Will you be his kitchen slut, after all?"

She slapped him, not even taking time to think about it. "Fine one to talk, you—still warm from Sally's bed."

"Just tell me you do not mean to lie with Sparrow, or I swear I will beat the snot out of him."

"Get your hands from me!" On a rush of rage, Rennie heaved him off and scrambled to her feet. "What I do, and with whom, is my affair."

"That is where you are wrong." He leaped up also, quick as lightning. "Stupid lass—what you do affects us all."

Chapter Sixteen

"This is a doomed enterprise. I am surprised you are willing to condone it," Sparrow told Alric in a grim undertone.

"I cannot count the doomed enterprises in which I have participated during the course of my life. Some of them, I dare say, even kept me alive. Besides, my son, it is only doomed if you declare it so."

"That is a fine sentiment for a sunny day, which this is not."

True enough. Rain pissed down, soaking their small party as they tramped toward Nottingham. The weather, or so claimed Martin and Wilfred, who had hatched the plan, would prove a benefit rather than an obstacle. Heavy rain tended to render the guard careless, and provided cover. Folk wished to be in out of the wet.

"Why do you accompany us," Alric asked, "if you think so little of the venture?"

Sparrow raised his eyes to Wren's back, some distance ahead of him. She looked less like a woman than a lad near-grown, tall and long of limb, walking with her bow on her shoulder and her hood raised against the wet. She strode beside Martin and yet, somehow, not with him. Between the two of them something ineffable had changed.

Sparrow could not place his finger on it.

"You know why," he said, gloomily.

"I think I do." Alric shot him another look. "You do not want my place."

"Your—? Oh, no, it is not that."

"Ah, then," Alric laughed softly, "it must be love."

"'Tis certainly no laughing matter."

"Forgive me. To be sure, it is not. I know that right well, having myself suffered its pangs in the past."

"You?"

Alric grinned ruefully. "Aye, lad. You look at me now, white-haired and with age in my limbs, and cannot imagine it, eh? But I have stood where you stand."

"Lil?"

"Ah, likely you do not remember her when she was young, either, but she was a woman to beguile a man's heart, full of wisdom, strength, and kindness—magic, too."

"And you loved her then."

"I love her yet. And now I must think on her languishing in some vile cell, shut away from the light she requires, awaiting pain and death. So, my lad, do not tell me what mad plan you would undertake until you need face that."

"I only wish Wren were not involved. Why must she go back into Nottingham? It is too risky. We cannot stand to lose her."

"Or yourself, or Martin. It is the three of you together that hold the magic, you see. That is something I learned long ago, when Lil chose Geofrey over me. I was equally important to her, only in a different way."

"You have powers of prophecy, do you not, Father?"

"Sometimes, when the gods let me see."

"Then tell me how this will turn out."

"If I did not think we had a chance of success, I would not be here. Yet"—for the first time the old man frowned—"there is something..."

"Danger to Wren?" Sparrow nodded at her back.

"Danger—aye, to someone we love."

****

"The weather could scarcely be more vile," Wilfred said earnestly. "And I know what happens on such nights when the dark comes down. Despite Sir Lambert's orders, the guards stay under cover and neglect their posts. I will part from you here, and go to admit you at the west gate."

Everyone in the little group nodded. Grim and silent, already wet to the bone, they made a miserable cluster of four after Wilfred slipped away: Sparrow, Wren, Martin and Alric—who would not enter Nottingham but meant to await them outside. Cedric, a man Wilfred swore was friendly to their cause, would meet them near the dungeons and lead them on to the cells and Lil herself. With luck and the right timing, they might not need to do so much as strike a blow.

The dungeon master rarely stayed on after his shift, and the guards who remained on duty suffered the woes of boredom. It would be Wren's job to distract them long enough for her companions to gain access to Lil's cell. And that was the part of the plan Sparrow did not like.

Now, standing in a close group and waiting for Wilf to open the west gate from within, he could feel her tension, and Martin's. Once again, he wondered what had happened between them. Just a day ago, they had been thick as thieves; now they scarcely looked at one another. Despite the perilous conditions, Sparrow's heart rose. Was there hope for him? Perhaps, if they got out of this alive.

"Hsst! Softly." The oaken gate opened with a creak, and Wilf's anxious face welcomed them in. Sparrow's tension ramped up another notch. His arm brushed Wren's shoulder and he received her feelings in a flash—razor-edged fear, and determination.

The guard room into which they were admitted was empty and steeped in gloom. Their wet boots made a disturbingly loud patter on the floor, and Wilf led them on.

"Not a word."

They entered a corridor, and Sparrow's heart began to beat up in his throat. Now they must be prepared at any moment for discovery, and combat.

Yet all Nottingham castle seemed to sleep under enchantment. They traversed passage after passage, Sparrow bringing up the rear and keeping watch behind, and descended more than one flight of stone steps. At the foot of the last, they met Cedric, who waited to conduct them on.

Another few shadowy corridors and they paused while Wilf conferred in whispers with Cedric. "There," Cedric said then. "The cells are just ahead. Can you find your way out, should I fall?"

Martin and Wilf nodded.

"I could not get duty, but wait while I see who did."

Cedric left them standing and disappeared around a bend in the passage. Sparrow's nerves tightened still further; Martin looked tight also, like a bow string, and

Wren stood shivering. Sparrow longed to put his arms around her.

After an interminable wait, Cedric returned, his expression grim. They all drew close and heard him whisper, "Bad luck. Two men on duty, and one is a right bastard. Wren, I hoped we would not need to use you, but—"

Without a word, Wren turned to Sparrow and handed him her bow and quiver. She pushed back her hood and shook out her sopping hair, tugged open the laces of her tunic to reveal a glimpse of pale flesh. As she did, Sparrow received a flash of her emotions, and caught his breath.

"Go carefully," he told her.

Her eyes met his, full of resolve and terror.

Cedric breathed into her ear, "Your target is the big brute on the left. Use any means you can to distract him."

She nodded and moved off, soundless. Sparrow, unbearably tense, listened to what followed.

A clank as of a mug being set down, the scrape of a chair being pushed back, then gruff voices expressing surprise. Martin turned his head and his eyes met Sparrow's, reflecting his agony.

They should never have brought her here, important though Lil's safety might be. Wren was too precious, and the risk too great.

Martin eased his sword from its scabbard. Ahead, Sparrow heard one of the guards say, "What ho! How did you get here, wench? No one is permitted below stairs. Get you off now, before there is hell to pay."

A second, rougher voice objected, "Just a moment, Rolf. Not so fast."

Wren spoke, her voice unrecognizable, low and seductive. "A friend led me in. I come, sirs, to ask of you a favor. I have learned my poor husband is held here and sentenced to die on the May Day. I pray you, let me see him for but a moment."

"You are mad." Rolf's voice. "Clear off before you get us all in trouble."

The second man spoke over him, an insolent drawl. "Your husband, you say?"

"Aye. He is accused of felling one of the king's deer. Falsely accused, at that. It was not he but Robin Hood's men who committed the crime. I have two small children at home."

"Why do you not apply to Robin Hood's men for succor?"

"Hsst, Albert," the first man warned. "Robin Hood is but a legend, as you know full well."

"And the arrows our men take in their backs every time they venture into Sherwood, are those legends, as well? Why are you clad that way, wench? You look like a wolfshead."

"How are my children and I to survive, if we do not take shelter in the forest? Our cottage was burned."

"I am going to fetch Sir Lambert," Rolf decided, and every man waiting in the corridor braced for action.

"Aye, Rolf, all in good time." Albert's voice dropped to a gravely growl. "'Tis a cold and lonely night, and who knows what the wench might do in return for seeing her husband? What you do, woman?"

"Anything you ask. Anything you want."

Sparrow closed his eyes and leaned his head against the rough stone wall.

"Is that so? Well now, Rolf, is that an offer we should refuse?"

Rolf made no answer.

"Go you, Rolf, and make sure no one is coming. I will take her first. You, wench, come here."

Wilfred nudged Sparrow, and Martin raised his sword.

Wren spoke. "If I oblige you, sir, do you promise I will see my husband?"

"Aye, so long as you do all I ask. Rolf, I told you, keep watch lest that bastard, Lambert, comes. If he does, he will want her for himself, and me, I do not like another man's leavings. On your knees, wench."

Rolf appeared round the bend in the passage, still looking over his shoulder to see what happened behind him. Wilf met him with open arms and smashed a palm over his mouth to still any outcry. Martin's sword made one smooth movement and gutted the man as neatly as a trout.

Sparrow pushed past both of them to peer around the corner. The guard room was no more than a wide place in the corridor, about which squat doors were set. A table and two chairs made bleak comfort, in light shed by a half-shuttered lantern. Sparrow saw a great brute—Albert—standing with his breeches open and his manhood exposed, and Wren forced to her knees before him. The cretin's hands were in her hair.

Sparrow's bow came up without conscious thought. He never remembered notching the arrow but noted the whispered twang as it flew true and took Albert through the throat. The man fell with a violent rumble that pushed the table aside.

Wren gave a cry and shied back. Sparrow reached

her in three strides and took her in his arms.

"Did he harm you?"

"Never mind me." Instantly, she freed herself. "Where is Lil? Which cell?"

The doors were waist high, built from thick oak, none with slots or other openings. No less than six of them ringed the alcove.

Cedric spoke hurriedly, "She is in the last cell on the right. Albert has the keys." He shoved Albert over onto his back with the toe of one boot and fished inside his tunic.

"Get her out quickly," Wren begged.

"Not so fast." Martin put out a hand and touched Wren's shoulder. "Cedric, how many prisoners are here?"

"I am not certain. Could be nearly a score."

Martin's eyes burned. "Open them all. I will not leave any of our folk in the hands of these Norman bastards. Unlock all the doors."

Wilfred scowled. "But you have yet to get away."

"Confusion makes a fine cover. Do it, man!"

Sparrow objected, "A horde of prisoners will surely draw the guards' attention."

"Aye, away from us." Martin stepped up to Sparrow, his temper evident. "Robin would not leave them here. Besides, it is not up to you."

"Nor you," Sparrow retorted.

They both looked at Wren. Her eyes filled with tears. "I wish only to get Lil free of this terrible place. Open them all, Cedric—hurry."

"She is here. I made sure of it this morning." Cedric had to stoop to the lock and bend double to enter the cell. Wren followed him, and Sparrow went close after.

A vile stench rolled out to meet them. The cell, half subterranean, had no windows, light or ventilation. Even though he had expected the worst conditions, Sparrow nearly gagged.

Faint light trickled in from the guard room and showed a space about eight by eight paces, not tall enough to allow a man to stand upright. Rotting straw dusted the floor, and four figures stirred. The fifth did not.

"Lil!" Wren dropped to her knees and crawled forward. She hesitated before touching the woman curled into a motionless ball. When she did, she stiffened and looked over her shoulder at Sparrow.

"Oh, Sparrow, we are too late. I fear she is dead!"

Chapter Seventeen

"You are freed. Go now, off out of here and away." Wilf's voice encouraged the occupants of the cell to scatter, but Sparrow spared them no glance. All his attention centered on Lil's motionless form.

Aye, and she did look dead—frail and, for the first time in his memory, old. He could feel Wren's emotions; she teetered on the very edge of devastation.

He reached out to touch Lil's cheek, but Martin pushed in and shoved him aside.

"No time," Martin gasped. "We need to move."

Without awaiting a reply, Martin gathered Lil's body into his arms and, hunched awkwardly, barreled out of the cell.

Out in the guards' alcove, confusion reigned. Freed prisoners milled about, spoke in hushed voices and grappled with their sudden liberty. One man kicked Albert's lifeless body viciously. A woman who had emerged from Lil's cell stared into Sparrow's eyes and begged, "Where are we to go? What to do?"

"Go home, Mother," he told her.

"I have no home. The Sheriff burned it, burned it all, and killed my man."

"Come," Martin interrupted the exchange. "Let us—"

"Wait." Wren put out a hand and stopped him. "Tell me, does Lil yet live?"

121

In the dim light shed by the lantern, they all peered at the woman in Martin's arms. Wren groaned. "What have they done to her? So many wounds!"

Lil's skin showed a livid mass of raw and angry injuries, some old and half crusted over, many still oozing puss and blood.

Martin swore viciously. "These are cuts, and burns. The bastards tortured her."

For days, by the look of it, Sparrow acknowledged. His stomach turned over, and he had to fight nausea. He placed a careful hand at the side of Lil's neck.

"Aye, but she lives."

Wren stared at him with a dawning of hope. "You are certain?"

"I am."

"Oh, thank heaven! Martin, get her away—at any cost, understand?"

Martin gave a hard nod. Wilfred gestured at them. "Hurry. The alarm has been given."

Martin moved off, scarcely hampered by his light burden. The former prisoners followed, crowding the passageway. Sparrow caught Wren's hand. "Come. And be ready to fight."

He did not like the fact that they must wend their way up from the very bowels of the castle, but he meant to defend Wren and Lil with his own life if necessary.

Wilf and Cedric had both disappeared, as had some of the prisoners. Others, seeming half dazed, lingered outside the cells without apparent direction. Sparrow and Wren, still hand in hand, ducked the intervening escapees and took the first flight of steps at a dead run behind Martin. The man had fearsome strength, Sparrow had to give him that. At the foot of the second flight he heard voices from above.

Shouting. Guards.

"Wait." He let go of Wren's hand and drew his sword. "Let me by."

His weapon of choice had always been the bow. He made barely half the swordsman Martin did. For an instant, he considered relieving Martin of his burden so he could fight, but saw there was no time.

He felt Wren press in beside him, her knife in her hand.

Martin protested, "Wren—"

"Just win Lil free of here."

A trio of guards, all heavily armed, appeared at the top of the stairs. These were men from the outer walls, intent on their duty.

Sparrow's heart began to beat high and hard. He cared not what befell him. He feared only for Wren and Lil.

One of the guards called down, "Stay where you are, by order of the Sheriff."

Some of the escaping prisoners ahead of Martin on the stairs obeyed the order, some did not. The guards met them with forged iron and cut them down, weaponless.

A sound very like a sob came from Wren's throat. Sparrow whispered a prayer and charged up the steps.

The foremost of the guards met him, blade to blade.

"Wolfsheads!" cried a second. "Wolfsheads in the castle!"

An arrow silenced the man. Sparrow, striving desperately to fight upwards, imagined Martin must have put down his burden in favor of his bow, but then

123

Martin came surging up past him with Lil still in his arms. Sparrow's opponent moved to block him, and Sparrow's blade took him between two ribs and through the heart.

Martin, with Lil, moved up and away, leaping around fallen bodies. Sparrow glanced behind to see Wren loose a second arrow that took the third guard in the shoulder. Her third penetrated the man's cheek, even as he fell.

Sparrow scarcely gave her time to shoulder her bow before he seized her hand again. "There will be more soldiers on the way. Come."

At the top of the stairs they met Wilfred, with a torch. "Sir Lambert has called up everyone on duty. Hurry—this way."

They followed him away from the stairs and through a narrow passageway that smelled of damp. All too soon they heard more cries behind them, but no immediate sounds of pursuit.

Under her breath, Wren sobbed, "They will all die. We never should have freed them."

"Better dead than trapped in those foul pits," Martin growled in response. "Wilf, where are we?"

"A service passageway, rarely used. One level up is the kitchen. There is an opening to a courtyard."

"I know it," Wren gasped. She tugged Sparrow's hand. "Come."

The following moments tormented Sparrow's heart with doubt and hope. The narrow passageway led to storage rooms strewn with rusted kettles and other cast-off kitchen trappings. They met no one and hurried still faster. Sparrow heard Martin's breath begin to catch in his lungs.

One last flight of stairs loomed before them.

"Kitchen is up there," Wilfred breathed. "And I cannot be seen with you."

"Seen?" Martin questioned.

"The kitchens are rarely empty," Wren explained. "Wilfred, we owe you so much. Come with us to Sherwood."

"I am more useful here. I will double back and take up my place among those hunting you, if I can." And he melted back into the narrow passageway, taking the torch with him.

"Come." Wren started up the steps.

"Stay behind me," Sparrow cautioned.

"Do not be a fool."

Only a flicker of light trickled down these stairs. They followed it to the yawning doorway of the kitchen.

Sparrow had been here before, of course, to call on Lil. He knew the place made up a community of its own. But he had not fathomed the impact of their sudden appearance with the woman who ran this world—Lil—fast in Martin's grip, her head hanging down over his arm.

Wren entered first with her knife in her hand, then Sparrow with his bloodied sword, and Martin after. Silence and a sea of stricken faces turned toward them. One or two of the kitchen wenches gasped. Some spoke Lil's name in horrified reverence. A young boy asked, "Is she dead?"

No one answered. Their boots pattered loudly as they crossed the flagstone floor, and someone near the outer door opened it for them as they approached. The cold dark and rain rushed in and seemed to pull at them, promising safety.

Outside, Martin faltered for the first time.

Sparrow turned to him. "Let me take her."

Martin shook his head. "We are nearly safe. Hurry."

They made it as far as the courtyard gate, which stood ajar, before the squad of soldiers appeared. With them was a mounted man who positioned his horse to block their way. Sir Lambert.

Sparrow felt Wren flinch. She drew her hood up over her hair.

"Halt!" Lambert bellowed. And, to his own men, "Take them."

Rapidly, Sparrow summed up the odds and his heart sank. Five armed men in addition to Lambert, a fine swordsman in his own right. He felt rather than saw Wren pocket her knife and take up her bow, and experienced a thrill of pride. Aye, that was the way of it. He sheathed his sword also, seized his bow and notched an arrow, all in one movement.

His first shot felled the man on the left, dodging inside his long shield and striking him through the jaw. At this distance, the force spun the man around before taking him down. He felt Wren shoot also but no one fell. Had she missed? But no—Lambert's mount shied. Her shot had brushed Lambert, himself.

"Wolfsheads!" Lambert shouted, having ducked Wren's arrow. "Do you think you can—?"

The soft twang of a bowstring heralded Wren's second shot, which took Lambert through the shoulder. He fell from his horse, and the animal pranced in distress.

Martin pushed forward, Lil now slung over his

126

shoulder and his sword in his hand.

Sparrow took aim at a second of the soldiers. They must get free of here before the entire guard descended upon them.

His second man fell with a loud cry. The other three rushed forward to engage Martin.

Wren shot one of them through the upper arm—his sword arm—and the man fell back. Trying to steady his aim in defiance of his pounding heart, Sparrow took out the next. That left one, crossing swords with Martin.

Wren gave a cry. Lambert was on his feet, sword drawn, with her arrow still protruding from his shoulder. Before Sparrow could blink, she rushed for the captain.

By all that was holy, was she brave or mad? Sparrow followed and was in time to land a blow across the back of Martin's opponent. Now only Lambert stood between them and the freedom lent by darkness.

Martin moved, sword extended, and pushed past Lambert's mount and away. Sparrow turned astonished eyes on Wren and Lambert. Wren, enraged and afire, had already marked Lambert with her blade, though Sparrow knew not how she had avoided the man's sword. But Lambert, known far and wide for his brilliance in battle, now turned on her with a blow, aimed at her head, that nearly stopped Sparrow's heart.

His sword intervened just in time and Wren danced back. Lambert faced Sparrow with a sneer.

"Wolfshead! You will not get away with this." He slashed at Sparrow murderously, and Sparrow barely succeeded in turning the blow. Sparrow tossed the hair out of his eyes, surprised to feel his own rage rise. Behind them, he knew, the whole kitchen watched the drama made by one of their own, facing one of their masters.

"We shall not go down to defeat," he grated, "for we fight in the name of Robin Hood."

"Fool!" Lambert bared his teeth. "Robin Hood is long dead."

"Nay, he lives," Wren cried. "Only look." She cast back her hood, defiant of both rain and danger.

Lambert glared at her, and his blade faltered. "You!" Rage flared in his eyes as he turned toward her and away from Sparrow. "Vile bitch—"

Sparrow swung his sword with all his might. A half-score voices cried out behind him. It might have been a fatal stroke but for the fact that Lambert's foot slipped on the wet stones as he spun. The sword struck both flesh and armor, and Lambert went down.

Without taking time to sheath his sword, Sparrow seized Wren's hand.

They fled and melted into the exterior darkness. Martin, with Lil, had disappeared as completely as if he had never existed. Sparrow could see no glimpse, either, of other escaped prisoners. Had they all been recaptured or killed?

He did see another squad of soldiers off to his right, all hollering. He pulled Wren in the other direction.

When they could run no farther, they stopped in the shelter of the outer wall and fought for breath. Sheets of rain washed over them, and Wren sobbed softly.

"Which way?" she gasped. "The gate—"

Sparrow no longer knew. Flight, rain, and darkness beguiled his senses. He felt Wren lift her head as if listening. She said, "This way."

"The gate will be guarded."

"I know. One more fight."

"I wonder if Martin got away?"

When they reached the narrow eastern gate, they discovered the answer: dead guards lay strewn in a spattering of blood. Martin, in fighting his way out, had done their work for them.

Wren wept even as they stepped over the bodies to freedom. "Oh, thank the sweet Lady for Martin."

Chapter Eighteen

"Sparrow, do you know where we are?" Completely out of breath and wet to the bone, Rennie dragged her companion to a halt. They had been running for what felt like half the night through dark forest, lashed by rain, raked by thorns and branches, Rennie's only anchor the strength of Sparrow's fingers in her own.

Now they paused for the first time, and she heard Sparrow gasp for air. Had they fled blindly, or had he led her to safety?

"We are deep in Sherwood, some distance east of where we need to be."

"How can you tell?" Rennie tipped her face up so water filled her eyes. She heard the wind in the trees but could not actually see them.

Sparrow admitted, "I am guessing from the direction we ran."

"We have seen nothing of Martin, with Lil. Do you think they will hunt him down, the soldiers, I mean?"

"Not until morning. They do not like venturing into Sherwood, even in daylight. And Lambert is sore wounded. Are you hurt?" His hands brushed gently over her skin.

"Scratches. You?"

"The same. We were fortunate, all round. Come daylight, I imagine Lambert will organize a search. But, come daylight, we should be able to find our way home."

Rennie shivered. "Not until then?"

"I fear not."

Rennie moved closer to him. Just days ago, she would have been terrified, finding herself lost among the trees. Now they had become a refuge, and she worried only about Lil.

"Do you think Martin truly did get away? And what of Alric, who was waiting for us?"

"Alric can look after himself, as can Martin. Trust him for that."

"Lil is in a bad way."

"Very bad."

"I cannot lose her, Sparrow. She is all I have." Rennie did not realize she wept until he pulled her into his arms. There, all at once, her courage—so bright when she faced Lambert—crumbled, and she sheltered against Sparrow's shoulder.

"Lil is strong, none stronger. But you are mistaken, Wren. She is not all you have."

Were those Sparrow's lips she felt on her hair, moving across her brow to her temple? She could hear his heart beating a deep, strong rhythm under her cheek, and once more his arms seemed as complete a refuge as Sherwood, a place she might stay forever safe.

"Surely you know I am here for you." His voice was a mooring place in the darkness. "And will always be."

So great was Rennie's need at that moment, she did not question his motives or intent, did not ask whether he spoke as had Martin, out of desire for the place at her side, or to hold strong the magical bonds that protected Sherwood. Blindly she lifted her face and his lips found hers, as naturally as a flower finds the sun.

Sensation exploded, one point of heat amid the wet and cold. She felt his emotions as intensely as her own, knew when the fire kindled and raced through his veins like life returning.

Need, pure and raw, engulfed, strengthened, and then possessed her. She pressed herself closer, desperate for his heat, for his essence. She wanted to be inside him; she wanted him inside her.

Helpless against her feelings, she did not protest when the kiss deepened. His tongue belonged in her mouth, searching and caressing. She let her own meet it, slide, and tangle delectably, suddenly wild for the taste of him. This went beyond comfort and even need to a mingling of spirit, the very reason she had been born.

She moaned, and his big hands drew her still closer. Her flesh seemed to leap for his until she barely felt the sopping leather still between them. His heat and the rain both beat on her with equal intensity.

Not until she was desperate for breath did Sparrow break the kiss. She felt his lungs draw air as if they were her own.

Raggedly, he said, "I have longed to do that since last I kissed you, wanted it every moment, both waking and sleeping."

"Then I think we needs must do it again."

The fire leaped still more swiftly this time. Rennie lost track of everything but the feel of his lips, his hands when they began to move over her body, exploring, then caressing and possessing. They warmed her flesh wherever they touched—the skin of her back, up inside her wet tunic and, still lower, her buttocks, which they cupped, starting a whole host of new sensations. Rennie raised both arms and wound them about his neck, tasting an abandon never before felt. She buried her fingers in his sopping hair and rode the current of her burgeoning need.

She never knew which of them spoke the words, "I want you." It did not matter, because their feelings had melded as surely as their tongues.

Sparrow caught her up in his arms and walked blindly through the windy darkness as if directed. Even as they went, she kissed him, little bites of kisses irresistible as comfort. She barely noticed when he set her down. The ground beneath her, though, felt soft and dry.

"Sparrow, where are we?"

"I do not know. Say my name again."

"Sparrow." She breathed it into his mouth and accompanied it with a kiss.

He begged, like a sob, "Again."

Rennie laughed in delight and reached for him. Did she remove his clothes, or did he? And what of hers? The sopping leather should have been difficult to remove, yet it melted away just like Rennie's uncertainty.

She no longer felt the cold; Sparrow's body became a shield, a defense, a place to dwell. Heat followed his mouth, exquisite in the darkness. She could see nothing, not even Sparrow, but could feel everything: the calluses on his broad palms, the whispered abrasion made by the hair on his chest when it caught her bare nipples and teased them deliciously, the gentle strength of his fingers that seemed to call something from within her body and lit in her the unprecedented desire to give him anything, everything.

Sparrow. She continued to speak his name in her mind, when her lips were otherwise occupied. And he heard.

Wren. His breath poured into her. She nearly wept when his mouth left hers, but then his lips whispered across her throat and lower still. Aye, Martin had touched her breasts, but that had felt nothing like this. For when Sparrow's hot mouth found her chilled breast and he began to suckle her, he called forth her very soul.

Time suspended; Rennie died and became born anew, a woman of sensation, existing only for this one man. When his hands moved over her again, when his fingers slid between her thighs, she opened to him eagerly. When they slipped inside her, she knew she had never wanted anything more.

"Wren." He raised his head from her breast. "I need—"

"Sparrow." She tangled her fingers in the wet silk of his hair and pulled his mouth to hers. "I need."

He kissed her with fearsome passion. "I would not hurt you, frighten you, harm you at all."

Gentle soul, priceless soul, her soul, hers. "You will not."

"Are you certain? From this, there is no going back."

She could not see him; he was but heat, sensation, a spirit in the darkness. "I need," she repeated helplessly.

She lifted her bare legs and wound them around him, drew him in. He slid into her as easily as if she had been made for him.

She had—oh, she had.

After that she did not know where her body left off and his began. She could not tell his thoughts and feelings from hers. His rush of pleasure, when he came, was hers also, triumphant.

Mine, mine, mine.

Her legs still draped around him, she kept him inside her, and felt complete for the first time in her life. Breath sobbed in her lungs, and she could feel his heart flutter, a bird held in her soul.

"Wren—"

"No need to speak, Sparrow. Only hold me."

He gathered her in, though in truth she could scarcely get closer.

Never let me go, she beseeched.

I will not.

Only after the vow was given did Rennie realize the words had not been spoken aloud. Amazement coursed through her, followed swiftly by delight. Their joining had been no illusion; he was with her, in her mind.

Can you hear me? she asked.

How should I not? She felt his surprise as he grasped the truth. His soul rippled with gladness that matched her own.

By the Green Man's horns, he said, *it is a miracle.*

"No," she told him aloud, "it is destiny."

"You believe that?"

"I no longer know what I believe in, save you."

"Wren—"

"Hush, Sparrow. The night is long, and I need you again."

Chapter Nineteen

"Sparrow, are you awake?" Rennie whispered the words even though she knew he slept still. She could sense his soul's repose, feel him dreaming, like flickers of butterfly wings in her own consciousness.

But morning had come to Sherwood. Light streamed in radiant bars through oak and beech, making an enchanted bower of the place where they lay. Rennie could see it now, for the first time: an earthen burrow beneath the shelter of a massive oak, perhaps a former animal's den, snug and dry.

And she could see the man whom she had welcomed into her soul.

Could a man be described as beautiful? She bit her lip in wonder, remembering how, the first time she had seen him in Lil's kitchen, she had considered him ordinary. No more: he lay with one naked arm thrown across her in a gesture of unconscious possession. Brown hair, still crumpled from the rain, scattered in wild disarray and fell against his cheek. A bare chest—naked save for that line of dark hair she had felt but never seen—and burnished shoulders that rippled with strength. A big man, he had nevertheless fit her in a way that still had the power to make her tingle.

Aye, he was beautiful, and she wanted him again—no, needed him the way she needed air. But the need to find Lil pulled just as strongly.

Yet, how to wake him? A thousand possibilities filled her mind and made her fingers itch. With a touch? With a kiss? With a call of the mind?

Sparrow.

His sinfully long black lashes fluttered, and he opened his eyes, dark and wise as those of a wild creature, the eyes of a hart.

My stag, she caressed him in her mind.

He smiled and reached for her, as natural as breathing. *Wren. Will you welcome me again?*

She would, had they not duty before them. Aloud she said, "Lil."

"Aye."

He sat up in one glorious movement, stealing Rennie's breath. She could see him now, oh, yes—and she might never be able to look her fill. Completely unselfconscious beneath her gaze, he sat with the morning light washing over him. Her eyes explored him freely, even to that part of him responding so magnificently to her nearness.

"Ah." Rennie sat up also, her only cover provided by her hair. Helplessly, she reached for his face, now rough with beard.

His fingers caught her wrist. "Wren, you do not regret what happened between us last night?"

"Can you feel any regret?" She dared him to use the sense that had been forged between them in the darkness.

He shook his head with a rueful smile. "Then let us get you home."

"Aye, but first—" She leaned forward and kissed him, something to hold against the fear and difficulty ahead.

****

They moved swiftly and almost soundlessly, their hands still joined. All last night's rain had flown, and the light strengthened around them as they went.

They spoke only between their minds.

Do you know where we are?

Aye, Wren. He loved repeating her name, and every time he did, it sounded in Rennie's soul, deepening the claiming. *Not much farther.*

I hope we find Lil well. Martin—

Martin.

Martin posed a problem from which they both flinched. Would Martin be able to tell what had happened in the forest? If so, how would he react?

But when they at last reached the camp site, they found chaos and upheaval. Alric and Simon came forward to meet them. The old man looked weary and grave.

"Children, I am glad you are come." His gaze dropped to their joined hands for a moment before he went on. "We have had word Lambert is on his way with a squadron of soldiers. We are moving camp."

"Lil?" Rennie managed but the one word.

Alric eyes filled with regret. "She lives, but only just."

"I need to see her."

"Aye, lass, I think you should."

Sparrow asked Simon, "Where is Martin?"

"Arranging Lil's transport. He is sore hurt, himself, and collapsed after he got her here last night."

"Madlyn has treated him as best she can," Alric added. "But the truth is, we need Lil's healing hand." He eyed them once more. "What of the two of you?

You are not harmed?"

Sparrow answered, "We are well enough." He released Rennie's fingers. "You go with Alric. Simon, take me wherever I can do the most to help."

Alric led Rennie to a shelter constructed of boughs, where Madlyn and Sally bent above a pallet. On the way, they passed Martin, who looked startled. He leaped to his feet and called, "Wren!" But Rennie did not pause. All her attention was on the swaddled form beneath the branches.

Lil. She looked so small lying there, scarcely bigger than a child. Her hair, pale gray, caught the light from above, but her face looked uncannily still. With eyes for no one else, Rennie dropped to her knees beside the pallet.

"Mother."

Lil did not seem to hear. Eyelids like the thinnest parchment remained closed, bluish lips still. Someone, most likely Madlyn, had tried to ease the wounds that marked her flesh, covering them with salve, yet they stood out like brands.

Rennie's heart twisted at seeing her so, this woman whose strength, wisdom, and indomitable kindness had made the one beacon in her life, yet now so weak, so frail.

Tears filled her eyes and threatened to choke her.

"Thank the Green Lord you have come," Madlyn said. "She has been asking for you."

Rennie reached out and touched Lil's hands. "Mother, I am here."

At that, Lil's eyes opened. They held a blank, distant look and did not sharpen until they found Rennie's face. "Ah." Her voice held relief. "Daughter."

They gazed at one another, and Rennie felt eternity rushing like a strong, oncoming wind. She had to swallow hard before attempting to speak again.

"Tell me what to do for you, so I can help make you well."

Lil shook her head, and terror speared Rennie's soul. "Please, Lil. I will do anything."

"You know what you must do. You have your father's courage, and your mother's kindness. It has been a privilege to know you, and to have had a hand in raising you."

Rennie's tears began to fall, hot and slow. "Do not speak as if my raising were all in the past, Lil—I need you yet! You are the strongest woman I know. You will recover from this." Even as she spoke, her eyes noted again the terrible extent of the wounds, and she faltered. "What did they do to you? Oh, Lil."

"Hush. Do not fret for me now. My days are run out. And do not try to hold me. I go to follow Geoffrey."

"No—oh, no."

"Would you deny me what you have found? Duty so often kept us apart in life. But I can feel he waits for me now."

A sob rose to Rennie's throat. Lil reached out, and Rennie took her hand between her own.

"You ask, child, what you can do for me. Take my place. Use your courage to fill it well."

"I cannot. Oh, Lil, I—"

"It is the role for which you were born. For the sake of any love you bear me, promise—and let me pass on."

Rennie struggled to speak around her agonized grief. "You know I would do for you aught you ask.

140

You have been everything to me, each day of my life. But do not ask me to go on without you, alone."

"Not alone. You have him." Lil smiled, and it transformed her, made her suddenly beautiful. Her eyes no longer saw Rennie but reached for something beyond, and Rennie knew what she saw.

"I will not hold you here in pain," she said, cradling the frail hand. "I will do my best to do as you ask."

"Thank you, my child. I love—" Lil sighed then. Her eyes gently closed, and her hand, in Rennie's, became light and lifeless as a dead bird.

For an instant the entire camp stilled. Men busy packing bundles turned their faces toward Lil and froze; all but Alric, who sank to his knees where he stood and covered his face with his hands. Life paused, and then began once again.

Madlyn wept, Sally lamented, voices cried inquiry and response. Rennie, still kneeling, looked into a gulf of blackness so bitter she shied from it.

"Come, love." Not Sparrow's arms, but Martin's lifting her up so Lil's hand slipped from between her fingers. She felt his kindness, his unexpected gentleness as he pulled her into an embrace and comforted her like a child. Instantly, his grief assailed her and combined with her own.

"There now, there—I know it is a terrible loss. But you will take her place, even as I will take Geofrey's."

Rennie could not tell him, not now, that someone already filled the place beside her. She closed her eyes and sheltered against the agony. Martin pulled her still closer, wrapped her in his arms. He murmured, "Together we will keep the magic strong, here in

Sherwood."

And so they would. Had she not promised Lil?

All about the camp, cries of grief and weeping arose. Rennie drew from Martin's arms and saw Sparrow on the ground beside Alric, seeking to offer comfort. The old man appeared broken, and Rennie knew how cruelly the bonds inside him had been severed. It would feel just so for her if she lost Sparrow—or Martin.

But now it was time for her to take her courage in both her hands. Time for her to do as Lil had asked. She drew a deep breath. "We cannot linger here," she declared. "Gather the rest of our things, and we will go."

Chapter Twenty

"We need to scatter," Martin declared. "We stand a better chance in small groups, for the Sheriff's men cannot pursue us all."

"What of Lil?" asked Wren, her face a mask of grief. "We cannot just leave her here."

"No," Sparrow agreed.

The three of them stood in a clutch with Alric and Madlyn, struggling to make last-moment decisions. Alric had pulled himself up from the ground, but the old man was clearly shattered, barely able to speak. Madlyn wept silently, and constantly. Wren—Sparrow could barely look at her, for what leaped up between them whenever he did. When he met her eyes, or even when he did not, he could feel her hands upon him, sliding over his naked skin, even feel himself glide again into her welcoming heat. This was no time for such thoughts, when emotions were raw and brutalized. Martin's control hung by a mere thread, and if Martin suspected the truth, hell would erupt.

Wren could not withstand that now. Sparrow's first duty was to protect her, even from Martin's anger, and even though he wished only to take her in his arms.

She spoke, brokenly. "We must take her body with us. I refuse to abandon her to Lambert's men. She will want to be buried beneath the oak, next to Geofrey."

"And that is impossible, now." Martin seemed to

143

think someone had given him the right to make decisions. Sparrow glared at him through narrowed eyes and felt Alric seize his arm.

"We will bundle and take her with us. Time to bury her later."

Sparrow stared into the old man's eyes and read his pain. Did Alric feel as Sparrow might, if he lost Wren?

"You will come with me, Sparrow," Alric told him. "We will take Lillith."

"Aye," Martin agreed quickly. "I will look after Wren."

Sparrow felt Wren reach for him with her mind. "No," he said, an instinctive reaction. "Wren will be safer with the both of us looking after her."

Martin spoke impatiently. "It is not safe for the three of us to travel together; we might all be taken."

"He is right, Sparrow," Alric agreed. "The protection of Sherwood now falls into your hands."

"Give me my bow." Wren stepped away from Martin. At least some of her grief seemed to have transformed into anger. She glanced at Sparrow. "We will meet later."

"Three days," Martin declared.

Three days—it might as well be three years. Sparrow ached to reach for Wren, to bury his fingers in her hair and hold her as he had last night. Yet she had turned her eyes away from him.

"Come," Alric said to Madlyn. "You and I shall prepare Lillith for her journey."

Martin touched Wren on the arm. "We will collect supplies and weapons. Swiftly, now."

Sparrow swallowed hard. Only moments stood between him and unbearable separation. Would Martin sense the feelings running rampant inside and guess the reason for them? Would he unleash his anger, then? Would Wren be safe with him?

He spoke to Wren in his mind. *Remember you are mine.*

With her face still turned away, she replied. *Aye, love. I am not likely to forget.*

Love—she called him "love," a word that had not yet passed her lips. It struck him to the heart.

Return to me, he told her.

I will. Even as she turned to follow Martin, her eyes gave the promise.

****

The three days, as Sparrow lived them, might have been thirty. Alric led their little group, which included Sally and two other men—Timothy and Roderick, who helped carry the burden—far deeper into the wood than Sparrow had ever ventured. The old man knew Sherwood like the landscape of his own heart, or, more precisely, as a man knows a lover.

The rain returned to dog them and, light as it was, Lil's body made a troubling burden.

On the second night, while Sally, Tim, and Roderick tossed in troubled sleep, Sparrow and Alric sat together without so much as the comfort of a fire.

"Perhaps we should bury Lil here, come first light," Sparrow suggested. "She grows—" Words failed him.

"No." Stubbornly, Alric shook his head. He seemed, in a peculiar way, to have shrunk since their flight began, shriveled in upon himself. Now he coughed fitfully. "I know 'tis not truly Lil we bear—"

"Then what does it matter where her remains lie?

145

Surely here, in the heart of Sherwood, would suit."

"She would want her bones to lie beside his. She did so love to lie with him." Pain weighted Alric's words. "And she had so little chance for it, in life."

"Aye, then we will do as you think best." Curiosity stirred in Sparrow's heart. "Alric, if you do not mind me asking—" Sparrow paused.

"Ask what you will, lad. You do not stand far off from where I once stood. And the time swiftly moves to when the three of you—Wren, Martin, and yourself— must take our places completely."

Sparrow stared blindly into the wet darkness. "How was it with you, then? Did you both love Lil?"

"As the both of you love Wren now, aye." Ruefully, Alric confirmed it. "Oh, do not think to hide what you feel. Things are as they were meant to be. Love it is that weaves the spell."

"The spell?"

Alric turned toward him, yet the dark prevented Sparrow from seeing what lay in his eyes. "Surely you know, Sparrow, only love can weave magic? Love—or hate. And we will have no part of that sort of spell. But it calls for strong emotion: for the world, for one another, for Sherwood itself. Robin bore that love, and others before him. Lil had great love. And I."

"But the love and desire of a man for a woman—"

"It is a force in itself. The intensity of the wanting calls up the power of the world. Do you see?"

Sparrow wondered if he did. "How was it for the three of you? How, when Lil decided?"

"Lil chose with her heart. She loved us both in different ways. I always knew that. For a time, I hoped she would choose me, but then I saw how she looked at him."

Sparrow thought of Martin. "And you felt no anger for that?"

"Anger? Lad, for a time my emotions were so twisted I barely recognized them. But it was a troubled time, just as it is now, and everyone's emotions were in discord. Robin had held so much on his heart, in essence inhabiting the place of leader and worshipper combined, linked to Sherwood through the Green God himself, as so many before him."

"There have been others?"

"So many others—since the time the first men came here and found the spirit that dwells in the wood and the wild."

"But when Lil chose Geofrey, you accepted it?"

"You must understand, Sparrow, when it happened we were not so young as the three of you. The blood no longer ran so hot. I had seen two score years. Three score, now."

"I see."

"And we both know youthful blood runs very hot, indeed—especially Martin's. Sparrow, do you dread taking my place?"

Not any more. All Sparrow need do was think of Wren—remember touching and caressing her, recall the look in her eyes at parting—for the warmth to come flooding. But he could not tell even Alric the secret he shared with her. Softly, he asked, "Is your place so terrible?"

"No. No, it holds its own reward. When I die, I will become part of what I love. What could be more magnificent?"

"Sherwood, you mean."

"I do—and the magic that exists here."

Sparrow hesitated. "Can you better explain it to me, Father? How was this magic born, and how does it continue? If we are asked to give our lives to it, I would know."

"Aye, lad. But it is difficult to explain the ineffable. Have you ever seen a book?"

Sparrow frowned. "Once or twice."

"Ever seen a man—a monk—write? The stylus leaves a trail on the parchment, and something of the thought behind the words then remains. Love is like that. It leaves traces of itself that can be felt and, sometimes, manipulated. Since men first came to our island, they have loved and worshipped the wood. That love has left its trace, and it is that Robin tapped into, when he came."

"But how did he know?"

"You would need ask him that, lad—or his spirit, for it dwells here still. Geoffrey, Lillith, and I never misunderstood that. I know, for he told me, that he communed with the god of the greenwood, in essence became him, and lay with his lady, before ever Marian joined him."

"Lay with his lady, the god's lady?"

"Do not sound so startled. I have lain with her myself, as will you, if you take my place. When I die, it is in her arms I shall lie."

"You are right," Sparrow admitted ruefully. "It is ineffable."

Alric laughed softly. "Be that as it may, the three of you must take up the threads of this ancient magic and spin it as you will. If you do not, if separation from the Green Man occurs, the Normans will eventually claim Sherwood. They will fear it no more, and the faith Robin kept burning will extinguish. Then will he die."

"I see."

"Do you, lad?"

"I feel your words even if I do not wholly comprehend them. The magic is our defense and our strength."

"Our defense, our strength, and our identity. If we lose that, we lose ourselves."

"And it is all held by love."

"Aye. Love of a man—or woman—for place, for duty, for one another. But that love must be manifest and it must be earnest."

"Father, may I tell you a secret?"

"Of course."

"Sally carries Martin's child. How will this affect our delicate balance?"

"Ah." The single word conveyed Alric's regret; he said nothing more.

Earnestly, Sparrow went on, "You speak of love: Sally loves Martin. How does that impact what happens between the rest of us?"

"A good question." Alric repeated what Sparrow had told Sally. "Children born in Sherwood tend to be special, even destined for greatness."

"I know."

"Soon she will need to tell him. Such a secret cannot remain long hidden. It will be the measure of the man, what Martin does then."

"I suppose it will." *The Lord and Lady help them all.*

Chapter Twenty-One

"Has Sparrow come?" For at least the third time, Rennie asked the question, and Martin sent her a sharp look. She drew a breath and struggled to control her emotions. For days now, she had kept them locked down tight, afraid to let them stray where they naturally wanted to go, for fear Martin would glean what she felt for Sparrow. She thought she had succeeded reasonably well. But on this, the third day, her resistance was in shreds. As the scattered parties slowly drifted to Oakham, prepared to lay Lil's body to rest, her uneasiness grew. Most of those now gathering had stories of pursuit and danger, tales of the Sheriff's men. Only Sparrow's group had yet to arrive.

"Nay," replied Madlyn, sounding as worried as Rennie felt. "Not yet."

"Oakham has become a perilous place," Rennie said, also not for the first time. She fidgeted like a woman dancing on hot coals; she wanted Lil safely laid to rest, and this thing done.

And she needed to see Sparrow, with an intensity that frightened her. Her eyes longed to rest on him, her heart wanted to be at home with him, her fingers itched to caress him.

She added, "We cannot linger here long. What if another troop of soldiers arrives?" They had already faced two small parties before finding refuge deep in

Sherwood—Rennie, Martin, Simon, and the two others who, along with Madlyn, made up their group had fought valiantly. Rennie remained unhurt, but Martin now bore wounds upon his wounds.

The three days had seemed three score long.

She glanced up to find Martin's eyes on her. All too aware he could sense her feelings even as she sensed his, she once more caught herself up, hard.

"Why do you fret so?" He sounded annoyed.

Rennie tossed her head. "We cannot have a burial without Lil's body, can we?"

Sudden awareness seized her then and turned her gaze northward into the wood. It pricked all over her skin and played like a song in her mind. Relief hit her in a staggering wave. All the time they had been apart, she had caught no thoughts from Sparrow's mind, not so much as a hint of comfort. But now—

Wren?

Sparrow, Sparrow, Sparrow.

Incautiously, she said, "They come," and ran to meet them.

Martin followed, as did Adam, now serving as headman of Oakham, with Madlyn in their wake. The party came slowly, Timothy and Roderick carrying Lil's swaddled corpse and Alric leaning heavily on Sparrow's arm.

The old man looked shockingly unwell. Gray in the face, his expression set in a stoical mask of pain, he appeared frail and almost powerless, his grief palpable.

Compassion struck Rennie, an overflow of Sparrow's compassion. Their eyes met.

Wren.

My love.

The worry seemed to lift from Sparrow like mist at sunrise. His shoulders straightened and his head rose.

Madlyn went forward and took Alric's hands. "Old friend, you look unwell."

Alric nodded soberly. "We gather here to bury a dear one. I shall not be long in following her."

"Do not say that." The words came from Sparrow. His beautiful, dark eyes held troubled concern.

Alric gave him a rueful smile. "Why not? There is always value, lad, in speaking the truth."

****

Lil, so well-loved, called forth floods of tears as she was laid to rest. The service was, perforce, brief. Alric kept himself upright until the end, when he sank to the ground above the grave. He was senseless when they lifted him up again.

"We cannot linger," said Martin, tense as a bowstring. "Should we be found here, Oakham will burn."

"I need time to tend him, if I hope to save him," Madlyn told her son. "I have not Lil's skill, but I will do what I can."

"Soldiers!" The cry came from the south end of the village. "They ride this way from Nottingham, with Sir Lambert at their head."

"You must scatter once more. Quickly!" Adam told them.

"Aye. Someone help me." Martin caught Alric up in his arms. Sparrow stepped forward to share the burden.

Wren?

I am with you. This time we will not be parted.

As so often before, the outlaws melted away by

twos and threes into the forest. This time, though, Rennie felt she left part of her heart behind, lying beside Geoffrey. How could she hope to go on without Lil's steady presence, her strength and wisdom? How could she imagine filling such emptiness?

Their group numbered but four in addition to Alric: Martin, Sparrow, Madlyn, and Rennie herself. Her bow on her shoulder and exhaustion pulling at her limbs, Rennie brought up the rear, keeping constant watch on their back trail.

Yet the wood held its silence. She caught no outcry from behind, no sound of mounted soldiers, no hint of smoke. Birds wove their songs overhead, and new, unfolding leaves rustled.

Rennie reached for Sparrow's mind.

My love, how I missed you.

And I, you. Your absence was a wound on my heart.

His thoughts sang in her mind even as the birds sang overhead. Rennie drew a deep breath and felt herself steady.

Martin glanced at her over his shoulder. Did he sense the connection, or did he but check their progress? Unsure, Rennie strove to rein in her desire. It had been one thing, keeping her feelings in check when she and Sparrow were apart. Now that they traveled together, could she hope to hide the truth from Martin? She determined she would not speak again to Sparrow in her mind.

Yet when they paused at last, too spent to go on, she had to fight her need to go to him, touch his hand, bury her face in his shoulder. He and Martin sat side by side, while Madlyn provided what care she could to

Alric, who had not yet regained his senses.

She went to Madlyn's side. "How is he? Can you tell?"

Madlyn glanced into Rennie's face and shook her head. "It may be his heart is tired. I cannot tell."

Martin spoke unexpectedly. "He has chosen to die. He does not wish to live without Lil. Can you not see that?" Rennie once more felt his gaze on her. "Now perhaps you begin to understand the strength of the bond between them."

Rennie turned her eyes on Alric. Eyelids like thin, withered leaves closed the doors to his soul. He looked peaceful.

Martin spoke again, sounding aggrieved. "The truth is we have no time to prepare ourselves for what is upon us. With Alric thus, we three must be ready to step into our places, whether we want to or no."

Wryly, Rennie said, "I barely understand my place, or what I am meant to do in it. It will be hard enough just going on without Lil."

"And Geofrey, and Alric," Sparrow conceded. "I would have given you more time, Wren, to get used to what lies before us."

"Decisions must be made," Martin declared hotly, "and one in particular. Until that is done, we cannot move forward."

That decision had been made, Rennie acknowledged in her own mind. But how would Martin react when he learned of her choice? She could feel his emotions now, barely controlled. What if he could not accept her choice of Sparrow? What if he could not bring himself to replace the man who even now lay dying?

****

The moon rose slowly through a wattle-work of tree branches, shedding an indistinct light. Alric never stirred, and Madlyn tended him as best she could before curling up beside him and falling asleep.

Weariness pulled at Rennie also, yet something else pulled still more strongly. She took her turn at watch even though the wood seemed almost uncannily quiet. And she awaited but one thing: for Martin to sleep.

Wren? The call penetrated her light doze and roused her instantly. Need flared brightly at the sound of Sparrow's voice in her mind. She sat up and looked at him.

He stood with his sword in his hand and his bow on his shoulder, his dark hair streaming down his back. Though he made a fine enough picture to make her catch her breath, his eyes were what held her, captured her heart like a bird in his hand.

Magic seemed to swirl around him, and Rennie's heart began to pound. Was this what she had always been meant to find?

She rose silently and went to him. His arms opened to welcome her, and she felt herself engulfed in protection.

Oh, Sparrow, oh god, oh god—

Aye, Wren, I know. I expected love, but not this burning need.

Need, yes. How did Lil and Geofrey ever stand it? She was so often away from him.

Sparrow stirred and sheathed his sword. His big hands claimed her and drew her still closer. *Alric and I spoke of that. I am not sure the feelings were so intense for them—or perhaps just as intense, yet less physical.*

Martin—

Hush, do not speak his name, else it might call him from sleep. Wren—

Rennie lifted her face, and he kissed her. It began gently, a mere brush of lips against lips, but then hunger came rushing. Rennie's heart, body, and spirit all cried out for him, and his answered.

"Wren." When the kiss ended at last, they both shook helplessly. Sparrow rested his forehead against hers. Barely aloud, he whispered, "I need—"

"As do I. Come with me."

"We cannot. I am on watch."

"Let Sherwood keep the watch."

"But there is Martin. And Alric lies dying."

"Surely Alric would understand."

For an instant only, Sparrow hesitated. Then he caught Rennie up in his arms and carried her away into the trees.

They coupled silently, passionately, two souls starving for one another. The spell of moonlight found them where they lay, washed silver over Sparrow's skin, made mystery of his eyes. Yet Rennie did not need to see what lay there. She held him, and filled him, even as he filled her.

"I cannot live without this," she whispered when they once more lay joined, her legs holding him tight, "without you."

"Beautiful Wren." His rough fingers caressed her naked breast and, as easily as that, brought her to life again. She gasped as desire speared through her and wild hunger for him quickened.

Yet she said, "Me, beautiful? My fine wolfshead,

you are mistaken. I am but a scullery wench, over-tall and often awkward."

"Beautiful scullery wench." Laughter and desire tangled in his deep voice. Both went straight to Rennie's head. "Shall I number the things that make you beautiful? These perfect breasts that just fill my hands, your hair that smells of Sherwood, and the eyes of a wild hawk, legs such as I never hoped to see, dangerously long." His lips brushed hers and coerced them open. She thrilled as his warmth, words, and breath all poured into her. "You are irresistible."

Only the moment existed, and Rennie wanted it to last an eternity. "Then, my fine wolfshead, do not try to resist."

His weapon, still inside her, had once more readied itself. He flexed his muscular body and began to move slowly. Every part of Rennie roused and gloried in the joining. So this is happiness, she thought. This is why I was born.

Out of the darkness, hard words came cutting through the euphoria that enfolded her. Martin's voice.

"Betrayer! On your feet, Sparrow, and face me!"

Chapter Twenty-Two

"So this is what it comes to—lying and deception and sneaking behind my back!" Sparrow had never heard such rage in Martin's voice, and that said something. Over the years they had engaged in countless quarrels and contests, but this threat sounded deadly.

"Have you no shame? The rest of us sleeping within reach, and Alric dying? Did you have to take her now?"

Sparrow did not know when he had been caught at such a disadvantage—Wren in his arms, himself still inside her and flagrantly hard, both of them half undressed. His back was to Martin, and he wondered if the man had drawn his sword. His own lay, with the belt he had shed, on the ground, barely within reach.

Wren moved, slipped from him and out of his arms, scampered up on those long legs. Her loosened hair swirled around her as she faced Martin, half naked.

"He did not 'take' me. I gave myself to him, full well."

The curse of their connection, Sparrow thought ruefully, was that he could feel her emotions and, to a lesser extent, Martin's. Sparrow felt the shock spear through Martin, followed swiftly by increased rage.

Sparrow got to his feet, snagging his sword on his way up. Martin did, indeed, grip his own blade, fiercely. But all his attention focused on Wren. "What? What did you say? But you are to be mine."

At that moment, Sparrow almost felt sorry for the poor blighter. For in the welter of emotions assailing Sparrow, Wren's love for him screamed aloud.

"Do not be a fool," he said huskily. "She chooses."

"Does she? Does she!" Martin's gaze raked him. "She is an untried maiden. How do I know what wiles you used upon her, to make your claim?"

"I *was* an untried maiden," Wren corrected.

Martin's jaw dropped. "This is not the first? Ah— when the two of you fled together, after Lil's rescue." He answered his own question.

Gravely, Wren inclined her head. She looked a queen standing there with her tunic gaping and her hair streaming about her—a goddess, strong with the essence of Sherwood. A breath escaped Sparrow; surely she would command the moment and prevent bloodshed.

But Martin waved his sword in a wild gesture. "Out of the way, Wren. I will face him as he deserves."

"No." She stood firm. "You will not."

"It is for him to answer, not you. Have you chosen a coward?"

"Should I let you kill each other? I need you both."

Martin used his blade to point behind him. "You expect me to take his place? I will not! Now, move aside, Wren. He and I will settle this between us."

"With me as prize? I think not. Go back to Alric and Madlyn, and wait for us. We shall speak together sanely."

"Oh, and should I go so he can finish rutting with you like a stinking boar?"

"What goes on here? What is all this shouting?" Madlyn appeared behind her son; her voice held concern.

"Go back to bed, Mother."

"I will not. Do you want to summon every soldier in the district to us? Oh." Her eyes must have deciphered the scene despite the gloom. She laid her hand on her son's arm. "Come away out of it, love."

He shook her off violently. "Get you gone, Mother. I mean to settle this."

"What is to settle?" Madlyn asked. "If she has chosen—"

"She has not chosen fairly. He has beguiled her."

"Sparrow, a beguiler? I think you have it wrong."

"Be gone, Mother. Go watch over the old man 'til he dies."

Madlyn recoiled slightly from the harsh words. Martin edged her aside and stepped forward aggressively. "Well, Sparrow, are you afraid to face me like a man?"

"Never." Sparrow's anger rose rampant. Perhaps Martin needed a lesson: the sun neither rose nor set on him, and his arrogance could not always blaze his trail through life.

But Wren objected. "No, I will not be snarled over like a—"

Martin's sword flashed round her and reached for Sparrow's. The contact made a sound like a chime there in the quiet wood. Sparrow knew Madlyn had spoken true; any of Lambert's men searching for them would come swiftly to that sound. But then he thought no more about it; he found himself in a fight for his life.

Martin's anger screamed in his every stroke, and he

came swift and hard, his face set in a grim mask of bitter determination. Even in the dim light, his blade flashed silver. At once, Sparrow knew he had no hope of matching such skill, yet his own emotions lifted him and let him keep pace at the start. He, son of shepherds and woodsmen, was not the man for the sword. Give him axe or bow and he did better. Martin, himself descended from a soldier turned wolfshead, possessed true ability.

Lightning fast, Martin made the first touch on Sparrow's shoulder. Wren cried out then, as did Madlyn, saying, "That is enough." The two men fought on, grimly now on Sparrow's part. Did Martin mean to kill him? He shook the hair out of his eyes and fought for breath. And did Martin's rage permit him to wonder what, then, would happen to the triad?

Martin struck again, a blow to Sparrow's left thigh, and Sparrow felt the warm blood begin to flow. Emotions battered at him, Martin's anger, his own tangled caution and determination—for his anger had flown—Wren's love and growing alarm.

Martin bared his teeth in a grimace and Sparrow felt he faced a stranger, not his lifelong companion and sometime friend.

He remembered Will Scarlet spending hours drilling at the sword with his son. Aye, and now it would pay off.

Martin raised his sword in a skillful, murderous stroke. Sparrow saw death coming on it—or at least, maiming. His own weapon came up just a tick too slowly.

Yet Wren moved swiftly enough. Before Sparrow could blink—or flinch—she leaped before him and stood, a shield of love and defense. And her flesh took the impact of Martin's blade.

Everything froze and sudden silence rushed in. Wren wavered where she stood, and Martin's emotions turned to horror. Sparrow's heart seemed to crumple in his chest. His sword dropped from his hand.

Wren fell in bits, folding in upon herself; Sparrow caught her as she went down, denial screaming a protest in his mind. Bright blood sprang out against Wren's pale skin, from collar bone to breast. Her gaze reached for him.

"Fool!" He shouted at Martin as he sank with Wren across his knees, her back resting against him. He cradled her. "Look what you have done."

"I did not mean— She stepped in!"

Wren's lips moved but no sound came.

"How grave a wound? Let me see." Madlyn pushed in. Sparrow had not seen such a look on her face since the day Will Scarlet died.

Blood now streamed down Wren's breast. Murder flared in Sparrow's soul. He wanted to lay her down, to get up and kill Martin with his bare hands, but he could not, because Wren needed him. He could feel her love and need, reaching.

He could also feel Martin's extreme dismay and regret, but he cared little for that. He raised his eyes to Martin's face. "Get out of my sight."

"Do not speak to me that way."

"Look what you have done! You have killed her." Even as Sparrow spoke, Wren's eyes drifted closed. His arms tightened around her. "If we lose her, we lose everything."

Martin's lips tightened. He gave a hard nod and

then, miraculously, withdrew.

Madlyn's hands trembled as she inspected the wound. "I have not the skill for this. We need Lil."

"She *is* Lil, now." Sparrow barely recognized his own voice. "If she follows Lil into the grave, our world is undone." And his life would be over. Sparrow knew that now, to the very root of his soul. He could not hope to live a day without Wren. Yet she lay senseless in his arms.

"Bring her." Madlyn scrambled to her feet. "I have bandaging and medicines in my pack. Please the god, it will be enough."

Sparrow began to pray as he swung Wren up into his arms and returned the few paces to where Alric lay. He spoke to the god he always addressed, the only god he had been raised to know—the Green Man, lord of the trees. The god represented life, here in Sherwood; to his heart, Sparrow believed that. Yet the god had not kept his father alive, nor his mother. Nor Robin. Why should he save Wren now?

Please, he beseeched even as he stretched Wren out beside the motionless Alric. *I will do anything, give anything you ask.*

The trees tossed restlessly overhead, even though mere moments ago there had been no wind. A voice seemed to speak from nowhere and everywhere, to seep through Sparrow's skin and sound within his mind.

Anything?

Anything, Sparrow confirmed. *Only save her, please.*

Chapter Twenty-Three

"Can you hit that mark?" Rennie heard challenge in the question, as well as gentleness and love.

She stood in the forest, green light filtering down through branches high above. Motes of radiance danced around her like magic dust, and she breathed them in effortlessly. Her bow sat on her shoulder, and the man beside her made her feel inexpressibly safe.

"What target? Where?" she asked.

"Dead ahead—the beech tree with the square of fabric pinned to it."

Wren narrowed her eyes and peered ahead; she could barely see the target, yet she slid her bow from her shoulder and eased an arrow from the quiver on her back, sighted, and shot smoothly.

"Well done. And now the next target, farther on."

"Where?" But even as she asked, Rennie saw it and loosed her second arrow. It flew true, and found its mark.

"And the next."

"But I cannot see that target at all."

The man beside her laughed softly. "That is where faith comes in play. Sometimes, Daughter, we have to trust blindly."

Rennie lowered her bow and looked at him in surprise.

"Surely you are not shocked to see me," he smiled.

"We have met here before."

So they had, and her heart quickened with gladness. He was Robin, her father, dead before she entered the world. He was the Green Man himself, god of this place. He was Sherwood.

"And we have met in dreams. You came and spoke to me."

His smile deepened and reached his eyes. "You are very like me, you know."

"Am I?" Her gaze, amazed and curious, drank him in. Was this, indeed, how he had appeared at the time of his death? An ordinary-looking man, some might say, yet with nothing ordinary about him: of medium height, not so tall as Sparrow, with hair the exact color of her own streaming over his shoulders, and a narrow, clever face. Did her countenance truly echo his, with its grace and fierce beauty, the humor and wisdom? She feared not. And his eyes were nothing like her golden wild-fox eyes but held a clear sapphire serenity.

She asked, quite reasonably, "Am I dead?"

"No, Daughter."

"But you are."

"Am I?" He shook his head and the shaggy hair slapped his back. "I think not."

"Can you die? Are you just my father, or the god, in truth?"

"Both." He smiled again and light filled his face, drew her to him. Was this that which allowed him to inspire folk and lead them, sometimes to their deaths? Was it this that kept his legend always alive?

"I am not sure I understand that."

"But you must be sure, or you will never hit the target."

"Ah. We no longer speak of arrows, I think."

"Wren, look around you." He waved a leather-clad arm. "What do you see?"

"Trees."

"No."

"No?"

He laughed again, and the sound made Rennie's heart rise. "Beyond the trees and inside them."

Rennie shook her head.

"Life." He supplied the word. "Endless life. It dwells in every tree, and it dwells in you. It dances like that light, and it cannot be defeated by so small a thing as death."

"Death, small? How can that be? I have lost to death everyone who should have been there to care for me—"

"Daughter, do you believe in the magic of Sherwood?"

"Well I must, since I stand here speaking with you now. Is this the magic of which you speak?"

"It is. Sherwood is a repository of belief. It is strong because it is a place where old faith dwells, like the great stones to the south, or the sea that surrounds our island. Do you know at one time England was all forest? And when the first men came, it was here they found the magic of being, of life, and called it God. Daughter, you must defend Sherwood because it is so much more than trees. It is a natural fortress of belief in the right of each of us, who shares life, to flourish above oppression. I fought the Normans because of the threat they represented to what makes England— England."

Rennie wrinkled her brow, struggling to

understand. "I am but an ignorant girl, raised in a scullery."

"Raised by Lil, you mean. Do not forget all she gave you—knowledge of herbs and spells, folk wisdom and history. You are well equipped for the role you must play."

Rennie did not feel well equipped. Yet reassurance flowed from this man the way radiance flowed through the trees. "And what role is that to be?"

"You must take my place, that of leader, guardian, champion of right and of life."

Panic struck at Rennie's heart. "But I thought I was to take Lil's place while Sparrow and Martin contested over Alric's and Geoffrey's."

"The balance has changed. There must be three, aye, forming a circle of power, an inviolable container for the magic that dwells here. Once it was me, your mother, and the Green Man himself, but the power was uneven, and when I died, it all fell apart."

"My mother gave up."

"I had carried too much of the burden, and she was ill prepared. Lil, Geoffrey, and Alric did a better job of distributing the load, but Alric will not survive long now without them. You, Sparrow, and Martin must find a way to share the weight evenly, and with strength."

"But Martin—what shall we do about him? He is so angry, and he does not want Alric's place."

"Then give him his own place. It is as I tell you, Daughter. With the three of you, the circle now takes new form. It does not matter where you stand, but so long as you do, my legend lives on and I continue to dwell here. Now, shoot your arrow."

Rennie still could not see the target. She raised her

bow, narrowed her eyes and used the knowing inside her to aim, blind except for faith. Loosed, the arrow flew and voices rushed in upon her.

"She wakes."

"Nay, she only stirs, still senseless."

"She hears us, she hears my voice."

"Get back away from her, you great louts, and let her breathe."

Someone took Rennie's hand—Sparrow. She would know his touch even blind. Anyway, she could feel his thoughts battering at her—and Martin's—both close at hand.

She squeezed Sparrow's fingers and felt his rush of relief. "She lives."

Rennie stirred; pain fell on her like a stone, searing across her chest. In spite of it, she opened her eyes.

Three faces hovered over her like worried moons. At that instant Rennie knew how dear to her they were—all of them. How strange that only a month ago she had known none of the three, yet now they encompassed her world.

She tried to smile.

Martin leaned closer. To Rennie's surprise, she saw tears in his eyes. "Wren, I am so sorry. I never meant…"

She reached her free hand to him. He took it, his fingers rough and warm, and Rennie felt the bond become complete, the link forged whole.

She spoke, her voice ugly and thin. "My father says we must learn to share this burden, the three of us together."

"Your father?" Sparrow looked startled.

"I have just been with him."

"By the Green Man's thorn," Martin breathed, "did I send her over the threshold of death?"

"He is not dead. Alive, here in Sherwood."

"Poor lass," said Madlyn, "she is raving."

"Is it not why we join together," Rennie whispered, ignoring Madlyn's opinion, "in order to keep him alive?"

"Aye," Sparrow murmured, "aye, Wren."

"We cannot fight amongst ourselves; that will only do the Sheriff's work for him." Rennie's eyes flitted closed against the pain.

She heard Sparrow say, "Martin, give her your strength."

"Eh?" Martin sounded startled.

"Pour it into her, man. Through your fingers. Do you not see how vitally we need her?"

Rennie tried to open her eyes and found she could not. Yet she felt strength begin to trickle into her, like warmth, through the fingers of both men. Slow at first, and uneven, it steadied until she could almost see, against her closed eyelids, the circle of power that connected them.

She knew, then, the triad had become complete, and she knew why. "Alric," she mourned.

And Madlyn spoke softly, "I am sorry, my dear; Alric is dead."

Chapter Twenty-Four

"We have been hunted like foxes these three days past. I have never known Lambert so persistent."

"Perhaps the Sheriff is dead at last. Can it be Lambert acts on his own, trying to earn a high place with the King?"

Rennie lay listening as the two men spoke in low voices, while Madlyn laid yet another poultice on her chest. Comfrey it was, this time, to draw the heat from a wound that had become inflamed. Rennie closed her eyes against the pain, her endurance nearly at an end. Could she go on another day? Since being injured, she had traveled mostly on foot, despite her weakness. Sparrow and Martin shared the burden of Alric between them.

Much of their conversation centered on flight, pursuit, and on where to lay the old man to rest. On his own, in Sherwood? Back where he had kept his hermitage, among the trees? Or beside those two with whom he had been so surely linked?

The three of them understood the bond so much better now that their own had been forged. It made them hesitant to bury Alric apart. Yet a return to Oakham meant danger. Twice had they ventured near, only to run into patrols of soldiers.

"Bold," Martin had muttered on the second occasion. "Do they fear Sherwood no more? If we could round up our own men, we could put them to the chase. But Lambert did his job too well, scattering us."

Now Rennie opened her eyes and turned her head. Sparrow and Martin sat together like friends, both of them showing obvious signs of exhaustion. Rennie caressed Sparrow with her gaze and received a resultant jolt of pleasure. Feeling her emotions, he swung his face toward her; their gazes tangled and held.

"There, now," Madlyn whispered, "lie still, lass, and let that do its work."

"Will she be able to go on?" Martin asked his mother.

Rennie answered before Madlyn could give her opinion. "I will."

Martin made a rude sound that expressed his doubt. He looked angry and aggrieved, with weariness under it all. Well, they all felt worried and tired unto death. "One thing is sure. We cannot linger here."

"Wren needs to rest," Madlyn protested.

"And we need to move on." Martin's gaze could have cut glass. "Gather your medicines, Mother, and let us go."

Madlyn straightened, sudden tears in her eyes. "You will kill the child, Martin. Is that what you want?" She seemed to realize what she had said only after the words left her lips. Martin's face froze, and tears flooded Madlyn's eyes. "I am sorry, I did not mean—"

Martin got to his feet, desperation in every line of his body. "Naught to be sorry about, Mother. 'Tis the truth." He looked at Rennie. "Do you wish to rest here a while?"

She struggled up somehow, trying not to let her agony show in her face. "No, best we move on. I have made a decision: we can wait no longer to lay Alric to rest. Perhaps, after all, he should lie apart from Lil and Geofrey, as he lived apart from them."

"Poor bastard," Martin muttered. "But where, then?"

Rennie lifted her chin. "We will take him to his hermitage. That was a place of peace for him, and it was there he found his own bride—the Lady herself."

Sparrow and Martin exchanged glances and nodded.

"How far are we from the hermitage?" Rennie asked.

"Farther than you will be able to walk," Sparrow told her. "Here with you, up on my back."

"Eh?" Rennie returned, startled.

"I will take you pig-a-back, if your wound can stand it. Madlyn, can you make a cushion to fold over my shoulders?"

"Never mind me bearing it," Rennie objected. "Sparrow, you cannot. We are all weary to the bones, and I am no tiny lass, nor an easy weight."

"There is nothing to you. Just tuck your arms round my neck."

"You expect to tote me, as well as carry Alric?"

Sparrow reached out and touched Rennie's cheek tenderly. His gaze engulfed hers, and Martin quickly looked away. Such exchanges still troubled him.

"Love, you are no burden."

They traveled much more swiftly with Rennie up on Sparrow's back, hampered only by Madlyn's ability to keep up. Rennie went with both arms and legs twined about Sparrow, so she could feel his every movement, the smooth strength in each muscle, and her cheek pressed against his hair. Unexpected desire stirred. Would they ever have another chance to be together, man and woman? Even sore and hurting, she cried out for it. But perhaps duty called them to be something more than lovers.

"Ah—" Martin, in the lead, stopped suddenly. "Someone has been here before us."

"No." Madlyn pushed forward. "How could anyone discover Alric's secret place?"

Rennie peered ahead and saw a small, cleared area in the wood, hard against an outcropping of rock where the land rose. The trees here, old and massive, stood guardian, and a spring bubbled up to form a rivulet that joined a stream farther below. Alric must have kept his few belongings in the alcove, but they were now strewn about, most smashed across the remnants of his last fire, and the ground looked trampled.

It struck Rennie to the heart, having brought the old man back to refuge only to find it defiled.

She slid down Sparrow's back and stood on her own feet. "But how could this place be discovered, so deep in Sherwood?"

"The Sheriff—or, more correctly, Lambert—must have inside information," Sparrow said uneasily. "But, from whom?"

Martin spat, "Curse him, whoever he is, to betray Alric—and us."

"Few knew the location of Alric's lair," Madlyn whispered, as if fearful someone still listened. "And he would have woven a strong spell of protection round the place."

"No matter," Rennie said. "They have come and gone, and snared no one. Surely they will not return

173

soon."

"If they do," said Sparrow grimly, "we will hear them coming. Let us lay Alric to rest at last. But if we stay here the night, Martin, we will need keep watch, in turns."

Martin nodded but said nothing.

Madlyn tidied away the mess, gathered shards of broken pottery, and collected what could be salvaged, while the two men dug a grave in the soft, loamy earth. They finished just as darkness began to gather beneath the trees. Solemnly, heads bowed, they stood over Alric's mound. Madlyn started to weep.

"Do not, Mother," Martin said. "We will exact revenge for all he has suffered. This I promise you."

"Son, I do not think it is about revenge. He was a good man, and I grieve at his loss, and the fact that I will never see him again."

And, Rennie wondered, did Madlyn also grieve because she believed her son must take this lonely path, for which he seemed so ill suited? Did Madlyn resent Rennie for choosing Sparrow? She had, so far, treated Rennie with nothing but loving kindness.

Rennie stole a look at Martin's face, just visible in the gloom. He stared down at Alric's quiet grave, his expression bleak. Did he even now suppose he stared into his own future?

She closed her eyes and attempted to pray, to ask for Alric's repose. Above her head a breeze stirred the leaves, just as if a breath passed through them. Something brushed her hand and then her shoulders— Sparrow, she thought, but it did not feel like Sparrow's touch.

She opened her eyes and saw their number had

increased by two. A spear of alarm went through her before she blinked and identified the new arrivals.

The light had nearly failed, yet Rennie saw both of them—Lil and a man who could only be Geofrey—standing with their hands linked, heads bowed. Her heart lurched and rose. So, Alric did not lie alone. How could she have imagined anyone was ever alone, here in Sherwood?

****

"We need a plan," Martin said insistently. "I refuse to continue running like a hare before the hounds, letting Lambert's men do as they will on our turf. We need to round up our men and make answer—and, if someone has indeed betrayed us, I would answer him, also."

Morning had come to the wood, and with it a feeling of renewed strength. Bright sunlight flickered through leaves that danced in a freshening breeze. Magic seemed to dance with it, and some of Rennie's vitality had returned. Her companions looked grave but resolved. With Alric at rest, the burden of responsibility had passed to them fully and completely. They must learn to make their own way now.

She nodded. "I agree. And I propose that the way things were done in the past may not be the way we need to go on. Roles and duties may change."

Both men looked at her in surprise.

Sparrow said, "I am not sure I understand."

She grimaced and waved a hand. "We have two examples before us. My father held the magic firm in his own hands, and carried most of the responsibility. My mother and the Green Man himself completed that circle."

"Who told you that?" Martin demanded.

"He did—my father."

Martin shivered but made no reply.

"When he died, the connection with the Green Man was severed, and my mother surrendered to her grief, unable to go on. Lil, Alric, and Geofrey took it up for the sake of Sherwood and those who depend on what Sherwood represents—they did a fine job, but they formed the circle according to who they were." She struggled with the ideas gleaned last night, above Alric's grave. "We are not them. And I believe so long as we maintain the circle, we need not take up their places, or identities."

"What places, then?" Sparrow asked curiously.

"We need to hold to our strengths. Martin, I cannot see you surviving here, amid all this quiet. It feels wrong—and I would not make of you what you are not."

He looked both relieved and wary. "What, then?"

"You need to embrace what you do best—I believe that means you should stand foremost for us. I would ask you to serve as my captain, even as Lambert serves the Sheriff. I also believe you should take the place as headman of Oakham, if that is acceptable to Adam, and if it does not prove impossibly dangerous."

"But—you have chosen Sparrow."

"So? Is there some magical law that says he with whom I lie must be a soldier, and skilled with the sword? I know Geofrey was headman of Oakham. But that circle is dissolved away."

"Well." Martin sat up a little straighter. She felt his rush of enthusiasm. Yet he asked, "Am I not destined to mate with and attend the spirit of Sherwood?"

"That was Alric's role, not yours. Anyway, Oakham is part of Sherwood, as good as. And will you not be attending Sherwood by defending its magic as you do best, with your sword if necessary?"

Sparrow asked softly, "What of us?"

She looked into his eyes and felt her heart stir. "We must find our way and our balance in this circle of power. I would not mind living here, or some place like it."

"You—to take Alric's place?" Martin asked, amazed.

"My own place," Rennie once more corrected, "among the spirits of Sherwood. You, Sparrow, could be my connection between the magic here and the work we must do in the world. And there is much work to do, beginning with what you just mentioned, Martin— regaining the upper hand. That is, if you both agree."

"I agree," said Martin, looking happier than he had in days.

"I agree," Sparrow echoed, gazing deep into Rennie's eyes.

She reached out and seized both their hands. "Then we will begin."

Chapter Twenty-Five

"How are you, Sally?" Sparrow asked in concern.
He thought the lass appeared unwell. Her once rosy
skin had turned pale, and her features looked pinched.
Sparrow feared the worst. During their time apart, had
she rid herself of Martin's child? And was there a
tactful way he could ask such a question?

A fortnight had passed since Alric's death, and the
outlaw camp had more or less reformed in a new, well-
hidden location. One by one, folk had drifted back,
along with new arrivals driven by the cruel punishments
visited upon Oakham. Each arrival had brought snippets
of information, and Sparrow had built a picture in his
mind.

The Sheriff lived yet, but he was so ill and spent
those about him expected each breath to be his last.
Word had been sent to King John. No one could guess
whom he might appoint as the Sheriff's successor, but
meanwhile Lambert acted with the King's authority and
proved a cruel and violent master. He had declared
himself determined to eradicate the outlaws of
Sherwood and all who assisted them.

Martin, who had stepped into his new role with
enjoyment, seemed more than ready for the challenge.
But in all this time he had barely glanced in poor
Sally's direction.

The lass now drooped, sad and wan. Even

distracted as he was by his own worries, Sparrow ached to do something for her. When he found himself sorting arrows with her, following a skirmish not far from Oakham, he decided to speak.

"How is your health," he asked, his voice a low buzz, "and that of your child?"

Sally shot him a warning look and her expression turned even grimmer.

Sparrow caught his breath. "I pray you, Sal, tell me you have not—?"

"I would have, given the opportunity. There has been no chance, with Lil gone and the rest of us in flight, all about Sherwood." She pressed both hands to the small mound of her stomach. "Now I fear it is too late. But you promised not to tell."

"And I have not." Sparrow had shared the precious knowledge only with Alric, and he now in his grave. "Sal, I cannot help believe 'tis best you have kept the child. But you need to tell Martin. Surely the truth will soon begin to show."

"And should I throw myself at him for such a reason, when his disinterest cries aloud?" Sally gazed across the camp to where Martin even now stood in conference with Wren. "I still cannot believe she did not choose him. Not that I say she is wrong in choosing you, Sparrow—we are good friends and I am that happy for you. But he—"

Sparrow smiled ruefully. "Aye, Martin burns very brightly, especially now." He followed Sally's gaze; Martin and Wren stood with their heads close together, the yellow nearly touching the brown.

Martin fairly oozed confidence, and Sparrow acknowledged Wren's wisdom in placing her faith in him and giving him purpose. It had gone far in healing the sting of her rejection, which Martin perceived as a slight.

Yet the position of headman, dangerous as it might be, allowed for marriage, did it not? He turned to Sally again. "Sal—he needs to know. It might make him risk himself less."

She shook her head. "That it will not. Martin is Martin, and will never change."

"We all know what it means to be without a father. But now that things are sorted between us he might well be able to help you look after a child."

"He does not love me. He no longer even wants me—he still wants her."

"A babe might change all that."

"No. When Martin's heart is set, it is set." Sally's eyes met Sparrow's. "I hold you to your promise. You will not betray me?"

"It is not a matter of betrayal. Soon Madlyn will ask why you appear unwell, and she is no fool, even if Martin is. Better the truth comes from your lips to Martin's ear."

"Lies can be told," Sally said stubbornly. "You just keep your promise to me, Sparrow Little."

Unhappy, Sparrow looked up again to see Martin watching him and Sally with an expression that boded well for no one.

****

Not until much later in the day, when the patrol had gone out chasing soldiers and returned again with the swords of no less than three, did Martin approach Sparrow. He came at a swagger, the gore of the fight still upon him.

Sparrow felt Martin's aggression break over him in a bold wave, even before he spoke. "So—one woman is not enough for you, is that it? You are not satisfied with winning what I wanted once but must do it again."

Sparrow, interrupted splitting kindling for the fire, straightened with the axe in his hands. "What are you on about?"

"I saw you earlier—you and Sal all cozy together, whispering. What do you want with her, when you already have Wren?"

Sparrow drew a breath. He had hoped Martin might have left his jealousy behind him, but it seemed Sally was right—Martin would be Martin. "Do not be a fool."

Predictably, Martin bristled. "Is that what you call me?"

"That is what you are. Have you no eyes in your head?"

"To see what?" Martin's gaze narrowed. If Martin guessed Sally's secret, so Sparrow told himself, that did not count as betrayal on his part. "Sally is my friend, only. And she is troubled," he said.

"Troubled? How so?"

"Is it truly so impossible for you to fathom? Her father has been killed, she has lost her home and is forced to take refuge in the forest, and the man upon whom she should be able to rely has forgotten to care for her."

Martin flushed with ire. "So she turns to you for comfort? Have you bedded her, as well as Wren?"

Sparrow laughed incredulously. "If you can suppose I want anyone but Wren, you are a greater fool than I thought." In truth, he burned for Wren, but had not lain with her since she took her injury. The stubborn wound refused to heal cleanly, and Wren insisted on doing too much. He nearly had to tie her down to make her rest.

Martin's eyes narrowed. "Why would you not want Sal? She is beautiful enough."

"She is. And she loves you with her whole heart, if you could but see it." That made no betrayal, being a fact everyone knew—save Martin. "Look at her. Truly look at her, man!"

Martin turned hard eyes across the clearing to where Sally stood speaking with Madlyn. The late afternoon sun caressed her form and outlined her increased shape. Martin's eyes widened. He turned to Sparrow with dread. "She is—" Words seemed to escape him. He stared at Sparrow accusingly. "Yours?"

"Of course not mine, you pillock."

"Who—?"

"You will need to ask her that. But talk to her, for the love of God."

With no further question, Martin crossed the clearing and joined Sally where she stood. He laid a hand on her arm, and they stepped away and then sat together.

Sparrow did his best not to watch; he went back to work splitting kindling, but dangerously, with one eye on the couple across the way. Soon Sally put her face in her hands and began to weep. Martin put an arm around her.

At last, Sparrow thought victoriously. He swung his axe and smiled to himself.

"You nearly removed your own fingers, there." Wren stood beside him. She looked weary and spent, yet her presence brought him a rush of gladness.

My love, he said, his mind to hers, and then, aloud, "How do you feel?"

"I keep telling everyone I am fine." She, too, looked across the clearing. "What goes on there?"

"I believe Sally confesses a secret, and high time."

"What secret?"

"'Twould not be one if I told you, would it?"

He felt her shrug before she leaned close. "I shall tell you a secret of my own, shall I?" Her breath tickled his ear and sent a shiver down his spine.

He gazed into her wild-hawk eyes. "Pray do."

"Sparrow Little, I cannot live without you one night more. I have been watching you ply that axe this long while and fairly burnt myself to cinders in the doing." She leaned still nearer and brushed her lips across his. The axe fell from his suddenly numb fingers and landed harmlessly on the ground. "Why do you not come to me where I lie?"

"You are hurting, and need to heal."

"Are you sure that is all?" She withdrew from him, and sudden doubt invaded her eyes. "It is not because my wound makes me ugly?"

"Ugly?" Sparrow could not conceive of the word in relation to her.

"Aye, Madlyn tells me there will be a scar, a great, hideous one. All these days of inflammation, and the flesh refusing to close, do not help. You know, the wound cuts clear across my chest, and onto my breasts. You called them beautiful, once."

"As I do still."

"You have not seen—"

But he had seen, when Madlyn changed her bandaging, back at Alric's hermitage. "Wren, you took

183

that wound for me, unhesitating, to save my life. How could it be anything but beautiful?"

"I wish I could believe you."

He caught her face between his hands. "Listen to me, Wren—I love you, and will until the day I die. Surely you can feel that. You can hear my thoughts; do you hear any lies?"

"No. But there is a difference between being compelled to love me, by magic, and finding me desirable, as once you did."

He laughed unsteadily. "You think that is why I love you, because Sherwood ordains it?"

"Is it not?"

"No, Wren. I told you, I loved you from the first moment I saw you in Lil's kitchen, when you came stumbling out of the scullery with your hair all loose about you and questions in your eyes."

"That is not desire."

"I never leave off desiring you."

A faint light entered her eyes. "I may need call upon you to prove that."

"Feel this?" He drew her close against him so she could not miss the burgeoning bulge trapped inside his leggings. "Woman, I scarce need the axe. I could split wood with—"

A cry echoed across the clearing and interrupted their affectionate exchange. Hand in hand, they spun to face Martin and Sally, just in time to see Martin explode in rage.

With a roar, he leaped up from Sally's side. She came to her feet also and stood with her arms wrapped about herself, her face white as bone.

"What has happened?" Wren asked.

Sparrow shook his head. Even Martin would not react so to what Sally must have told him. Yet Martin, flushed with anger, now charged across the camp, calling to men as he came.

"You—Gerald, Micah, and Dennis—go find your brother." He called on the best of his men. "We leave at once." He virtually skidded to a halt in front of Sparrow. "I need you, also. Bring your bow and as many arrows as you can carry."

"Why?" Sparrow shot a look at Sally, who stood wearing a dreadful, shuttered expression. Their eyes met. "What goes on?"

"We go after Lambert, and I will not rest until that bastard lies dead."

"Calm down, Martin, I do not understand." Wren laid a hand on his arm. "Explain!"

"Sally just confessed the truth to me at last," Martin raged. "That villain's attacked and had his way with her. She is with child. His child!" Martin struggled to gain control of himself and failed entirely. "I tell you, he needs to die."

Chapter Twenty-Six

"Martin has gone mad, I am convinced of it." Rennie breathed out a sigh of pure exhaustion and threw herself down on her back beside Sparrow, who lay sprawled with his eyes closed. With her hand, she caressed his bare arm and then clasped his fingers. She ached from head to foot, yet still she wanted Sparrow and needed to touch him. "Have you ever seen him like this?"

"No," Sparrow grunted. "He will kill us all."

It was Rennie's fear also. She bit her lip, twined her fingers more closely with his, and frowned at the green leaves dancing overhead. For how much of this did she carry the blame? No sooner had she conveyed upon Martin the title of headman than he had taken on this intention to see Lambert dead. And now they engaged in nothing less than war.

For the past seven days there had been a series of running battles. The troop of outlaws Martin favored had gone out to find, intercept, and battle Lambert's soldiers whenever possible. The fierce ploy had the advantage of driving the soldiers from Sherwood, but they plagued the towns about its perimeter still. Lambert seemed particularly determined to take out his revenge upon Oakham and its surviving denizens.

And it had cost the outlaws dear. Already they had lost two men and had a score of injured.

"I do not deny we need to fight Lambert," Rennie murmured now, her eyes narrowed. "He is a hard-hearted blackguard and must be stopped from using other women as cruelly as he has poor Sally."

Sparrow's fingers twitched violently in hers, and she turned her head to look at him. "What is it?"

There was an advantage in virtually being able to hear her lover's thoughts. Rennie knew how Sparrow felt nearly all the time, even when they were apart. But she also knew when he kept something from her.

He closed his eyes, displaying his sinfully long, black lashes. Like everyone else, he looked tired beyond measure, yet she loved every line of his face—the proud nose, broad forehead, well-defined chin. She might gaze at him forever, would life only slow down and give her the chance.

"What are you holding from me, Sparrow? Surely Martin is justified in his campaign against Lambert. Did not Lambert very nearly do the same to me as he did to Sally? Poor lass, she never leaves off weeping."

Sparrow lifted his lashes and looked at her. His eyes—liquid, dark, and wise as a hart's—reached into her soul. "I am not at leave to say what I would, Wren."

"Why not?

"When I give a promise, I keep it."

"Oh. Then do not speak as you should not. Whisper it, from your mind to mine."

"Do you not think I wish to? That would still be a betrayal."

"Do you believe so?"

"I do. By any road, once you know, you will fly off into anger, and then Sally will know I have revealed what I swore I would not."

187

Rennie lowered her voice. "This secret concerns Sally, then?"

Sparrow blinked once.

Well, Rennie thought, the gods love Sparrow and his honorable heart. But he should at least tell her, since they in essence shared one mind. Plumbing the depths of that connection now, she picked up a few tendrils of information. Sally had lied about something, but what?

No lie that the lass was with child. She now seemed to increase by the day—a big strong child it was, no doubt. Rennie had spoken to her, or attempted to, thinking Sally might wish to confide in another woman her age. All Sally would say was that Lambert had caught her one day in the forest near Oakham and attacked her most vilely. The rape had occurred before Sally's father died, but she had not told him, nor anyone, until now.

Rennie frowned in thought, her gaze still holding Sparrow's. "It must have something to do with Martin."

An answering spark. "Because she is in love with him and she confided in him. Or did she confide in you first?"

Sparrow said dryly, "Words confided may not all be truth."

"Ah, so she lied to one of you. Yourself?"

The slightest shake of Sparrow's head.

"Ah, to Martin? You mean, the child she carries may not be Lambert's?"

"Keep your voice down. And, you did not learn that from me."

"I did not." Rennie raised Sparrow's fingers to her lips and brushed them with a kiss. "It seems I need to speak to Sally again."

"Or to Martin. As it is, he will not rest until Lambert lies cold and dead. I have no quarrel with that, but I suspect it may prove costly to achieve, more so than we can stand. Have you heard his latest scheme?"

"I have not."

"Best speak with him about it, for it has even our most hardened men quaking with dread."

Reluctantly, Rennie released Sparrow's hand and scrambled to her feet, her few stolen moments of bliss flown. "There is, as Lil used to say, no time like the present."

****

Martin looked like a wild man. Rennie acknowledged that as she approached him where he stood giving orders to a scouting party. The men—a group of five—looked at Rennie imploringly and then scattered, their bows upon their shoulders.

"Wren." Martin favored her with a nod before turning back to an outline he had scratched into a patch of cleared earth. She saw it was a map of Sherwood, with various points marked with Xs.

Her brows lifted. "That is a fine piece of work. What is its purpose?"

"It tells the men where to search and where to lie in ambush." Martin's voice sounded fierce and his eyes blazed—a man with a cause. So close to him as this, Rennie could clearly feel the emotions raging inside him, burning bright with violence.

"A useful tool," she acknowledged cautiously.

"We shall catch him out where he least expects, see if we do not."

"We will," Rennie agreed, "if the god's hand is in it."

189

Martin promptly exploded. "With the god or without. Where was the god when Sally was attacked and plundered?"

Rennie drew a breath against the power of his emotions. "Peace, Martin. When is the last time you ate a meal? Or took rest?"

He snarled, "I will not rest until Lambert feels the full weight of my sword."

"And do you care how many lives that costs?"

"Eh?" He stared at her, his blue-gray eyes aflame.

"These attacks you launch are costing us men."

He bristled. "Wren, do you question my place as captain? It is the one you, yourself, granted me."

"I merely question the present campaign. Open warfare is not our way. We have not the weapons nor the men."

Martin's expression turned ugly. He sneered, "You chose this, Wren. You chose him. You want your place of peace with him, hidden away as Alric was. You must then live with the consequences."

Rennie's ire flared in response to his. "You know I never meant to hand over to you all the power."

"You should be more careful, then. But you would rather lie with Sparrow than fight for justice. And I supposed you a worthy daughter of Robin Hood."

"So I do strive to be!"

"Well, I think you had better strive harder. And it comes to me you possess less of Robin's courageous heart than your mother's—she who gave up in the face of pain."

"I will not second guess my mother's choices." Rennie could not imagine how she, herself, would survive if she lost Sparrow. Just the thought of it stole her breath and threatened to still her heart. Could she fight on? Or would she, too, wish to retreat from the world? Marian had abandoned Rennie to Lil—her own child, Robin's child. That argued unbearable pain.

She struggled to keep her head, and her temper. "I think you should consult with Sparrow and me before planning these excursions." She gestured to the map in the dirt. "That is all."

"So the two of you, together, can vote me down? I think not. This is no time to hesitate. Lambert needs to be hunted and killed before the Sheriff dies, else he will acquire still more power. He thinks he can use folk however he will, that a lass like Sally does not matter. But I am here to say she does."

"Have you spoken to her about it? Is this war what she wants?"

Martin stared. "Need I ask her if she wishes the blackguard who raped her struck down? Besides"—his bright eyes fell suddenly—"she will not talk to me. She does nothing but sit and weep. Lambert broke her, that is what."

Rennie drew breath to speak, but he rushed on, "I will fight Lambert and all his ilk until the day I die."

"Or until everyone for whom you care does?"

"Wren, do not be soft. The Normans would have us believe they are our overlords. They steal our land, our rights and our women. What is our purpose, if not to teach them differently? Is that not worth the dying?"

"Yes," Rennie answered softly. "Yet I would be sure I am truly fighting for what I believe. Talk to Sally," she urged again. "Quite possibly she would rather have you alive than have her vengeance."

"Have me?" he asked, clearly baffled.

Rennie leaned toward him. "You might wed with her, make a father for her child."

"Raise a bastard of Lambert's?" he howled. "I tell you, Wren, I would far sooner die."

Chapter Twenty-Seven

"Mistress Wren, Mistress Wren! Martin has been captured, seized by Sir Lambert's men—taken alive, we think."

The man who spoke had blood on his face and more splashed across his tunic. He still bore his bow upon his shoulder, but his quiver hung empty across his back, and he cradled his right arm close to his chest. His name was Micah.

He, in the company with three other members of Martin's patrol, stumbled into camp just before dark, the sole remnants of the party Martin had led out shortly after dawn. All day long, Rennie had felt uneasy, half her mind on the escapade from which Martin refused to be turned. Now, hearing these words, the tension within her broke. Had it been the danger to Martin that dogged her?

She felt Sparrow stiffen beside her but did not take her eyes from Micah's face. "What happened? How badly are you hurt?"

Micah ignored the second question in favor of the first. "We had information a party of merchants would be on the York road, light guard, and enough goods and coin to pay the taxes of everyone in Oakham for the year. We went out early and lay in wait—but we were betrayed. 'Twas Lambert's soldiers who came, led by the man himself."

Swiftly Sparrow asked, "From whence did Martin get this information?"

"He never said. Someone from inside Nottingham castle, he let us think. Though I can guess—" Micah caught himself up and his eyes, filled with pain, searched Rennie's face. "Do you not know, mistress? It was by your orders we went."

Rennie cursed herself. The man spoke truly: she should have known every detail. She had trusted Martin, given him altogether too much leave, and now her people paid for it. "How many dead?" she asked grimly.

"We were a party of a half-score. You see, Mistress, how many have returned. Dead or captured, the rest. Lambert's men took Martin and two others."

"Four dead." Rennie grieved it. She had failed them. "And yon fellows, are they hurt also? Go you to Madlyn. See what aid she can give."

"Aye, mistress, but—" Micah reached out and seized her sleeve with bloodied fingers. "I saw Simon."

"Eh?" Rennie had believed the lad killed during the last flight from Oakham. Had he been captured, instead?

"He rode with Lambert." Micah spat the words.

Rennie's stomach clenched hard, and dismay filled her heart. She liked the lad and flinched from the suggestion he could have betrayed them.

"Mistress, what about Martin and the others? My own brother, Trent, makes one of their number."

"Leave it with me, and Sparrow," Rennie told him. "We will make a plan."

"What plan?" Sparrow asked as soon as Micah walked away.

Rennie met his gaze. "We need to rescue them."

"Are you mad?" Sparrow caught her by the arms. "That is just what Lambert wants. This was a trap from the start, and Martin, with his hot head, fell right into it."

"It is my fault; I should have done a better job of curbing him."

Sparrow tossed his head. "No one curbs Martin. If you do not know that, you know nothing."

Rennie stared into Sparrow's eyes and became very still. So rarely did she sense rage in him, she barely recognized it now. Sparrow did a far better job than Martin of controlling his emotions, yet she could feel the ire boiling up. "You are angry with me."

"Not with you. With Martin for getting us into this, with that twisting adder, Lambert, and with Simon, if what Micah implies is true."

"And with me." Rennie did not dodge his gaze. "Do not lie."

His gaze softened. He reached out and touched her cheek, and she shivered. "I am incapable of lying to you, Wren. It is just that I know you, and I fear you will place yourself in danger. You are barely healed, yet you will rush within reach of Lambert's hands. Have you paused to consider what he will do if he catches you?"

Rennie did not want to consider it. She swallowed hard. Yet she knew she existed only to fight their oppressors. How could she turn away? Helpless, she told Sparrow, "I cannot leave our men there. I cannot abandon Martin to his fate. He is part of us."

Sparrow turned away from her. "Sometimes I think you are as impossible to deal with as Martin himself."

****

Word came next morning, soon after first light, in the person of Micah's brother Trent. He stumbled into camp, breathless and injured. Rennie heard the sentries she had posted cry out, and arose from her restless bed to meet the man beside the now-dead fire.

"How did you get here?" she asked. "Were you followed?"

He shook his head, and his eyes sought hers. "I made sure of that. Sir Lambert released me in order to bring a message. The others who were with me—" His voice broke.

Micah, now heavily swathed in bandages, reached for his brother's arm even as others, roused from their sleep, crowded in.

"Thomas, taken with us, is dead," Trent said bitterly. "The bastard, Lambert, killed him in the courtyard of the castle soon after we arrived. As an example, I think." Trent blanched. "I have never seen a man killed so. He screamed and screamed."

Rennie's stomach wobbled and turned over. She managed to ask, "But Martin—?"

"Alive—badly hurt. They beat him every time he protested Thomas's treatment—and he did protest. But Lambert recognized Martin from past encounters. He knows he has a prize. So he sent me to you."

Doubt flickered in Trent's eyes. "Only, he does not know you are *you*, mistress, if you take my meaning. He sent me with a message for Robin Hood."

A soft gasp traveled round the onlookers. More steadily than she felt, Rennie asked, "How is that? He believes my father is still alive?"

Beside her, Sparrow grunted. "It does not matter what he believes. He is a clever man. He knows the people believe Robin is alive and behind the resistance here in Sherwood. So he calls Robin out. He would destroy the legend itself."

Trent nodded. "He has issued to Robin Hood a challenge: appear at noon tomorrow—that is, today—at Nottingham Castle, to contest for Martin's freedom."

"No," Sparrow spoke instantly.

Rennie turned her eyes on him.

Passionately, he went on, "I know how you are, Wren—of what you are made. You will want to play the role, go there pretending to be Robin. You will be discovered—"

"I cannot forsake Martin. He is part of the circle, part of us."

Trent broke in. "Lambert says Martin's trial will begin at daybreak. That means it is starting even now."

"Trial?"

"By torture, there in the forecourt, where all can see."

A cry rang out. Sally's knees gave way, and she sank to the ground. Madlyn, pale as death, hauled her up and into her arms. "Here, lass, strength!"

"But it is my fault," Sally gasped.

"How is that?" Rennie asked.

Sally hid her face against Madlyn's shoulder and did not reply.

"It is Martin's own fault," Sparrow said, harshly for him. "I do not want to see him pay this price, but, Wren, I refuse to risk you in an effort to save him."

Agonized, Martin's mother protested, "You cannot just leave him there."

"I shall not," Rennie vowed. "We will plan a rescue."

"Rescue him from the forecourt of Nottingham Castle, with every soldier on alert?" Sparrow burst. "It is mad."

Rennie ignored his words. "We will form a party." She looked into the surrounding faces. "Volunteers?"

"I will go," Micah offered.

"And I," said Trent.

Rennie shook her head. "You are both too sore injured. Anyone else?"

A few hands lifted into the air. Even Rennie knew they would not be enough. She bit her lip, her heart torn.

How could she risk these brave souls in what must be a near-doomed cause? Yet how could she leave Martin in Lambert's hands to suffer unbearably, no doubt hoping for rescue that never came?

How could she abandon someone who, for all his rashness, was part of her?

And what would Robin have done in this situation? What wisdom lent, were he here?

I am here. The voice sounded within Rennie's heart, echoed in her mind. Warm and strong, she recognized it from her dreams. *I am alive in Sherwood, and Sherwood is alive in you.*

Her eyes widened, and she leaned toward her listeners. "Hark, all of you. I think I know what we must do."

Chapter Twenty-Eight

"I cannot believe you intend to risk your life—for him." Sparrow could hear the anger in his words even as he spoke them, and felt them hit the wall of Wren's resistance. He did not know when he had been so enraged—he fairly trembled with it, as with a sickness. He spat, "And you refuse to listen to me."

"I am listening," Wren replied, even as she donned the hooded leather jerkin and checked the contents of her quiver. She sounded calm, but Sparrow could sense her riotous emotions as clearly as his own. "But what should I do? I have told you, I cannot abandon him. Would you want me to abandon you?"

"Aye, if the only alternative was a mad rescue attempt that could cost your life."

"Well, I could never do that."

"Wren, look at me." He seized her shoulders in both hands and turned her to face him; her emotional turmoil poured into him as his eyes caught hers and held. "I cannot lose you. I would not be able to go on."

"I know." Sudden tears filled her eyes. "And so, we cannot lose Martin—"

Unreasoning jealousy licked up, cutting through Sparrow's other, tangled emotions. "So you love him?"

"Of course."

"As you love me?"

"Oh, Sparrow! I will never love anyone as I love

you." She leaned in and pressed her lips to his, sweetly. Need leaped up, and his heart turned desperate. For several breathless moments their lips held; then Wren drew away again.

"But, Sparrow, whatever happens, I will always be with you, even as my father is with me now."

"Your father?"

For the first time, Wren's gaze avoided his. She looked down and adjusted the belt at her waist. "It is Robin Hood Lambert wishes to meet—and Robin Hood I take to him. I will carry him inside me."

Sparrow gasped. "You do this thing on a fancy? You are as mad as Martin."

She stepped away from him and raised her hood. "How do I look? Will I pass for the legend himself? I am tall enough, I think."

"You mean to walk into that lion's den and declare yourself Robin Hood?" The audacity of it stole Sparrow's breath. "Aye, you might fool them for a moment, until they lay hands on you. Lambert will know you all too well, then."

"I shall not give him the chance to lay hands on me. I mean to issue a challenge—Robin Hood to stand against the best of his archers, the prize Martin's freedom and my own."

"He will never agree to it."

"His arrogance will not let him do anything else. How can he refuse the challenge? He must save face."

"And if you are wrong? If he seizes you as soon as he sees you?"

"He will not."

"You do not know that, and I refuse to let you risk yourself so rashly."

She paused in her preparations and laid her hand against his cheek. "My love, you cannot keep me."

He could. Sparrow knew he had only to lay hold of her and restrain her forcibly. She might never forgive him, but at least she would be alive.

He grasped her hand in both of his. "Please, Wren! What of Simon? Have you forgotten he may play the part of traitor? He will surely recognize you."

She shook her head. "You still do not understand. I go cloaked in magic. I do not go alone."

"You are right, Wren. If you insist upon this, I go with you. In fact, let me play the part of Robin. Not to boast, but I am the far better archer. You know that is true. I am nearly as good as Robin was."

"Nearly as good."

"Even if your plan works, Wren, you must stand against the best of the Sheriff's archers and win."

"Not I. The legend of Sherwood."

Sparrow stared at her, his eyes narrowed. She truly had lost her wits, and her sense; the strain of events must have turned her mind. He opened his lips to speak, but just then Sally pushed in upon them, her eyes wild.

"Wren, I need to tell you—Martin is in danger because of me. I lied—"

Wren turned to Sally, and Sparrow felt her strive to gather her patience. "This is no time for tears, Sally."

"No, it is time for the truth. Can I watch you sacrifice yourself even as Martin has, all for an untruth I told?"

"What untruth?" Wren challenged.

Sparrow cringed at the agony in Sally's pretty eyes. But she lifted her chin bravely. "Martin went out in anger, wishing to thwart Lambert, because I told him

Lambert had attacked and raped me, and I carried his child. It is not true. It is Martin's own child I carry, and now he may die for my falsehood, and you also."

"But why lie about it?" Astonished, Wren turned to Sparrow and saw the truth in his eyes. "You knew this? Why did you not tell me?"

"It was not my secret to tell." Sparrow had hinted, and bidden her talk to Martin. But she did not remember that now.

Quickly, Sally said, "Do not blame Sparrow. It is not his fault. All the blame lies with me."

Sparrow felt Wren's anger flare. "Foolish girl! I hope you can live with the consequences, however dire they may be."

Sally's eyes filled with ready tears. "Should Martin be lost, I will suffer every day for my sins. But I will raise his son, or daughter, the best I may. I pray, Wren, please forgive me. What I did, I did out of fear, and love."

Wren turned away from her and gathered her weapons, without another word.

Sparrow caught her arm. "Wait, Wren. I will come with you."

She whirled to face him. "You will not. I need you here, in case the worst happens. You will have to carry on."

"I have just told you, I cannot—not without you." Was this the terrible price the god had levied, when Sparrow had begged him for Wren's life? If so, he found he could not stomach it, after all. "You cannot go alone."

"I do not. I go with those who have volunteered."

"I volunteer!"

"No, love, anyone but you."

He tightened his fingers on her arm. They gazed into each other's eyes, and so deeply the edges of reality blurred that Sparrow no longer knew where his touch left off and hers began. Her heartbeat became his own, and her breath as well.

Her gaze abruptly softened. "Do you not see, Sparrow? We can never be parted. That is the true magic of this place. And so I will return to you, whether it be living or no."

Sparrow closed his eyes on a rush of pain. He wished he might lie with her one last time—possess her completely—and then realized that, aye, in the truest sense, he did.

He whispered, "I do not think I can bear watching you walk away from me."

"I go first to the forest, to pray and prepare myself." Her love poured into him. "Come with me, if you will."

They linked hands and walked away from Sally, into the shadowed forest, where the silence closed around them.

****

Morning light trickled through the trees like sifted holiness. Sparrow sat with held breath and watched the woman he loved transform.

Her prayer seemed less supplication than the evocation of a trance. She sat with eyes closed, the hood thrown back onto her shoulders, her hands folded together. Her breathing quieted until he feared to speak and break the spell.

For spell it was. He felt her spirit call, and other spirits came in response: those of the trees, the forest itself, and the creatures that inhabited it, and the memories of those gone. Nay, more than memories.

How did Wren know to command such magic? Had Lil taught her? But no, for this ability flowed naturally as the light, and it filled Wren, and changed her.

Sparrow saw her lips move as if she spoke inaudibly to someone. Her back straightened and her head lifted. When she once more opened her eyes and looked at him, he was not sure what he saw.

"Wren?"

She got to her feet, moving with an ineffable difference. Wonder suffused Sparrow, even as a chill shivered down his spine.

He had to ask, "Is it you?"

"Of course."

But the eyes looking at Sparrow were no longer Wren's eyes, not entirely. Sparrow knew this woman. He had held her in his arms, caressed her with his hands and tasted every part of her. He had become accustomed to feeling her emotions along with his own, and of speaking to her with his mind. He felt her still, yet someone else looked at him along with her.

She adjusted the quiver across her back in a movement both practiced and foreign to her. Sparrow stood gazing at her, torn. He wanted to run from this and at the same time longed to touch her. He had never beheld such fierce magic.

Yet even so deep a spell might not keep her safe.

"Reconsider this," he implored her. "Do not go."

"I must." Even her voice sounded different, deeper, its timbre changed. Aye, and so armed she might carry off the ruse in the forecourt of the castle. But that did not mean she would get away again. Even the man she pretended to be had met his downfall.

"Peace, Sparrow," she said softly. "I will return to you. Is this not proof of it?"

Aye, but Sparrow wanted her in truth, not some intangible form conjured by magic. He wanted her in his bed, wanted to tease and laugh with her, wanted to share children and old age. But maybe that dream had never truly been available for the two of them. They carried the gift, and the duty, of Sherwood on their backs, and on their spirits.

She smiled, and it was Wren's smile mixed with something more, both wise and kind.

"I go, Sparrow, to salvage a third of our circle. You stay here and keep your third safe."

Inwardly, Sparrow grimaced. He had lived his life in an effort never to lie, especially to those he loved. He had promised, in particular, never to lie to her. But she asked, now, the impossible, and his lips moved in answer to the demand of something far beyond intention.

"Aye, Wren, and so I will."

Chapter Twenty-Nine

"Remember, now," Rennie urged her companions, "we go boldly and with confidence. Robin Hood would not doubt himself, and nor shall we."

Four men—all those who had volunteered and were sound—looked back at her with a variety of expressions: fear, trepidation, determination. Rennie herself felt a disturbing level of disquiet, but beneath it, and underlying all, she harbored certainty.

She could do this thing; she had no choice.

Ahead, just across an open field, lay Nottingham Castle. Already she could feel the life contained there, surging—the energy of many minds. She had grown there, was once used to it. But in her time away, the silence of Sherwood had seeped into her and spoiled her tolerance. Now it seemed a great clamor. Yet this, too, must be faced.

And stealth would get her nowhere.

"Think of Martin," she told her men. "And believe I am Robin Hood."

Two of them—Edward and Stephen—nodded. Henry and Alfred stared with bulging eyes; she hoped they were not going to bolt.

"Mistress, are you sure you can win the challenge?" Alf asked.

Edward answered for her. "Of course she can, dolt. She is Robin Hood."

"But she—"

"You just heard her say."

Alf looked unhappy.

Kindly, Rennie told him, "You are free to turn back, if you wish. I will not force you to this."

He shook his head.

"Then remember our purpose," Rennie said firmly, "is to get Martin away, at any cost."

Edward's eyes widened. "Any? Even you—"

"Especially me."

"Sparrow will not like it," said Henry, grimly. "Are we to return to him without you?"

"Return with Martin, and let me take care of myself."

They nodded reluctantly, and Rennie turned toward the castle and tugged her hood further forward to shadow her face. "Then, let us go."

****

Even from a distance they could hear the commotion in the forecourt. It seemed every denizen of the castle had gathered, with a susurration of voices like a tide, and above it all, the screams.

Even the guards at the gate seemed distracted, all their attention turned within. Perhaps they had orders to admit anyone coming from outlying holdings, for they barely looked at the party of five before nodding them through the yawning gates.

A trap. Every one of Rennie's senses declared it. She felt within for the presence that was, and was not, her own. As soon as she found it, she steadied and strengthened.

Edward muttered in her ear, "That cannot be Martin. He would not bleat so."

It did not sound like Martin's bold voice, rising and falling in a song of agony. Rennie, her men at her back, pressed forward through the outskirts of the crowd, though she did not truly want to see.

A lake of humanity spread before her—serfs, knights, and nobles, all cheek-by-jowl and caught in the drama before them. Rennie narrowed her eyes and stretched herself still taller and saw—

Lambert. He stood on a platform built in front of the castle's main entrance, along with two other men. Two men, and also a strange contraption from which suspended something bloody, that swung slightly in the fetid air.

Rennie's stomach contracted and roiled within her. At her ear, Alf swore viciously. "Martin!"

So it was, though barely recognizable now as a man. He had been stripped down to his trews and hung from the wooden frame by his arms, every exposed inch of flesh marked by wounds.

Rennie stepped forward instinctively, pushing other onlookers aside, and Martin's emotions reached her, assaulted all her senses, a crashing wave of agony. She gasped, wavered, and fought to withstand it. She pushed harder against those in the way, who glared and then let her through. In such fashion, with eyes only for Martin, she battled her way to the front of the crowd.

And became aware of a voice speaking over those gathered, pronouncing statements with the authority of a king. She fought the distraction of Martin's pain in an effort to comprehend the words.

"...are not exempt from the King's law. No one is exempt. Those who think they can rise above and defy it, who set out to steal what rightfully belongs to the

Crown, will meet but one fate."

Lambert. Dressed in a deep blue cloak that flowed over polished armor, his stern features twisted into an expression of arrogant superiority, he stood beside the unspeakable figure hanging from the frame. He swept one arm over the crowd in a grand gesture and then pointed viciously at Martin.

The two other men on the platform—torturers—bent to their work.

Agony arced through Martin and, simultaneously, through Rennie. She quailed, stiffened, felt Martin valiantly strive to ride out the pain. Nay—no coward, Martin Scarlet. But streaks of blood curtained his bare hide, making his surname all too apt, and his eyes were wild.

"Behold the price paid," Lambert bellowed. "And payable by all who breach the King's law."

The torturers' blades bit deep. Against his will, Martin screamed. His staring eyes raked the crowd—was it possible he could feel Rennie here?—and found her.

He knew her. How, Rennie could tell not, for her visage remained shadowed and her very form changed by what resided within. Yet he knew her through their connection. His hope flared, and then trailed swiftly into despair.

She pushed forward another step and fed his hope back to him. *I am here. Endure, and leave it in my hands.*

His head drooped between his straining arms, and his eyes closed. Had his senses deserted him? No, for she could feel him still, a rush of pure love.

Save yourself. I am lost.

Not yet, you are not.

He groaned, and she felt it all through her body.

Lambert took up his rant. He spoke of those who defied the Crown, who took the King's laws into their own hands, who dared steal in the name of rebels who should have been defeated long ago.

"Like this man." He pointed once more at Martin. "A rebel. An outlaw—a wolfshead." Lambert sneered the word. "What is fit punishment for such a man, who spreads lies and unrest, whose heart is untrue? I say that heart should be cut—living—from his chest."

Horror—and some eagerness—suffused the crowd. Martin's gray-blue eyes came open again, and Rennie experienced his flash of fear. Aye, and Lambert would see it done—here, before everyone.

She drew a deep breath, fought down her rising sickness, and called out into the ensuing silence, "And, high sir, would you wager his life on a challenge?" Her voice did not sound like her own. It had deepened, and it carried an edge of boldness—the voice of her father as she had heard it in her dreams.

Lambert's head swiveled until he located her.

Martin cried out in his mind, *No—no—it is madness.*

She sent him a strong wave of love. *Hush. Let me do this.*

"Who speaks?" Lambert demanded.

"I—Robin Hood."

Voices arose all around the courtyard, eager and disbelieving.

Lambert lifted his head arrogantly. "You are not Robin Hood. Robin Hood is dead."

"If I be a shade, then you need not fear to accept

my challenge."

"I stand here in the authority of the King. I fear nothing."

Rennie shifted her bow purposefully and pointed at Martin. "You say, Sir Lambert, men such as he have no right to freedoms not granted by their King."

"I do."

"And I say justice gifts a right granted by God, and higher than any earthly authority. I say that a man be a man, and worthy of dignity in his own life. I say if this man, here, exists under God, you have no right to hold and treat him so cruelly."

"Cruelly?" Lambert's sneer twisted his features into an ugly mask. "Should I then let wolfsheads such as this run the King's roads? Kill the King's deer? Steal from the King's coffers with impunity?"

"I say we let God decide the matter of his fate, here and now. I come here as his agent—"

"The shade of Robin Hood, an agent of God? Enough of this nonsense." Lambert waved a hand at her. "Seize him."

Not so much as a guard, listening, moved.

Rennie called, "Do you, Sir Lambert, fear God's justice?"

"I declare that a wolfshead such as you brings it not!"

"If that be your belief, what need you fear in my challenge?" Rennie glanced at Martin. His eyes, now well open, stared at her with burning passion. "Should I lose, you may finish the King's business and pluck his heart."

"And should you win this proposed challenge?"

"Then I win his freedom, along with the safety of

myself and all who came here with me today. You give your word to our safe conduct back to the forest."

You are mad, Martin shouted into her mind.

Faith, she returned. *Believe.*

Lambert glared around the crowd. He had to sense the intense interest of all gathered, the power of the spell being woven. And most of all, he could not be seen to fear a mere wolfshead, either living or dead.

"And the nature of this challenge?"

Rennie tossed her head and lifted her bow in her hands. "Bring your best archer—set up any target of your choosing—and I will best him."

Chapter Thirty

"Clear a path and make some room. Give us a sight line. And send at once for Master de Breche."

Lambert's voice boomed through the castle forecourt, the first thing Sparrow heard as he passed between the gates. His eyes narrowed on the scene within, and his mind struggled with disbelief. A virtual sea of people lapped at the castle entrance, all focused on the unfolding scene. Even the guards had virtually deserted their posts and barely noticed Sparrow as he pushed in.

And Wren—Sparrow's senses sought her amid all the rampant distractions. Emotions beat at him from every side and tangled with his own. When he saw the figure hanging from the frame on the platform, virtually naked save for blood, his stomach heaved.

Martin: Sparrow's rival, lifelong companion, sometime friend. Sparrow knew Martin almost as well as he knew himself, and had never seen him other than bold, daring, full of fire. Now fear gripped Martin, as well it should, for he hung in Lambert's power, and on the knife's blade of death.

Even upon that thought, Martin twisted his head painfully, and his eyes found Sparrow and knew him. And in that instant, Sparrow knew Martin's fear was not for himself.

Stop her, Martin beseeched.

Eh?

Wren—

Lambert's voice boomed again, cutting through the fragile communication. "Master de Breche is foremost among my archers, wolfshead. He has won tournaments in York, Lincoln, London, and Normandy. By great good fortune, he arrived at Nottingham not two days since. Now whom do you think God favors?"

"Bring him hence and we shall see." The answering voice was, and was not, Wren's. Sparrow pushed against the intervening, resistant backs, and began to force his way forward.

And he saw her. She stood, hood well raised and bow in her hands, at the very front of the crowd facing Lambert on his platform. Sparrow's heart began to thump in his chest, and his gaze narrowed still further. For all around her, encasing her from head to foot, he saw a glow of soft radiance. And a trail of it, like a single ray of light, extended to Martin.

Could the others see it? Sparrow did not think so; he suspected that, like the emotions that linked them and the sometimes audible thoughts, this was something only the three of them shared.

"Wolfshead, Robin Hood," Lambert called out, with hard mockery, "will you meet any challenge I set, in order to win your prize?"

Sparrow shuddered with foreboding as he heard the reply, "I will."

Stop her, Sparrow. Sparrow! Martin called again. Sparrow could feel his pain, his desperation.

His love.

The last was almost strong enough to knock Sparrow down where he stood. In that moment he knew

Martin, perhaps the strongest man he knew, was willing to sacrifice himself to save Wren, and that humbled Sparrow to the heart.

How? He cried the word into the void. Before him, the crowd shuffled aside, bunching impossibly to clear the room Lambert demanded. Not a soul departed the scene.

"I am here." De Breche. Even in Sherwood, folk had heard of him—a knight of renown and an archer beyond compare. They said King John had once pitted him against the King of Spain's best man, to settle a land dispute, and won. And now he would face off against a legend—the people's hero—for a far greater prize.

Sparrow reached for Wren with his mind and hit a wall. Aye, she was there, but another spirit wrapped around her, enfolded her. Neither seemed aware of him.

Amazement suffused Sparrow, along with awe. To Martin he said, *She has brought her father.*

And Martin raged, *She risks her own life.*

All too true, but she did so in an act of heroism such as Sparrow had never witnessed. If she succeeded, it would be the thing of fame and story. If she failed: terror hit him, staggering him. If she failed, far more than her life, and Martin's, would be lost.

De Breche stepped out onto the platform, a polished bow in his hand. He wore a cloak of bright blue, and confidence rode his every movement. Sparrow looked from him to Wren and felt a jolt of shock: she no longer looked at all like Wren, and her confidence matched that of the Norman.

To Lambert, she called, "We are agreed? If I win, all who belong to me leave here, free?"

An ugly smile curled Lambert's lips. "And if Master de Breche wins, I cut out this wolfshead's heart personally—before putting you in his place."

And, Sparrow thought gravely, the rest of the Sherwood party would never make it out of the forecourt alive, most likely including himself. For he would stay and fight for her, to the end.

Lambert spoke to one of the torturers, who spoke in turn to a lad standing by. The lad went running. Lambert and de Breche consulted, their heads close together.

What was afoot? Sparrow did not trust the man.

The lad swiftly returned with an unidentifiable object in his hand. He passed it to Lambert, who held it high. "You see what this is?" He addressed Wren, not the crowd, but everyone there leaned forward. "A mere lump of raw meat, fit only for the Sheriff's dogs. A fit crown for the head of this wolfshead you value so high, Sir Legend."

Sparrow strained to see. The chunk so described was little more than a morsel, perhaps the size of a fist, an ugly knot of gristle and bone.

Lambert stalked, with his rooster's walk, to where the prisoner hung suspended, and set his trophy on Martin's head. "Do not shake it off in your trembling," he warned. "If it falls and is not shot cleanly, your life is forfeit."

Wren called, "That is no part of our bargain."

Lambert gestured. "My ground—my rules. So, Master de Breche, are you satisfied with the challenge? First man to shoot the target cleanly, without putting an arrow through the wolfshead's forehead, wins."

The crowd inhaled as one. An impossible

challenge, for Martin dangled, swaying slightly, and his head drooped in pain.

De Breche made no answer beyond a nod, and Wren called, "Who shoots first?"

"My setting, as I say—my champion shoots first."

De Breche leaped down from the platform and took up a stance at Wren's side. A tall man, he nevertheless topped Wren by no more than a hair, and Sparrow marveled. Aye, Wren was tall for a woman. But just who stood there beside the Norman champion?

He looked at Martin, who strained to keep his head upright, and knew that Martin's fear was all for Wren. Wren looked at Martin also, and the current of light that linked the two of them wavered, and then strengthened.

If Wren protested the favor that allowed the Norman to shoot first, she did not say so. De Breche lifted his bow and notched his arrow in one beautiful movement.

From where Sparrow stood, the target looked impossible to hit cleanly. The shooters stood below the platform, making a difficult angle. Sparrow doubted he could make the shot, and he had been the best Sherwood had to offer since Robin's death.

Sparrow closed his eyes and began to pray. The courtyard fell silent, so silent he heard de Breche release his shot.

The crowd roared; Sparrow's eyes flew open.

Martin swayed slightly on his ropes. The gory lump of gristle rested still on his head.

Wren stepped forward and set her shoulder toward Sparrow. He could not see her face, but her hands looked sure, far steadier than his would have been. The onlookers hushed again. The glow around Wren that connected her to Martin brightened unbearably, and Sparrow knew it for what it was: pure magic.

Wren raised her bow, she notched her arrow, she stood posed with power in her every line. The breath caught in Sparrow's throat—he knew he saw a legend a score of years dead.

Robin Hood.

The legend drew back his bowstring with a grace that caught at Sparrow's heart. The arrow flew, following the path of light that connected the shooter to the target. Martin lifted his head and his eyes went wide; the arrow seemed to aim for the very center of his forehead.

It brushed his hair instead and lifted the lump of meat from his skull, as cleanly speared as if impaled on a knife.

The crowd reacted with thunderous cries. Voices rose, wild and ragged, leaving no doubt as to where rested the sympathy of the onlookers. Did these folk know what they had just seen? Could they feel the magic now crackling through the air?

"Cut him down." Robin Hood's voice silenced the clamor.

Sir Lambert did not move. Still on the platform, he stood apparently frozen in disbelief.

Robin drew his bow again, his second arrow aimed at Lambert's heart. "Is a Norman noble incapable of keeping his word? Must I end this differently?"

Lambert looked at him, and he added, "Do you doubt I will loose this shot?"

Lambert moved suddenly and gestured at the torturers. "Cut him down."

They hurried to obey. Robin—or was it now

Wren?—spoke to the rest of the Sherwood party. "Bring him."

Martin fell to the platform with an ugly thud; Sparrow shuddered in responsive pain. Wren's men gathered him up and brought him down from the platform onto the courtyard.

"Take your prize," Lambert taunted, "and go, proof that I keep my word. It is not as if we do not know where to find you."

"Go," Wren told her men. She turned to follow the struggling party, for whom the crowd cleared still another path, and de Breche, standing beside her, reached out casually and pushed the hood back from her face. There stood Wren, indeed, her hair bundled in a knot and her golden eyes wide with sudden alarm.

"You!" Lambert seethed. "Wench!" His hand went instinctively to his cheekbone. "Impossible. You are no wolfshead. And you are no Robin Hood."

In answer, Wren loosed her arrow. It cut so near Lambert's ear he ducked wildly and fell from the platform. Chaos broke out then; hastily, Sparrow turned to follow Wren, who fled in the wake of the departing outlaws.

The courtyard seemed a mile long, the gates an immeasurable distance. Behind him mayhem reigned. He could hear Lambert calling orders. Would he break his word after all? If he did, Sparrow would stand in his place at the rear of the party, to fight to the death if need be. But no, they gained the gates, still struggling under Martin's weight.

And there, quite near the gate, a face Sparrow knew—a figure hesitating as if not sure whether to stay or go.

Simon.

Wren's head spun as the name sounded in Sparrow's mind. She must have heard him—she knew Sparrow was here. And she, too, saw Simon. Her eyes speared him and her anger flared.

Bring him, she told Sparrow. *And, by the god's light, get yourself safe away.*

Sparrow bulled his way through the crowd to collar the lad roughly. "You—traitor, come with me."

Chapter Thirty-One

"You must keep strong, Martin. I know just how strong you can be." Rennie spoke the words out loud as she walked alongside the rough litter hastily formed out of two tree boughs and borne by her men. At the same time, she plumbed the reaches of Martin's mind. No response. He still breathed, shallowly, but his thoughts had sunk far beneath her reach.

She felt spent, drained, utterly exhausted. Her father's spirit had deserted her at some point after Martin's freedom was won—even she could not be sure when. The shot that skimmed Lambert's ear had been her own. In going, Robin seemed to have taken something of her with him.

Now she survived on residual tension and worry. Lambert had tortured poor Thomas to death; one of the first things he would have ordered his torturers to discover was the new location of the outlaws' camp. Lambert had also seen Rennie's face. That meant she, and those for whom she cared so dearly, balanced on the bright blade of danger.

And she did care for them, she who once cared for so little. During her days spent suffering in the scullery, she had loved Lil, and squandered the remainder of her energy in anger and resentment. Since coming to Sherwood, she had changed. She now loved like a tide out-flowing—loved the folk of the forest, with their courageous hearts, loved Sherwood itself.

Loved Martin.

Every time she thought of him, her heart faltered. A powerful bond had flowered between the two of them there in the forecourt. Her love enfolded him still.

And, what of Sparrow? Even now he followed them through the forest. Rennie could not see but felt him. He had risked himself to follow her to Nottingham—she would worry about that later. For now, she knew only Martin's need.

He could not die. She could not let him. Was this what poor Alric had felt, when losing Lil? No wonder he had laid himself down and surrendered.

The men who bore Martin muttered among themselves, as exhausted as she.

"Camp, just ahead."

Home, but no refuge. Rennie groaned inwardly. She would have to mobilize everyone this night, once more send them scattering into the safety of the trees. Her heart quailed at the very thought.

Lambert would come.

She shivered, remembering the look in his eyes when de Breche unmasked her—the look of a man who would not rest until he had revenge. Aye, well, she was capable of seeking revenge also. And what he had done to injure her folk far surpassed any blow to Lambert's face or his pride.

They entered the camp and were met by waiting arms and an outcry of dismay. Madlyn came and laid both hands against her son's cheeks, and her own turned white as milk.

"What have they done? Oh, Martin—" She drew a breath and stared at Rennie. "I possess not the skill to mend this. We need Lil."

"You will do as you must, Mother, and I with you," Rennie told her. She began calling orders. "Make for him a pallet, as quickly as possible. Bring water and bandages. Hurry, we cannot stay here long."

"Cannot stay?" Madlyn echoed, daunted.

"Lambert tortured his prisoners. He knows all Thomas knew before he died."

"But—" Madlyn's lips parted. "We cannot drag my son through the forest in this condition. He will surely die."

"It is the forest that will save him, and you. Tend him as best you can before we depart. You travel in my party."

But Madlyn did not move. She stood with her hands resting against Martin's face while tears came, filled her eyes, and spilled over.

An agonized cry sounded behind Rennie. She whirled to see Sally, who stared at the man on the litter in dawning horror.

"No—"

"Catch her," Rennie said to no one in particular, "before she goes down."

Several hands were in time to snare Sally as she sank to the earth. Rennie's tension ramped up another notch.

She turned her head sharply. She could feel Sparrow coming up from behind—he had escaped safely. The knowledge was her only available comfort.

"Send word to Oakham," she told the nearest man, "and to the other hamlets sympathetic to us. Lambert will be coming, and when he does, he will burn them to the ground."

****

Sparrow arrived in camp only moments later, with his prisoner in tow. Rennie, bent over Martin's pallet, watching Madlyn bathe his wounds, heard the furor of raised voices and sharp exclamations. She got to her feet.

Seldom had she seen Sparrow look so grim. And the young man caught in his relentless grasp—Simon—the lad looked like a trapped animal, paralyzed by terror. Rennie's anger flared when she saw him. She leaped forward and met the pair beside the fire, with half the camp looking on.

"You! Traitor!" Her fingers moved of their own volition and struck the lad hard enough to sway him in Sparrow's grasp. "Do you know what you have done? Do you see what you have cost us?" She pointed at Martin. "The deaths of many good men—and him!"

"Wren," Sparrow said softly.

"I know. Forgive me—I had no choice." Simon choked on the words.

"Lambert has his mother." Sparrow spoke in sorrow. "He threatened to throw her to his guards, like a bone."

"She is lost now. Better dead!" Simon began to sob.

The anger left Rennie in a rush, to be replaced by grief. For an instant she saw it all so clearly—the injustice and pain, endless wrong and suffering. As if, for an instant, she looked with her father's eyes, she viewed the cause and the need, knew why he had chosen this fight at any cost.

"Oh, lad," she said to Simon.

"I tried to save her, I did. I told Sir Lambert

whatever he wanted. But it did not matter, in the end." He broke down completely and wept in Sparrow's arms. Those watching drifted away, and Rennie fought to control her own emotions.

Sparrow's eyes met hers over Simon's head.

What to do now? he asked her silently.

Aloud, she said, "We must flee this place. Best take him with you."

"With us, you mean. I go where you go, Wren."

Rennie felt Sparrow's emotions so clearly, his love and determination—the same feelings that had drawn him to Nottingham in her wake. But she shook her head. "I go with Martin."

"But—"

"He needs me, Sparrow, to give him my strength."

Sparrow's face grew tight. "And your love?"

Rennie realized Sparrow had felt what took place there in the forecourt. She could not help that now. "If need be. I will give him whatever he needs to survive, whatever I have."

"Including yourself?"

"I cannot let him die. You cannot, for all that. He is part of us, part of this—of Sherwood." She gestured wildly to their surroundings.

"Fine, then." Sparrow's voice turned brittle. "But I come with you."

"No."

He opened his lips to speak, and Rennie rushed on. "We dare not be taken all together, the three of us. Do you not see that?"

"If two of us be lost, the spell is destroyed anyway," he answered gravely.

"Or one of us, for all that." She glanced over her

shoulder at Martin. "I do not know if he will live." Terror touched her at the thought of the alternative. "My strength is nearly gone."

"Then take me with you," Sparrow told her, "and let me give you mine."

Chapter Thirty-Two

"She chose me." Sparrow despised his own selfishness even as he reminded himself of that fact once again. He did not feel chosen. Instead, it seemed Wren had virtually dropped him from her awareness.

She thought only of Martin.

A full day had passed since they broke camp and fled, in groups, deeper into Sherwood. Their group was larger than Sparrow liked and consisted of Wren and himself, Martin, Madlyn, and Simon, with the unfortunate inclusion of Sally. When they moved, Sparrow and Simon toted the litter. Sally wept.

She wept silently and without ceasing. Sparrow could not say he blamed her. There were moments in plenty when he felt like joining her.

Such as now, when evening came down and Wren sat, devoted, at Martin's side and held his hand. They dared not have so much as a whisper of fire, even here in the trackless reaches of the forest, and already the night damp crept in.

Sparrow knew Martin wallowed in pain and his life hung by a thread. He could feel Martin's weakness, virtually taste his agony; Sparrow knew how he flickered in and out of consciousness.

To Sparrow's misfortune, he could also feel Wren's emotions—he did not even have to touch her to do so. They poured off her in tangible waves: warmth, caring, strength—love. It was as if part of her reached inside Martin to call him back from the dark place he had gone, and then held him.

Sparrow shivered, feeling his own chill at the edge of the circle, even as he paced their stopping place on watch. He glanced over his shoulder at the scene.

The three of them made a changeless tableau—Martin stretched on his litter, looking like a dead god with his fair hair all tousled and his wounded arms thrown out; Madlyn with her simples and her visible fear that her skills would not suffice; Wren—

Sparrow's heart faltered within him as he observed her. She glowed. The same light he had seen around her in the forecourt at Nottingham now surrounded her and burned steadily, extending to and fully enfolding Martin.

Ah, so that was what love looked like to eyes that could see it. And Sparrow, linked closely to the two of them as he was, could see.

By the god's horns, how could he be so selfish as to mind? But he did—he did, for he loved her with a depth that terrified him. It surpassed the mere physical, though that did not keep him from aching for her moment after moment. He longed for her touch even in passing, and suffered from being deprived of it. He perished for the taste of her. It might have been better had he never known her at all.

No, not that. He cherished every memory of what they had shared together, alone in the forest—that which he feared he might never know again. For he could not rid himself of the belief that Wren had now given herself, in some inexplicable, incomprehensible way, to Martin instead.

But she chose me, he whined to himself piteously, yet again. Could it happen? Could Wren choose him and then change her heart? Could it be changed by Martin's need?

Disgusted with himself, he spun on his heel and nearly collided with Sally, who stood at his elbow.

"What is it, love?" As if he need ask. Sally's grief and desperation nearly matched his own.

"Sparrow, I think I should tell him."

"Eh?" Fully distracted, Sparrow did not at once grasp her meaning.

"I wish to tell Martin I carry his child. He should know, in case—" Sally's throat spasmed and her voice died.

"Lass, I do not know that he can hear you, or will understand. He is far beyond our reach." But not beyond Wren's—for she held him fast. Kindly, he added to Sally, "And just as well. It shelters him from some of the pain."

And such pain it must be. Sparrow's very spirit flinched from it. He had to admit only Martin's great strength could so endure.

Two more tears coursed down Sally's face. "Will he die, Sparrow?"

"Not if Wren has aught to say about it."

Sally gazed at the group of three. Sparrow wondered if she could sense what he felt, if she minded, but then she burst, "I would do anything for her—anything—could she but save him."

And there, Sparrow thought, was love at its finest—no selfish emotion. He caught Sally's hand. "Come."

They approached the threesome quietly. Wren

glanced up, and Sparrow felt her attention slide over him and away again.

"How fares he?" Sparrow addressed Madlyn instead of Wren.

New, deep lines furrowed Madlyn's face. She looked exhausted. "He weakens." She waved her hands helplessly. "So many wounds."

"He will endure, Mother—you know how strong he is."

Madlyn's head drooped, her only reply.

Sparrow spoke. "Might we have a moment alone with him, Sally and I?"

Wren's head lifted sharply. Her nostrils flared, and her fingers, clasped around Martin's, turned white. "Why?" Her voice sounded rough, that of a defensive she-wolf. *Mine*, it said.

Sparrow summoned a painful smile. "We would give him something to live for." A child was that, at least to Sparrow's mind. What would he not give for one of his own? If the news could reach Martin—

Wren's eyes narrowed with caution. "I do not know that he will hear anything you say. I have been calling him. It becomes more difficult." She considered Sally, and her demeanor softened almost imperceptibly. "But if you think you can tell him aught that will help—"

Sally sank to her knees beside Martin, and Wren surrendered Martin's hand to her. Sally would not have her moment alone, but it seemed she cared little for any listening ears.

"Oh, my love, my dear love," she began. "Can you ever forgive me? This is my fault, all of it. You went seeking revenge because of what I said, the lie I told."

Wren's face once more tightened. Sparrow ached to touch her but dared not—she, like Sally, fought hard for control.

Sally's agony continued to pour off her. "Perhaps I do not deserve your forgiveness. But should my lie cost your life, should you pass from this world, you need to go knowing the truth: I do not carry Lambert's child. He never waylaid me nor touched me. That was a tale I told. My child is yours, my love—yours."

She collapsed in tears, Martin's hand clutched to her cheek.

Sparrow felt Wren recoil from the display. She got to her feet and stepped to his side. Her eyes, merciless as those of a hawk, raked his face. "She blames herself, but this is your fault as much as hers. You knew the truth, Sparrow. You knew, and yet you let him go seeking his revenge. You could have kept him from spending himself for a lie."

Sparrow sucked in a breath and winced as if she had slapped him. "No one in this world can keep Martin from spending himself, once his mind is set."

Her eyes narrowed, "Yet you could have said—"

"No." Sparrow clenched his jaw. "The secret was not mine. Had it been, I say to you again, it would surely have been told. But not even my feelings for you, Wren, will make me break my word given in good faith."

Her brows flew up and her look cooled still further. "So, for the sake of a foolish girl's secret, you have risked everything."

"No, Wren—for the sake of my honor."

"Your honor?" she burst. "And what is that, if we lose him? What happens to the cause, if the circle shatters? You might at least have confided in me. I thought we shared everything."

"As did I." His gaze touched Martin. "But I perceive I was wrong." He moved to turn away, and Wren seized his shoulder, her touch far from gentle. He had longed so for her to touch him, even a simple brush of her hand, but now the contact only served to emphasize the distance between them.

"What do you mean by that?"

Sparrow stared at her, mute. A muscle jumped in his cheek.

Her eyes widened suddenly. "You do not begrudge my time with him? He lies dying!"

The hard honesty inside Sparrow made him reply, "I begrudge not your time nor even your caring. But I saw—felt—what happened between the two of you at Nottingham—"

"What? I upheld him. I sustained him!"

"You love him." Sparrow was ashamed of the words that followed but could no more hold them than stop his breath. "More than me?"

She, in turn, looked as if he had struck her. She actually reared back, and her hand fell from his shoulder. He saw the thoughts move in her beautiful eyes: doubt, anger, scorn.

She seethed. "I was not aware that we meted out amounts of love the way Lil once measured her simples. And I did not know I had lain with a mere boy. I thought you a man full grown, wise and deep of spirit."

Sparrow felt her barb enter him, an arrow to the heart.

"Is this, then, your love?" she challenged. "This

narrow, ugly, and spiteful thing?"

Sparrow's throat worked before he spoke. Never had he been accused of selfishness. All the years of his growing, he had been the giver who considered the feelings of others, even while Martin did as he chose without regard. Aye, he felt jealousy now, but for Wren to denounce him for it went beyond bearing. Hoarsely, he said, "You do not understand."

"You are right. I do not."

"I need you."

Her eyes flashed. "*He* needs me. Be gone from my sight."

"By the god's mercy, Wren, do not ask that."

"I do not want to look at you—I cannot bear it."

Sparrow shrank into himself as her disdain found its deeper mark. He stood, frozen, as she began to turn away from him, back toward Martin. Only then did he call, not with his voice but with his mind, *Wren, I love you.*

She made no reply.

Chapter Thirty-Three

"I fear we are being trailed," Sparrow told Rennie, a new, guarded expression on his face. "I think we need to break camp and move on once more."

"Who could follow us, here? Who would have the ability?" Rennie asked. Exhausted to the bone, she could barely face the prospect of picking up and pushing on.

Sparrow swept her with one intense glance before looking away again, and his emotions assaulted her: hurt, grief, and need as great as her own. She ached from the rift between them. It yawned inside her, a deep gulf she had no idea how to fill. These many days past, while they fled ever deeper into Sherwood, she had poured so much strength into Martin, trying to keep him alive; she feared she had very little left for enduring her own agony.

"I hoped we might linger here a while. It is unwise to keep moving Martin. He burns with fever." Wearily, she added, "Perhaps you are mistaken."

"Perhaps." But Sparrow did not sound uncertain. He hesitated and then said, "It is possible Lambert has intercepted one of the other parties that lit out from camp when we did. Micah or Trent would have the skill to track us. Or one of the woodsmen from Oakham—"

Rennie struggled to think; her mind moved as slowly as a spoon through treacle. "Surely none of them would betray us."

"Who knows what a man may do under threat of torture to himself or to those he loves?"

Rennie rubbed her forehead, where a constant pain dogged her. Another pain lodged near her heart, a burning weight. "If we move on, will they not just continue to follow? We cannot move very quickly."

"I have been thinking about that." Sparrow glanced round at the trees. "I suggest we gain some distance and then sue the assistance of an ally upon whom we have not yet called."

"Ally?" Rennie lifted her brows at him.

"Aye. Sherwood itself. The magic of Sherwood is at the center of our triad, after all. Should we not take advantage of that?"

Rennie felt a rush of surprise, and a stirring of awe. This was the Sparrow she so admired, he who now felt so far from her. Suddenly her need to have him back again was so great she nearly staggered. But she said only, "How?"

"It will take the three of us together, I think—joined."

"But Martin—"

Sparrow shook his head. "It does not matter. Wherever he is, surely he rests closer to the god than we."

"Very well. It is worth the attempt. When?"

"We will move on a ways. You set the pace and let the forest lead you, Wren. When we stop, we will ask for protection."

Rennie gave another nod, even though the idea of again gathering their few possessions together made her long to lie down and weep. They were all spent; Simon, pressed into helping Sparrow carry Martin's litter, usually fell down in a stupor whenever they stopped walking. He had paid a significant price for his betrayal.

She resisted the impulse to reach out and take Sparrow's arm merely for the sake of touching him. "Aye," she whispered, "we will go where Sherwood leads us."

****

The sun disappeared into a haze of clouds and green branches, and shadows came down. Rennie could not be sure if the resultant soft gloom heralded rain or merely a deepening of the forest. Few folk could ever have trod where they now went. These trees, haunted by birds and animals, soared like great pillars in a cathedral and were alive with awareness that teased all Rennie's senses.

Despite her weariness, she did as Sparrow asked and chose their way by pure instinct, called by the flash of a bird's wing, a glint of light or a fancied whisper. Silence settled round them as they went, and when she stopped moving at last, it was with knowing in her heart.

"Here," she said, her voice hushed.

The place was a sheltered dell among the towering trees, formed where one had fallen long ago, steeped in deep green light. The remains of the giant beech still lay like a moldering corpse, and to one side ran a trickle of stream, clear and pure.

All the trees whispered to Rennie's mind, "Welcome."

Simon lowered his end of Martin's litter to the ground, and Madlyn hurried to tend her son. Rennie just stood, drinking in the stillness.

Eyes half closed, she felt Sparrow take his place at her side. Every impulse in her leaped toward him. Whatever she was feeling included him, somehow.

"A wise choice," he murmured. "There is power here."

"Aye. He is near—the Green Man."

Sparrow gave her a sharp look. She returned it, seeming to see him—really see him—for the first time in days. "Were we followed?"

He shook his head. "We lost the pursuers halfway here; I can feel them no more."

She held her hand out to him. "Then let us do what we can."

****

When first Lil had brought Rennie to the forest, she had spoken of magic. Real magic, she had called it— the sort connected to life itself. Rennie, battered and overwhelmed, had not understood what that meant then, but the knowledge had come to her slowly, perhaps the most important lesson she would ever learn.

Since then she had felt the magic when she listened to the wind in the trees, when she looked into Martin's eyes, and whenever she touched Sparrow. But here, at the very heart of Sherwood, it beat at her, a veritable wall of power. A presence.

For all that, though, Martin's condition had worsened. Passed from fever, he now lay waxen and far too still, his skin almost cold to the touch. Despite all Madlyn's care, some of his wounds had poisoned. If he survived, he would be marked by many scars, no longer so beautiful.

No matter, Rennie told the trees, speaking to the

source of that power—he must survive.

She sat with her eyes closed, one of her hands clutching Martin's cold fingers, the other clasped tight in Sparrow's. So did they form a rough circle, there beneath the trees. Their three companions rested at some distance, Simon already asleep, Sally face down, and Madlyn working over yet another batch of herbs.

Rennie could feel Martin. Even though he seemed so far beyond her reach, when she sat touching him this way she connected with his spirit, the one she knew—fiery and heedless. Her heart rose on a surge of gladness.

With her eyes closed, she could also feel Sparrow, even more clearly—all the gentle strength she loved in him, backed by a wall of hurt. *Oh, Sparrow*, she thought in sudden longing. Her compassion flowed to him as well as to Martin. Pure love, combined with the light of Sherwood, gathered itself and rose.

Something like a sigh issued from the trees and stirred the hair on Rennie's brow. She felt the shadows—or perhaps the spirits—of birds flutter by. Small creatures, and then larger ones, approached and ringed them, felt but unseen. Everything held its breath.

There was a fourth presence.

Rennie's entire being leaped in response to it. She felt Sparrow's fingers clench around hers; Martin's strength suddenly flared.

And the light grew, spun, brightened, and took form. Rennie opened her eyes.

A figure stood at the center of their circle, tall and still.

Sparrow swore softly in awe. Or perhaps he spoke the god's name. It was hard to tell.

The Green Man.

The name appeared as if by magic in Rennie's mind. She blinked, striving to comprehend what she saw. No, not the god but a stag standing upright on its rear legs; a beautiful woman with streaming green hair, who laid her hand on Martin's heart. No—it was her father, Robin Hood.

He smiled at her, the smile she remembered from her dreams. His eyes glowed blue, picking up the light that surrounded him—radiance that streamed from Sparrow and Martin, and Rennie herself, that mingled and combined to make a circle of power.

Light is love. Love is power. Rennie knew not who spoke the words. They danced through the air and she inhaled them. They took form in her heart. Magic arose, blinding.

Ah, so this was what Lil had tried to tell her—what she, Geoffrey, and Alric shared. This marvel formed the very fabric of Sherwood.

Martin stirred. Rennie felt his spirit rear up in gladness, and for an instant she could not tell what had called him, life or death. At that instant both were one. Or, rather, she saw death for what it was—a mere altering of form.

Lil was there, and Alric—Geoffrey also, and a woman with long, tawny hair and eyes the color of Rennie's. *Mother.*

"Protect us." Rennie spoke the words aloud. "Confound those who follow us." She savored the strength that flowed through her. "Save us."

Her father stepped forward and touched her head. A current of power flowed into her and called upon what she already felt within.

"None shall find you here." His voice echoed. "Gather yourselves and harbor your power. For the fight is not over. You must return and carry the magic with you. By love shall freedom be won."

"Martin—"

Behind Robin, two more figures stirred. One, a man with a wild, yellow mane, stepped forward and crouched over Martin's prone form. He laid a broad hand on Martin's forehead, even as Robin touched Rennie.

Will Scarlet. The name appeared in Rennie's mind an instant before Scarlet raised his gaze and met hers, all iron-gray fire.

And the other—

"Da," Sparrow choked, beside her. The giant of a man smiled. A wild beard obscured most of his face but did not hide the fierce, gentle strength that suffused him. Like his two companions, he reached out and touched the head of his child.

The brightness flared. It rose like a tower of fire that consumed all doubt and all distinctions between the possible and the impossible. The magic of Sherwood streamed up from the ground, through the trees, and reverberated like the chime of a silent bell.

The past had come again, and the circle stood, triple strong.

"Rest now and heal," Robin said, "and strength find you in your sleep."

Chapter Thirty-Four

"Sparrow, are you awake?"

Wren's voice called Sparrow from the depths of a sleep so profound it verged on death. He lay for a moment with his eyes opened to the vast darkness of Sherwood, trying to remember his dream. It had contained light and magic, and those gone before him. His father—

Only it had not been a dream.

His heart sped upon the memory, sounding great, deep beats, and he struggled to sort fancy from reality in his mind. The forest lay utterly quiet, the only disturbance Wren's whisper. Did their entire band sleep? Someone should have stayed on watch. He should have. But nay, surely they lay in safety, here? For a shield of power surrounded and protected them.

"Sparrow." Wren spoke his name again and moved into his arms, warm and close in the darkness. Sparrow's entire being rose up in gladness. His arms enfolded her and drew her hard against him.

"Can you feel the magic?" he whispered. It curled all about them the way a mist might, rising from the ground, twisting and twining up through the trees. He lifted his hand before his face. So complete was the dark, he should not be able to see it. Yet his fingers were outlined by faint radiance. Bemused, he turned his eyes on Wren, in his arms. Slivers of faint light slid over the length of her hair, her shoulders, and outlined the curves of her face. It danced from her flesh to his the way distant lightning leaps through the sky both before and after a storm.

Against his cheek, Wren whispered, "We lie in the very womb of Sherwood." She stretched her body against his and desire rushed at him out of the darkness. "Will you love me?"

"I always love you." He knew himself helpless in the grip of what he felt for her, caught like a trout in a net, driven by the current of the stream. He loved her with every breath he took, with all his being.

"I mean, will you love me, Sparrow, now? I would have your child. I would have it conceived here." Her hands moved over him, leaving him no doubt. His senses, already heightened by the magic so lately experienced, responded almost painfully. Yet a question lingered in his mind.

"Martin." He knew what she felt for Martin, had experienced the edges of it and seen it blazing bright. Aye, she had chosen him, Sparrow. But in the forecourt at Nottingham, had her heart changed?

Wren went very still in his arms. For an instant he was sure she stopped breathing. Then her sigh brushed across his lips like a kiss. "He needs me."

"I need you." By every god ever worshipped in the heart of man, he did. His heartbeat required hers, and his existence rested in her hands.

"It is my strength holding him, now." She hesitated. "My light."

"Aye." Sparrow knew that to be true also.

"We are, after all, three," she told him, beseeching now. "Can I forsake him? Abandonment, Sparrow, is the worst of things." Her lips moved over his cheek, brushed his jaw. She spoke into his lips. "But I want you. I choose you. I would have your child."

Sparrow's heart twisted in his chest. Could he share her? He did not know, yet his hands began to move of their own volition, slid over her body and up under the leather tunic she wore, encountering flesh smooth and warm.

She reared up, outlined by her own radiance. "You heard what my father said. We must take the magic of this place back to those who need it, whatever the cost. But first, Sparrow, please love me."

****

Darkness, fire, sparks of light flared as warm skin grew hot, sliding against naked flesh. Strength filled Sparrow, along with desire, and birthed in him a profound need to give. He had not missed the significance of Wren's words—this might be the last time ever he loved her. He meant to make it a precious memory.

She trembled in his arms, all need and yearning and tenderness wrapped together. She touched him everywhere with both fingers and tongue, leaving behind a trail of fire on his skin. Radiance moved about them in the soft dark, little glimmers of magic in two colors—the gold that Wren shed and the deep blue that seemed to come off his own skin. They combined together to make a shower of green, the color of light in Sherwood.

Sparrow had never felt so helpless, or so empowered. He lost his head with the taste of her even as he vibrated with certainty that he had been born for this, and for her. A beginning and an ending came

243

together with their coupling, and he knew time stood still.

Not until the act was complete and he lay with the breath surging in his lungs, and Wren still caught tight against him, did Sparrow glean the true meaning of what had just occurred, and why.

She said she had chosen him—perhaps not as the love of a lifetime, but as a father for her child. She said they must go back and face the danger that awaited them. Sparrow lay on his back and stared with wide eyes, watching the last of their shed radiance settle around them. He knew all too well how Sherwood worked. It took as well as gave, and sometimes took most from those to whom it gave most. He need only count the costs so far—Robin, Marian, Scarlet, his own Da, Lil, Geofrey, and Alric. The hard breath caught in Sparrow's throat. All these had been called upon to sacrifice themselves. Would he, Sparrow, now be asked to do the same?

The magic of Sherwood dealt in circles. And the next triad had already been founded. Sal carried Martin's child. And Wren asked for his. He had a sudden, vivid memory of Alric and Lil walking away hand in hand—linked—following Geofrey's death. Would not Wren go on with Martin, should some ill fate befall Sparrow? She had so surely bonded with both of them.

"What is it?" Wren's lips brushed across his. "You are very still, and you guard your thoughts from me." She shifted in his arms, naked flesh abrading naked flesh in incipient delight. Desire curled once more deep in his belly. Aye, Sherwood gave.

"I am but thinking."

"Do not waste time in thought. Love me."

"Again?" Even at the suggestion, the desire flared and stretched itself throughout his limbs.

Her long legs tightened around him and her hands slid down his body, finding and caressing every muscle, treating him as if he contained immeasurable worth. Her touch slid ever lower, followed by her mouth.

Still helpless, Sparrow groaned and leaped to life. But he needed something more from her than passion. He wanted something more.

Firmly, he pulled her up into his arms and held her tight. "Speak to me, Wren."

"This is not the time for words, Sparrow. It is a holy night."

"I need to know what is in your heart and your mind."

"Surely you can feel what I feel. I give you all of myself, everything I am."

Except the part devoted to Martin.

Sparrow swallowed hard. It should not matter. His rivalry with Martin was an old one and mostly good-natured. And the circle itself should be the most important thing.

Only—he was human and he could not deny it did matter.

He raised both hands and caught her face between them. He slid his lips over her lips and spoke into her mouth. "I love you, Wren—forever. No end."

She trembled. He felt his words course through her, and all about them the magic stirred.

"Forever," she repeated.

"And whatever is called upon me to do for your sake, I will—unstinting."

"What should you be called upon to—?" She sounded genuinely puzzled.

Sparrow gave a soft, wry laugh. "Ah, love, you do not know Sherwood and its demands as well as I. For a gift so grand as this, there must be a high price."

"You do not know that."

"No?" He drew her still nearer, greedy for ownership of her even if for only this one night. "Just know, Wren, I will not count the cost, even should it prove to be my own life."

He felt fear spike through her, closely followed by desperation. "No. Not that. There is no reason to think—" Her voice trailed away as her mind strove to plumb the depths of the unknowable. When she spoke again, her voice sounded broken.

"No, Sparrow. It is not fair. I want to live with you peacefully for all the years to come. I want to raise our child with you. Our children. I want your strength and your gentleness, your humor."

"Surely you know, after what we have experienced, I will always be here with you, in Sherwood."

"Aye, but I want you—you!" It was a cry of defiance. Her hands gripped and shook him, as if she might keep him with her by force. Sparrow knew, then, how she loved him. And that knowledge must be enough to carry him forward through whatever might come.

"If this is to be the last night ever we have together," he told her, "I would make it count."

"Aye." He felt her strive to master her fear and uncertainty; the defiance remained. "We cannot know what the future brings for good or ill. But I know what I have here, between my hands. You have already loved me well once, Sparrow Little."

"I have."

She bent to him and the desire flared once again. "But me, I am still a great believer in the power of three."

Chapter Thirty-Five

"They burnt the village of Oakham to the ground. Sir Lambert is furious, on a rampage. They say he has sworn vengeance and will not rest until he has you in his hands."

Rennie stood, drooping with weariness, and heard the words repeated yet again—the same story, more or less, recited by every soul they had encountered during their return from the depths of Sherwood. This time it came from a lad not much younger than Simon, one of many who had fled to the forest after his home was destroyed. He wore the shocked look of everyone they had met.

They had found the boy, with a number of others, when they reached the former site of the wolfshead camp. God knew this location probably was not safe, but it seemed to have become a kind of gathering place. People had nowhere else to go. And had not those from Oakham already lost everything except their lives?

She cast a glance at Sparrow, remembering his words when they lay together in the forest—there was always a price to pay. The residents of Oakham had, indeed, paid a high price for their past support of the outlaws.

"And," the lad went on with relish, "they say the Sheriff teeters on the very edge of death. King John is on his way."

Aye, Rennie thought, and when King John arrived, Lambert would want to present him with an impressive result, an answer to the current unrest, and proof that he was worthy of his place.

She sighed. She did not know when she had felt so tired; even her bones ached, and her mind moved sluggishly. Only one thing gave her hope: Martin was much improved. Since that night when the spirit of his father had come to him out of the forest, Martin's strength had steadily increased, and his vigor had begun to return. His injuries, though still horrific, no longer threatened his life.

No, two things gave her hope: Sparrow was still at her side.

She asked the lad, "Who is in charge, among the folks from Oakham?"

"Well, Adam Cooper survived, Mistress, but he is not here. There is another group of us camped farther off."

"Can you lead us to him?" Rennie could barely face the prospect of trudging on. But she had no time to rest, and a war for which to prepare.

Madlyn spoke up. "We shall stay here, with Martin." She indicated Sally, whose head drooped.

Rennie considered the women and nodded; the past days had proved easy for no one.

Madlyn lowered her voice. "What of Simon? Do you mean to punish him for his betrayal?"

Rennie looked at the lad who, utterly spent, had once more lowered himself to the ground as soon as they stopped walking. Just that morning she had caught a glimpse of his hands, a welter of sores and burst blisters from carrying Martin's litter.

"I think he may have his punishment already, do you not? Ask someone to keep an eye on him for me, please, Madlyn. And take care of Martin."

"I will."

Rennie turned to Sparrow, who stood firm as a rock beside her, silent. At the sight of him so, his dark eyes wide, emotion trembled through her heart. Indeed, he was her rock, and she could no longer imagine existing without him. She prayed to the Green Man she never must.

"I will go search out Adam," she told him. "You stay here. Rest."

He smiled ruefully. "You think I could, away from you?"

"Then I would be grateful for your company." She turned back to the boy. "Your name, lad?"

"Giles, Mistress."

"Lead us to Adam, swift as you can."

Giles chattered as they went, the words flowing from him like ale from the cask once the stopper is pulled. "There have been attacks every day by the Sheriff's men, a different place always, not just Oakham. Farms have been overridden and cottages burned. Lambert leaves always the same message—he will not rest until you and those who make up your band are given over to him."

Rennie felt Sparrow stiffen at her side. She laid a cautionary hand on his arm, which felt hard as iron.

"He seeks your betrayal," Sparrow growled, "and from folk hurting and desperate. It is not safe for you here. We should go back into the forest."

Rennie turned her eyes on him. "And do what? Allow others to die in our fight? It is our fight,

Sparrow," she added softly. "You felt the torch pass, as clearly as did I."

He closed his lips in a mutinous line, and Rennie felt emotion surge through her again—either his or hers, she could no longer tell for certain. But since that night when last they lay together, she knew how Sparrow loved her. Oh, yes, she knew, to her very soul.

Humility touched her, along with gratitude so deep it surpassed expressing. To know the love of this strong, wise, gentle man even for a short while was a gift beyond measure.

Giles spoke on, reciting a litany of Lambert's sins. Rennie wondered fleetingly if Sir Lambert hunted her so assiduously in the desire for personal revenge or, indeed, for the glory. Both, no doubt.

Adam and most of the surviving villagers from Oakham were gathered in an area just within the arms of Sherwood. A dangerous proposition—they would not be difficult to locate, for anyone who dared. Fires burned, children and women wept, and men spoke in guarded tones. The overall air was one of despair.

Adam did not look pleased to see Rennie and Sparrow, though he did grasp Sparrow's arm when the younger man offered it.

"Bad work, this," Sparrow told him, looking about.

Adam nodded. Like Madlyn, he appeared to have aged overnight, and his blue eyes looked stark with grief.

Softly Rennie said, "I am so sorry about this, Adam. How many have you lost?"

He shrugged. "Who can say? When the soldiers came through the village, folk fled and scattered. It is difficult to know where they are. Many met up again, here in the forest, but not all. We would go back to Oakham and search the ruins, but soldiers keep watch." He cast a look about and added, "Folk are fearful and grieving. We cannot even bury our dead properly." Disconcertingly, his eyes filled with tears. "I have not been able to lay my own wee grandchild to rest."

Rennie reached out to him. "It is a hard thing to bear."

"Impossible to bear. Mistress Wren, you know our people have long supported the cause, the wolfsheads, and your father before them. I was proud that his work should live on. But this…" He lifted his hands. "I do not know that we can survive."

Sparrow spoke unexpectedly. "The trouble is, Adam, if Lambert wins in this, if he succeeds in crushing Robin's cause and our spirits, it will not make an end to the heartache and sorrow. Is that not why Robin chose the fight in the first place? To put a stop to the floggings, the rackings, the severed hands, the burned homes? If Lambert defeats us now, he will be at liberty to ride over us roughshod. That will be all your children know."

"My father, and the memory of him," Rennie reminded Adam, "has been a force standing between the folk he loved and the Normans' tyranny."

"Aye." Once more Adam looked about. "But your father, lass, is a long while gone. And, pretend as we may have done this while, he will not return."

"That is where you are wrong." Sparrow leaned toward the headman. "He is here." He looped an arm about Rennie's shoulders and conviction poured from him. "Can you not see that? For all true purposes, here he stands."

Adam's gaze softened. "I can see you believe that, Master Sparrow, and I have naught but the greatest respect for you. But look at us. These folk had little in their lives, and have lost all of that."

"Save hope," Rennie appealed earnestly. "Without that, they are truly defeated."

Adam shook his head, but before he could speak, Sparrow said, "Only give me leave to go among your people and ask those willing to stand with us to step forward, a force for good."

"An army to stand against the Sheriff's soldiers, with their swords and armor? I will not stop you, but I will say any who choose to stand with you must be mad."

"Aye, well," Sparrow conceded, "a mad army is better than none."

****

"Martin asks for you, Wren. Will you come?"

Madlyn appeared at Rennie's elbow even as she stood watching Sparrow drill his new recruits. Ten men and, surprisingly, two women, both widows, had stepped up and offered to fight. Brave souls, they were nevertheless farmers, far better suited to having a hoe than a bow in their hands. And there was so little time.

It would not be enough.

Rennie pushed that conviction from her heart even as she turned to Martin's mother. "Of course I will come at once. How is he?"

"Hurting and refusing to admit it. Angry and frustrated."

Rennie smiled in spite of herself. "Martin as we know him, then?"

Martin lay half propped up on his pallet, his eyes

open and wild. Rennie, relieved to see at least some measure of his energy returned, hunkered down next to him. He reached out fevered fingers and clasped her arm.

"Wren, I need to tell you—I dreamed." As soon as he touched her, she felt his emotions clearly. They tumbled through her in a confusing rush: wariness, dismay, consternation—even a hint of fear. That last knocked Rennie back on her heels and made her blink at him. Was this the Martin she knew? Possibly not. Covered with half-closed wounds and in continual pain, he almost looked a stranger.

But his eyes held hers, single-minded and intent. "Must tell you. I dreamed I sat with my father, and yours. Talking."

Rennie nodded, trying to remain calm even as foreboding touched her. Was it so hard to believe Martin's father remained near him, after what had happened deep in Sherwood?

"He told me—he told me..." Martin's fingers contracted painfully on Rennie's flesh. "One of us may be required to make a sacrifice. One of us three."

"Death, you mean?" Rennie lowered her voice. Sally worked not far away at making bandages.

"You must help me get off this accursed pallet." Martin waved wildly at Sally and Madlyn. "These women will not let me get up."

"You are not yet ready to get up." Rennie strove to soothe him. "You have suffered much."

He gave an odd shudder, almost as if he shook himself, and Rennie blinked; when he moved she saw a faint shimmer of magic around him. "The body's hurts are nothing. I must fight. We must stand against

Lambert's men when they come. For they will come. I have seen it."

A responsive shiver passed through Rennie. Martin's eyes were those of a man who had looked beyond mortal life.

"They will come." Rennie thought of Sparrow's pitiful band. "And we will meet them."

"You will die," Martin declared flatly.

"Do not say that." Rennie felt a sudden conviction that saying it could make it so. Was that not one of the things Lil had tried to teach her about magic? That with belief the picture in the mind held true? "You must hope for victory."

"I do hope." Martin sat up straighter, despite his wounds. "But if one of us must die, it cannot be you."

"It shall be as the god chooses." Yet, Rennie thought, if she carried Sparrow's child, might she not be meant to survive?

"Listen to me, Wren." Martin's eyes burned on hers. "There in the castle forecourt, I felt what you did, how you held me. You gave me your strength, like light. It lifted me, shielded me. You saved my life then—I will not hesitate in spending it to save you, anon."

"Martin, you are not fit—"

"No," he cried loudly enough to turn Sally's head. "You must help me up. Give me your strength once more—you are the only one who can. Because if you send Sparrow to this fight without me you will lose him."

"I begged you not to say—"

"I know how you love him. I felt the strength of your love for me, there at Nottingham. You love him

255

still more."

"Martin, this is the fever talking."

"Do you deny the bond that joins us? You and me; you and him; even me and him?"

"I do not deny it."

"All of us, and Sherwood." Martin blinked at her. "Whatever Sherwood asks of me, I will give. Now, help me up."

Both Sally and Madlyn had left off pretending to busy themselves and now stood, watching. Martin clasped both Rennie's hands, hard. She felt his spirit pull at hers, even as his weakness demanded her strength. Slowly, his gaze a fixed demand, he rose from the pallet, first to his knees and then, with a mighty surge of will, still farther, until he stood swaying.

All around them, heads turned. And power sparked like the dust of the stars.

"Now," said Martin, breathing hard, "take me to Sparrow."

Chapter Thirty-Six

"You must let me help," Simon begged Wren passionately. "Give me a chance to make up for what I have done. I can prove valuable to you, Mistress, for Sir Lambert does not know I have turned."

The sense of disquiet that had haunted Sparrow for days flared once again. He spoke before Wren could. "But what of your mother, lad? Surely you are better off keeping out of it?"

Simon turned empty eyes on him. "My mother is dead—word awaited me when we returned from the forest. There is naught I can do for her now."

"I am sorry, lad," Wren said with quiet sympathy.

Simon drooped where he stood. "Everything I did was for her sake. I betrayed those who cared for me. I betrayed Robin's memory."

"We act as driven, in the cause of love." Wren cast a look at Sparrow before extending her hand to Simon. "I will be grateful for your help. Sparrow and Martin have their army, such as it is. You and I, lad, shall go to Nottingham."

"Eh?" It was the first Sparrow had heard of any such plan, and alarm raced up his spine. "Nay, Wren. We have not spoken of this—"

"Sparrow, I need to get inside. Simon is at liberty in the courtyard, the hall. I can gain access to the kitchens."

"It is sheer madness," Sparrow hissed. "All it needs is for one person to betray you—one, out of the many. Why take such a chance?"

Wren narrowed her eyes. "Word from Nottingham says the King arrives tomorrow. I must gain access to him, to seek an audience. The Sheriff is not expected to live until dawn—"

"An audience with John? Now I know you are mad!"

Wren seized both Sparrow's hands. "You know as well as I do the Sheriff's authority is all that has kept Lambert's brutality in check. An appeal must be made to the King, lest he decide to elevate Lambert in the Sheriff's stead. You know what could happen then."

Sparrow thought of the scene in the castle forecourt, Martin brought to the finest throes of agony. He thought of Oakham burned, its folk slaughtered, right down to the children. Aye, Lambert represented Norman tyranny at its worst.

Yet he shook his head. "You cannot hope to appeal to John."

"The barons did." Her golden eyes widened. "They persuaded him to sign that charter to their benefit. What of us?"

"The barons had power."

"And so have we." She linked her fingers with his and raised the joined hands between them. "Of a different kind."

"You think magic will help us?"

"I think Sherwood will, if we believe strongly enough. Believe for me, Sparrow."

Sparrow felt her will and her emotions tug at him, yet he held back. Had she asked him to risk anything else, including his own life, he would not deny her. But his heart remained unsure. They possessed only an army of twelve, a lad who may or may not betray them again, himself, Wren, and Martin, who existed only on will and should not even be on his feet. How could it be enough? He had but one secret hope in his heart.

Last night he had spoken at length with Martin, the two of them with their heads close together in the dark, while Wren slept. Martin's body might be sorely battered, but his heart remained strong as ever. It was his heart that made him believe he could still fight—that, and his conviction that one of the three of them might yet be required to pay the ultimate price.

"And if that is so, Sparrow," Martin had vowed to him out of the darkness, "it should be me. Or you. Not Wren."

Finally, something on which he and Martin agreed. And if Wren now carried Sparrow's child, did that not mean she was protected—at least until that child, member of the next triad, was born? Perhaps so—but only should he or Martin prove willing and prepared to sacrifice himself. Oh, aye, Sparrow had learned well how worked the magic of Sherwood...

"Aye," he had told Martin, there in the darkness, "you or I—not Wren." And they had clasped hands on it, almost like brothers. Just so long as Wren remained safe.

****

Time for leave taking. The last that he and Wren might ever share? Sparrow could not but wonder. He stood ready with his bow on his shoulder and his quiver across his back. He had blessed every one of his arrows as he slid them into place and, somewhat to his surprise, had both felt and seen the magic that crackled around them.

Sparrow: the arrow. It was as if he could hear his father's voice again, full of warmth, love, and laughter for the young child Sparrow had been. *Look at him. He grows straight and long as an arrow. May he always fly as true.*

Aye, he had flown true—straight for Wren's heart. From that first moment when she came bursting into Lil's kitchen with her wild eyes and wilder spirit, igniting both the night and something within him, her heart had been the one place he wanted to dwell. And now he must bid goodbye to her, possibly forever.

All around them, other leave-takings echoed theirs. Both parties—Wren with Simon and Sparrow with Martin and their small band—were to set out at the same time.

Husbands parted from wives. Madlyn wept. Not far off, Martin and Sally stood together with their hands clasped. Of what did they speak? Did Sally tell Martin all he needed to know?

"Do not look like that," Wren chided Sparrow. "I need you strong and sure."

"'Tis difficult." He had never spoken truer words. "You walk into the lion's den. I still call it madness. Will you not reconsider?"

"Sparrow, we are lost indeed if you cannot believe in me. I need your belief now more than anything."

Sparrow knew that. Yet letting her endanger herself was the hardest thing he had ever done.

"What can you say to John that will make him listen? Why should he even agree to give you audience?"

"Why, indeed? He must be made to see that if he heard the demands of the barons, he owes as much to the rest of his subjects."

"You are no baron." Sparrow reached out and touched her cheek. "You are the woman against whom Lambert has sworn vengeance, a serf, the one I love."

"I am the daughter of Robin Hood. Shall he have spent his life in vain? Shall all the others have wasted their hearts' blood? What did they buy, if not my right to hold my head high and speak to my king?"

"Do you think John cares for your pleas, against a tyranny that has brought him all he holds?"

She clasped his hand, and green light flickered between them. "Believe for me, Sparrow. Believe in me. I cannot survive if you fail in that."

"I do believe in you." As in nothing else.

"Then kiss me once, for luck." She leaned in to him and her lips reached for his, greedily. The magic leaped between them, bright and strong. "Once, twice, thrice," she breathed, following suit and blessing him with kisses. "Believe in the power of three."

****

The two groups departed in separate directions not long after. Martin walked at Sparrow's side, silent, and Sparrow concentrated on catching his last glimpse of Wren's brown head as she disappeared into the trees. He started when Martin spoke, his voice rough.

"Did you know?"

"Eh?"

"That the child Sal carries is mine."

Sparrow turned his head sharply. Martin went with his hood thrown back onto his shoulders, at least here among the trees, with every half-healed wound on

261

display. Twin furrows marked the sides of his face and traced his hands, like red worms. He looked a different man, yet his eyes were the same, fierce and iron-blue, demanding.

"She told you, then?" Sparrow asked.

Martin grimaced. "She claims she told me before, when I lay dying. I do not remember. That is not a thing a woman wishes to hear—that a man does not recall such a telling." Once more he raked Sparrow with his eyes. "You should have told me. You might have kept me from flying off after Lambert—not that the bastard did not deserve it."

"It was not my secret to tell," Sparrow said yet again. "And I would have thought any sensible man might have guessed. You bedded Sal all winter."

"Aye, but I was not sensible, was I? I was taken entirely with Wren and this thing between us." He waved a hand and corrected himself. "Among us."

"So what will you do then? About Sally, I mean."

"Do? What can I do?"

A bit uncomfortably, Sparrow said, "She loves you, man. She sickens herself with it. Surely that is worth something?"

Martin gave him an odd, measuring look. "You would have me give her my heart in return? It is not worth much, Sparrow. It is blackened and twisted, and consumed by old anger—and better than half of it belongs to Wren."

Sparrow swallowed hard and Martin laughed ruefully. "No, you do not like that answer, do you? You do not want to share her, even in my heart. But I ask you, how can I fail to love her?" He widened his eyes and leaned toward Sparrow. "Or she fail to love me?

'Tis the nature of what we are, is it not?"

Sparrow rued the bitter feelings that stirred inside him, and that Martin could doubtless feel. He did not want to go into this day with any darkness on his soul. But even now he could not help himself. He asked, "Why can you not just love Sally with whatever part is left?"

"I do. I care for her as well as I am able. But you cannot expect me to make Sally promises."

"Why not?" Sparrow demanded.

"Because"—Martin gave him a long, hard stare—"I go away to die."

Chapter Thirty-Seven

"Rennie, is it you? I scarcely believe it!"

The words cut across the bustle of the kitchen with the effectiveness of a scream and put a stop to all chatter and movement. Rennie, who had paused just inside the doorway that led from the courtyard—scene of her original encounter with Lambert—saw every head turn in her direction as silence fell.

Mistress Moll had spoken, she who had trained as first assistant under Lil and now looked to be in charge. With her elbows cocked and her round cheeks red as apples, she stood at the center of the large room, apparently directing the chaos that extended from the lads turning the spits to whoever now inhabited Rennie's old place in the scullery.

Her eyes met Rennie's and narrowed. "Why have you come back? You know Lil is gone."

"I do." Rennie's voice came hard. Being here again stirred up a lot of conflicting feelings, despair and longing. She was no longer used to the organized racket, after the whispering susurrations of Sherwood, not even used to the skirts she now wore for the first time in so many days, borrowed from poor Sal. This place had once made up the extent of her life; no more.

"You do not wish to be found here," Moll informed her a bit uneasily. "Sir Lambert has been after you these many weeks."

"I know that, also." Rennie turned her head and peered into the scullery. Two maids blinked at her from its dim doorway. One, she knew—the daughter of a kitchen worker, and fatherless. The younger girl she did not recognize.

"Your replacements," said Moll, seeing her look. Her expression softened a bit. "We needed two to do the same work you managed."

So that place was only Rennie's in memory, now. Much as she hated the dank room with its constant drudgery, much as her heart now reached for Sherwood, she trembled inwardly. Truly she could not go back again. Everything she had been was gone.

Moll stepped toward her and lowered her voice. "Why are you here? It is dangerous to us, as well as you. And we are too busy for nonsense. I prepare a feast for the King."

Aye, Rennie thought, a sore responsibility, especially with Lil gone. She nodded. "I seek only shelter for a time, a place to wait. Because that is why I have come—to see the King."

Moll stared, and what little activity had picked up in the room ceased again. "You are mad," Moll breathed. "'Twas always rumored about you; now I believe it."

"I must get near him, for I seek audience. I thought you might let me help serve."

"'Twould be worth my head. What, when Sir Lambert sees you? When he accuses us of helping you?"

"He will not. Any blame will fall on me. Moll, I would not ask were it not of vital importance."

Moll tossed her head. "If you wish to see the King,

the great doors will be open. You may peer in at him, like the rest of the peasantry."

"I must get close to him, near enough to speak."

"Why?"

Rennie lifted her chin. "I would appeal to him for justice not only for earls and barons but for all who claim this land of England."

A ripple of amazement and awe ran around the kitchen. Folk drew breath and gaped.

Moll cast a look about and then said, "Fine words, those. But all here know there is one England for the gentry and another for the likes of us. Our places in this kitchen keep the wolf from the door. Why should we risk them?"

Rennie returned swiftly, "For those who have no place, and no door from whence to shoo the wolf. For those who huddle in ditches after their huts are burned, who lose their hands after stealing a crust for their starving babes, whose daughters are taken against their will by those they must still call 'sir.' I would speak to King John for them."

Another current of emotion ran around the room, of a different nature this time.

"Let her, Moll," someone whispered.

"Let her."

"Help her."

"Stand with her."

Moll stiffened her round frame, and her cheeks took on a still-redder hue. She did not look, Rennie acknowledged, much the heroine. Yet Rennie had learned, at last, not to judge by appearances.

"You will lose your head," Moll declared. "But you can carry in the sweetmeats at the end—the King will want those. He always does."

****

The crowd bustled unbearably, a crush of peasantry seeking to catch a glimpse of their betters, including that great man who held the power of life and death over them.

Sparrow and Martin, hoods raised and jockeying for position, had become separated from the rest of their group but managed to keep together, so close their shoulders often collided. Every time they touched, Sparrow received a flash of Martin's emotions, bright, edgy, and barely contained. He knew that, beneath his leather cloak, Martin's fingers clutched his sword. The guards outside had shouted at Sparrow, telling him he must leave his bow if he wanted to go within. But then the press of people had distracted them, and Sparrow had merely allowed himself to be pushed by the tide of humanity. He stood, now, with his bow on his shoulder, but damned if he could imagine how it would do him any good.

At their backs was the forecourt where Martin had been tortured. Ahead, through double doors tall as two men together and thrown wide, they could see the great hall set for the King's reception and feast. This area between, measuring perhaps three hundred paces by three hundred, was so packed with people Sparrow could barely breathe.

Just ahead of him stood a group of squat farmers who smelt so redolent of manure it stung Sparrow's nose. Ahead of them he saw what looked like tradesmen. Beside Sparrow on the right stood a couple with a young child held high in the father's arms. The tot had dimpled cheeks, shining curls, and large, solemn brown eyes that made Sparrow wonder about his own child—his and Wren's. Did Wren carry that child even now into danger? Would Sparrow live to see it born?

By the god, why had he not stopped this madness?

Because Wren was Wren, made in her father's image. He could not change her and love her, both. He could only hope the magic that encircled her would be strong enough. For it was difficult to imagine her getting into that room up ahead and away safely again.

Much easier to believe they would all die within the next hours.

Sparrow fought to draw a breath and calm himself. Martin shot him a crosswise glance. Did Martin feel what he felt? And Wren—where was she now? Where was Simon?

"Pray," he growled at his companion, and Martin's eyes widened before he nodded.

Up ahead something was happening. Two guards stood at the entrance to the great hall, a supposed barrier against the encroaching humanity. Now they braced themselves as a clarion played and a voice rang out clear and true.

"His Majesty King John!"

The crowd around Sparrow stirred. Inside, far too distant for Sparrow's liking, a party appeared.

"Look, pet," said the man beside him, lifting the child still higher, "there—the man with the fair hair—it is the King."

John traveled with his own dignitaries yet was not difficult to recognize. No knight, this, like his brother, Lionheart. He wore his sand-colored hair loose upon his shoulders under a circlet of rich gold, and his body looked spare and thin. Truth was, Sparrow thought, had

John been plucked from his fine raiment and put into a sark and leather jerkin, with a hoe in his hands, he would be indistinguishable from those clustered here for the privilege of glimpsing him.

Beside Sparrow, Martin twitched, and Sparrow, tearing his eyes from John, saw why. Lambert had just entered the hall. Clad in finery that rivaled the King's yet still with his sword at his side, Lambert moved like the undisputed lord of the place.

Music struck up in one corner of the hall, beyond Sparrow's sight, almost drowning out Martin's muttered curses. Sparrow could feel Martin's anger burning so bright he feared everyone around them would sense it also. They must remain under cover for a time.

He nudged Martin with his elbow. "Careful."

The King, surrounded by select of his nobles, had seated himself at the center of the head table, which sat on a dais directly ahead of the double doors. Lambert hovered at the King's elbow, and a swarm of servants milled about. Without further fanfare, service began.

So, Sparrow thought bitterly, the King's humble subjects—many of them starving, yet supposed to feel themselves fortunate in gaining entry here—were now expected to stand and watch their betters stuff themselves on fatted piglet and roasted swan, were they? An echo of Martin's anger touched him, and for the first time he understood in full why Wren had come.

But where was she?

Raising his eyes, he suddenly saw Simon. The lad was employed in running after the servants with a cloth over his arm, a dogsbody, no doubt prepared to swab any vile spills. For naught could be allowed to mar the overlords' bright perfection.

"Look, pet," the man next to Sparrow spoke to his child again. "Look your fill, for this is something you may never in your lifetime see again."

Chapter Thirty-Eight

"There, take that, and go carefully."

A platter of sweetmeats was placed in Rennie's hands: stuffed and sugared figs, they were, and pastries overflowing with compote. Each made a small, perfect treasure, but Rennie's hands trembled so violently she feared she would drop the tray.

Ahead of her, two other servants went with varied platters. One held bowls of spiced wine and toast, the other stewed pears aromatic with nutmeg. The richness of the meal that had just passed before Rennie's eyes—and nose—fairly made her senses swim after weeks of Sherwood's plain fare.

Yet could anything be richer than the clear, cold air and the sunlight sifting through branches in shafts of pure gold? Was it deprivation to live on only what the forest gave?

Would she see that place, for which her heart now yearned, ever again? Aye, well, she had not come here to worry about herself.

Moll glared into her eyes. "Steady, girl. If you drop those, I shall kill you myself."

Rennie nodded and sucked in a breath. Feeling as if her feet floated some distance above the floor, she followed the server ahead of her out from the kitchen, along the lengthy flagged hallway and thence to the great hall, which roared with sound.

Servants gathered at the entryway from which every prepared dish had issued, and to the left, beyond the yawning doors, Rennie could see a press of humanity, all come to gaze upon one man. Looking to the dais, her eyes found him without difficulty; he sat at his ease, speaking to the noble who claimed the place of honor beside him, ignoring those onlookers and, indeed, his servers, as if they did not exist.

Terror flashed through her. She would have to stand and gain that man's attention, speak and persuade him that the laws he offered his nobles were deserved by all. Ah, but her knees trembled so badly she could no longer be sure she could climb the two steps to the dais, and the ability to speak seemed to have flown.

She looked up and saw Simon staring at her, hard. He stood already on the dais, a cloth over his arm, and the sight of him reassured her somehow. Were Sparrow and Martin here, also?

She looked farther and saw Lambert. Head turned away, he stood at some distance, beyond the King. Dismay seized her heart. The attempt was doomed before it began, for the moment Lambert noticed her she would be seized and would never have the chance to speak.

Even as those thoughts claimed her, she saw Simon lean forward and speak earnestly into Lambert's ear. The man looked at Simon sharply and spoke in return; Simon nodded. Lambert then spoke to King John before hurrying from the dais and from the room.

And Simon smiled at Rennie. Making up for any past betrayal, he had just given her a chance.

Her only chance.

The server ahead of her climbed the dais, and

Rennie followed. Her heart pounded in her ears so hard it was deafening, and her mouth had gone dry. Her courage, hard won, threatened to desert her.

And so, with each step, she thought of Martin, whose courage burned ever bright, and of Madlyn, whose courage was love. She thought of Sparrow, whose courage made up the bedrock beneath her feet, and of her father, Robin of Sherwood, and the fact that she, too, was of Sherwood, and Sherwood could never die.

The King's table gleamed with riches, covered in snowy linen and more food than any man could ever hope to eat. In his place of honor, John looked bored, chin resting on one bent arm, staring at nothing.

Rennie bent toward him and offered her platter. "Sire—My Lord King—I would speak."

****

Sparrow stiffened like a pony with the whip laid on when he saw Wren enter the hall and climb the dais. She looked impossibly distant from him, a sea of people and tables between. How would he ever reach her in time if she needed him?

Beside him Martin also tensed. His arm bumped Sparrow's and lent a flash of emotion: protectiveness, rage, and determination. "Where has Lambert gone," he seethed, "the bastard?"

A sudden cry went up from the dais. A number of men started up, and the unseen musicians in the corner ceased to play. Both chambers went silent.

Into the sudden hush spoke the noble beside the King, who had leaped to his feet. "You insist? Get the wench out of here and have her whipped. Where is Lambert?"

Sparrow's heart spasmed. Would it end so quickly? He supposed a whipping was the least for which Wren could hope. At least she would probably survive that, and they might hope to get her away again.

There was always a price to be paid.

He saw Wren set her platter on the King's table and bow her brown head. Her voice came, too faint to hear the words, but John made a gesture, and then another, to the offended man beside him.

In a carrying, high whine he said, "Nay, but let her speak. She is a pretty thing, and may amuse us."

"Bored," Martin muttered under his breath. "He is frigging bored and wants to relieve his tedium."

Sparrow tensed still further, though he would not have thought it possible. He watched, disbelieving, as Wren lifted her head and stood before the King, holding herself now like a queen.

When she spoke again, her voice came strong and echoed around the room. Aye, she had found her courage. The faint glimmer of hope in his heart died, however, when he heard her words.

"Great lord and king, I come to you on behalf of my father's people, who are also your own."

"Your father, child? And who might he be?"

"A high lord indeed, sire—the Lord of Sherwood. They call him Robin Hood."

There came a general outcry, and John stiffened where he sat. "What?" His whine turned into a roar. "We have been told that Robin Hood—wolfshead, outlaw—is dead."

"No, sire, he lives yet, a good steward to his people, and seeking your wise justice for them."

"If he lives, why does he not appear here before us

himself? Why send his daughter, however lovely?"

"He comes not, precisely because the name 'outlaw' has been settled upon him—unfairly, sire, since he has never done aught but be a good guardian to those who rely upon him."

"He has done naught save kill our deer and steal our gold!" John sneered. "Aye, we have heard what goes on in Sherwood. If your father be so faultless, lass, why is the price of a wolf's head settled upon him?"

"Unjustly, sire! Would you not do whatever you must for the sake of your subjects? No less he. Like a good father, he provides how he may."

The crowd around Sparrow stirred, feeling the weight of those words. He and Martin were pressed forward a few steps as the onlookers strained to hear.

"We are not here to debate morality." The whine had returned to John's voice, but he no longer looked bored. "Speak as you will, and do not waste our time."

"Aye, sire. In Sherwood, we have heard of the great charter you have ordained, that which honors you above all men and, indeed, above all kings who have ever reigned in this land."

"Have you, by God?"

"Sire, men down the ages will sing praises of your wisdom and the fairness of your heart."

"Our heart, is it?"

Beside Sparrow, Martin swore. Sparrow could feel his hate. But he began to think Wren might just get away with this madness.

"Sire, your laws will be declared peerless for their fairness and mercy. But I say they should be available to all men—the noble in his castle, aye, but also the woodsman in his hut, the shepherd in his wold, the landsman in his village. For are they not all born of this great land? And are you not King of all England?"

Mutters erupted all around Sparrow, a low-voiced current of approval. The crowd pressed forward yet again.

But John came to his feet as if drawn by reins. "Do you ask us for justice—for serfs?"

And Wren answered, her voice vibrating, "Sire, it must be available to all, or it is nothing."

"Do you dare tell us what to do?" John's question became a screech, but the damage had been done. Everyone there, from the high to the low, had heard the words spoken, and the idea Wren presented trembled in the air and glowed bright.

Beside Sparrow, the jubilant father had gone silent, his eyes wide with awe. And all around, Sparrow felt emotions surge like wonder. They had heard and seen the impossible take place. The lowest of the low, a server from the castle kitchens who also, somehow, claimed the place of a forest lord's daughter, had declared that they mattered. Robin Hood's own child gave them leave to own their worth.

The pure courage of it flared and infected everyone present. Sparrow's spine stiffened, and he wondered if this single moment might not be worth Wren's life and his own. Because this idea, now unleashed, would never fit back into the Normans' sack of repression.

"Nay, sire," Wren answered the King. "I pray only that you will extend your justice to one and all—"

"The Sheriff of Nottingham is dead!" The words burst onto the scene and cut the air between John and Wren like a sharpened sword. They turned every head toward the speaker and had the effect of silencing even the King.

Lambert, the bearer of said tidings, stood white as a ghost, his eyes fixed on his King. For an instant everything froze, and then, belatedly, Lambert bent his head.

"Forgive me interrupting, sire, but I have just come from the Sheriff's chamber, where he has breathed his last."

John parted his lips to speak. But before he could, Lambert's gaze moved to Wren and narrowed. Emotions chased one another across his face.

"You!" he shouted. "Guards, here to me. Seize that wench!"

Chapter Thirty-Nine

"Move!" barked Martin, at Sparrow's side. "Do not let them seize her."

The fear in his voice matched that in Sparrow's heart. Every protective instinct Sparrow had ever possessed rose up, howling. Should Lambert succeed in hauling Wren away to the dungeons or elsewhere, he might visit upon her any vile punishment he chose.

But an impossible barrier of humanity prevented their movement forward. The guards at the double doors had been engulfed, and strained at their places. The tableau on the dais remained mercilessly displayed.

He saw the King speak to Lambert, who now gestured wildly at Wren. He saw Lambert speak forcefully in reply, but he could no longer hear their words because the crowds in both chambers had become restive, their muttering grown into babble.

Wren stood as if pinned in place by Lambert's glare, her back straight as a spear, displaying no emotion. But Sparrow could feel her terror and dismay; even from here he could. As must Martin; somehow, despite the press of bodies around him, he drew his sword, and Sparrow felt his courage flare.

"Let me through. Out of the way!" And, like magic, the crowd in front of Martin rippled, folk pushed and crumpled, and Martin moved forward.

Just as quickly as that, he and Sparrow were

separated. A glance behind gave Sparrow no glimpse of the rest of their band. Nor could he now see anything of Simon, just Martin's hood, well up to shield his face, migrating steadily to where the guards attempted to hold the doorway.

Sparrow pushed forward, but a solid wall of backs and shoulders prevented him. The gap Martin had formed was gone. Frustration raced through Sparrow, and sweat broke out all over his body. He could not stand here and watch the woman he loved far more than his own life die.

The crowd at the doorway rippled violently, and another outcry arose. The little girl beside Sparrow, still in her father's arms, began to wail.

One of the guards went down. No one on the dais even noticed—they still argued loudly. The disturbance that was Martin moved forward. Would he be in time?

"Guards! Guards!" King John's voice rang above the general rubble of sound. Sparrow saw Wren take a step backward as if to leave the dais. No guards had responded to John's call, but the nobles around him, all armed in their own right, rose up.

He saw Wren take up the platter of sweetmeats from the table and swing it wildly at the nearest baron. Figs flew everywhere, and the platter broke across the man's nose. General chaos broke out: John shrieked, Lambert bellowed, and half a score of voices demanded Wren's seizure.

"I challenge you! I challenge you for her freedom."

Martin's demand cut across the thunderous noise like a clean wind. For an instant, everything fell silent. Each face on the dais turned, and Wren spun about.

Miraculously, Martin had won the steps to the dais.

He raised his sword, and scarlet dust seemed to spark off the length of it and dance about his form. The breath caught, hard, in Sparrow's throat.

Quite possibly, Martin Scarlet had been born for this one moment, all his anger, all his courage stored and sharpened like the blade in his hand, allowing no refusal. He climbed onto the dais, and no one prevented him. He took the place at Wren's side to face Lambert, and no one questioned his right.

This, Sparrow knew, had been Robin's dream: that all men might stand equal on blessed English ground.

From what seemed an incredible distance, he heard Martin's words. "Show me your sword, Lambert, if you be man enough."

Lambert snarled. His blade came to his hand as if by magic, and he leaped the table, overturning it as he went.

A thousand thoughts now poured through Sparrow's head. Wren should take advantage of the distraction and get away, disappear into the seething crowd below. But she stood as if rooted, far too close to the fight which, as soon as the two swords crossed, turned so vicious it once more silenced the onlookers.

All his life Sparrow had watched Martin fight, seen him work countless hours at the blade, both with and without his father's instruction. But Martin had not yet recovered from his dire injuries. Even now, as he flung the mop of fair hair out of his eyes, and his hood with it, his wounds stood out, vivid, upon him. They were wounds laid at the order of the man he now fought so desperately, and Lambert's furious expression left no doubt he recognized his opponent.

But whose hate might prove stronger? Lambert, a

knight and a noble, possessed skill honed by every advantage. No one, however, could match Martin Scarlet's capacity for sustained rage.

Through their shared connection, Sparrow could feel that rage and hate alive in the room. It danced around the two men who fought with raw and deadly intent. Martin had never fought so well, yet step by step Sparrow saw Lambert, his face an ugly mask, force him back to the edge of the dais.

The final blow came in a flurry of muscle and movement, a surge of impossible quickness that drove Lambert's blade forward into Martin's chest and out through his back.

The crowd howled and Wren screamed. The red glimmer Sparrow could see around Martin winked out, and he fell backward from the dais into the crowd, pulling from Lambert's sword as he did so and leaving it in the knight's hand, stained scarlet.

No! The word bellowed in Sparrow's mind even though he made no sound. Rival, tormentor, companion, brother—Martin had been with Sparrow from the inception of his life and his world. Whatever he was, he could not be dead, for then how could Sparrow go on?

Unbearable grief rushed through him, rending and tearing his spirit. At least half of it was for Wren because, with all his undeniable courage, Martin had not succeeded in saving her.

Instead, Lambert—now on the same side of the overturned table as Wren—reached out and seized her, drew her back hard against him and raised the gory blade to her throat.

"Silence," Lambert roared. "This woman is an

Laura Strickland

outlaw, wanted for her crimes. She dies now."

Quiet fell, enough to let Sparrow hear John's indrawn breath as he spun.

"Do you usurp our authority?"

"No, sire. But this woman committed an assault upon me. She then fled to the forest and sought to lead others in the name of the outlaw Robin Hood. She is condemned by her own presence here."

"That is for us to decide. Take her into custody— she will stand trial."

"Forgive me, sire, but I do not agree." A bright edge of madness now colored Lambert's voice. "The Sheriff is dead. He passed to me his authority—"

"All authority in this realm is ours!"

Aye, and that about said it, Sparrow thought desperately. Yet Lambert's desire for vengeance had hold of him and looked beyond reach of even the King's reason.

"Sire, you do not understand. She will employ magic. If I leave hold of her now, she will flit away. There is but one answer for it."

His sword arm jerked and the blade, smeared with Martin's blood, bit the skin at Wren's throat. She shrank against Lambert as a lover might, but her eyes ranged over the crowd, beyond desperate.

And found Sparrow.

He felt the connection flare despite her terror, her certainty she was going to die. In that instant, he felt her emotions as clearly as his own.

I love you. I will never leave you. You will hear my voice in the trees, forever in Sherwood.

Not yet, Sparrow returned. *Stand still. Do not breathe!*

He jostled his bow down from his shoulder. It came to his hands effortlessly, and with a feeling of strength. He never remembered snagging the arrow from the quiver or notching it. Silently he asked those pressed around him for room and, as they had for Martin, they moved aside just enough.

Just enough.

Though there was no time, though the scarlet blood had begun to trickle down Wren's neck, he closed his eyes.

He stood again in the greenwood with his father at his side.

"I tell you, lad, you will never make the mark if you try too hard. You need to become what you are—what I named you. The speeding arrow—Sp'arrow. Do you see?"

Sparrow saw. He had to become what he had always been: intent, born of love.

He opened his eyes and shot the arrow. A shower of blue sparks erupted, and it flew over the heads of the crowd, past the guards at the double doors, above the gathered nobles. Sparrow dared not fail: Lambert held Wren with her body covering most of his. The barest twitch would end her life.

The arrow flew true, truer than any Sparrow had ever shot. It whispered as it went, the voice of Sherwood, the glimmer of light, the flicker of leaves, and embedded itself in Lambert's right eye.

And it screamed aloud: *This for justice.*

Laura Strickland

Chapter Forty

"By God, by God, by—" Someone breathed the words: a prayer. Rennie discovered they came from her own lips. She staggered and nearly went down as Lambert fell away from her like a heavy cloak. She put a hand to her throat, and her fingers came away red.

She could no longer see Sparrow in the crowd. But Martin lay at her feet, and scores of eyes watched her, from the dais and below it.

The King spoke and she heard him not; her ears were stopped, filled with rushing music. But no—that was the sound of her own blood and her own heart, both pounding. She lived still.

The King moved toward her but remained on the far side of the overturned table. She spared one look for Lambert, sprawled on his back with one of Sherwood's finest arrows protruding from his eye socket, along with a welter of blood.

She leaped into the crowd.

Hands welcomed her—not hard, punishing hands, and not noble hands. For the barriers at the doors had broken, and the common folk—her folk—now invaded the nobles in the great hall. She recognized several faces from the kitchen, some she had known most her life: the two lads who had been in the yard the day Lambert tried to force her, the boy who turned the spit, a bevy of women who worked now under Moll, the server who had climbed ahead of her onto the dais. They reached for her because she had spoken for them and because she was one of their own.

Behind her, John still shouted conflicting directions. "Stop her. Close those doors. Kill her. Attend our Lord Lambert."

Those who had Rennie in their charge listened not. They sheltered her, and their whispers poured into her ears.

"For Robin."

"For Lil."

Rennie knew, then, it was love that defended her.

Martin's body lay at the very edge of the dais. She turned back and reached both hands, begging her rescuers, "Please do not leave him here. Bring him."

More hands bore up Martin's still form. The tide turned and the sea of faces parted before them.

Where was Sparrow? Rennie still vibrated from that moment when their eyes had met among the many, caught and held. She had felt what he felt then, had been flooded with his love for her, and fully realized hers for him. Now, impossibly, she had lost track of him.

"Come."

Lifted by the will of the many, she gained the double doors and then the room beyond. The outer gate drew near, and with it Sparrow's face. She fell into his arms, and he swung her up as if she weighed nothing. He spared one glance for Martin, who hung between a score of hands, head lolling. *Dead.*

Suddenly the rest of their band surrounded them and accepted the burden of Martin. They passed into the blessed, cool air while behind them voices cried for

Laura Strickland

pursuit. Rennie stole one look over Sparrow's shoulder; it showed her the crowd had once more closed, tangled, and filled the space behind them like a rushing wave.

They began to run, Rennie's head bumping against the bow on Sparrow's shoulder. She could feel Sparrow's emotions surging through him as if they were her own.

****

"Down! Stop and put me down. I would see if yet he lives."

"Love, he does not." The breath came harsh in Sparrow's lungs, and Rennie could feel weariness riding him hard. But they were now well away into the cover provided by the trees, as safe as they were likely to be. Sparrow panted, "Farther yet—he will be coming."

"Who will? Who, Sparrow? Lambert is killed. You felled him."

Sparrow stopped running so abruptly he stumbled. Those toting Martin paused, sagged, and lowered him gratefully.

Rennie slid down Sparrow's body, her hands lingering on him, caressing his face. She realized, belatedly, she was weeping.

"No one will find us," she babbled through the tears, "not before this is done. Martin—"

Sparrow made no reply, but his dark eyes burned on her. She dropped to her knees beside Martin and laid both hands on him. His tunic was sodden with blood, and his chest was motionless.

He looked like an angel lying there with the new green leaves arching above him, his face so fair despite its half-healed wounds, and devoid of anger. His lashes

286

formed tawny golden arcs on his cheeks; his wild hair made a halo.

"Martin." She began to massage his chest. "Martin, return to me."

"Wren," said Sparrow, his voice broken, "it is too late."

"No!"

"Lambert's blade passed right through him. We all saw."

Rennie looked up at the man she loved, who stood grave and still, and at the others who ringed them—outlaws and outcasts, true hearts. Then she turned back and tore open Martin's tunic with hands that shook. The garment fell away and revealed the wound, a grievous thing.

Ragged and gaping, it leered at her, the mark of Lambert's hatred. Rennie placed her hands, one to either side of it, on Martin's skin, as if she could expunge, mend, heal.

"Wren," Sparrow breathed again.

Above Rennie's head, a bird sang. The trees stirred, and Sherwood whispered. It sounded like Lil's voice, like Robin's voice. Under her knees, she felt life flowing, and under her hands—

"He is not gone yet. Here, Sparrow, here to me."

Sparrow stood as if frozen, his eyes wide with shock.

She reached up reddened fingers and seized his hand. "I need you. This will require both of us. Call him, Sparrow. Call him back!"

"Wren, he is dead." Sparrow had landed on his knees, across from her. Martin's body lay between them.

She stared into his eyes. "He is still here. He is here! They are all here, in Sherwood."

She pressed Sparrow's hands to Martin's naked bloodied chest. His eyes widened still farther as he felt what she felt.

"Call him," she bade. "Tell him how we need him."

Sparrow gasped and bent his head. Rennie saw the blue light begin to gather around him, pure as water or the sky at night. She felt his strength begin to flow into Martin's body.

She pressed her own hands tight, fingertips just touching Sparrow's, closing the wound, and began to spin golden light, drawing it from the air around her, from the trees, from the very soil of Sherwood and its waters. She breathed it in with the air, and sent it in a current into Martin's stilled flesh.

Fine job, that, said Lil, beside her, with a smile in her voice. Rennie had always been able to hear Lil smile.

Will Scarlet knelt at Martin's head, his eyes burning silver fire. *Son, arise. Your work is not done.*

Blue sparks erupted from Sparrow's hands, gold streamed from beneath Rennie's fingers. They sifted together, and the world turned green.

Arise! Will Scarlet shouted.

Martin jerked beneath Rennie's hands. His eyelids twitched and he drew a deep, shuddering breath.

Sparrow opened his eyes. Rennie raised her head. They, and their band, were alone, both Lil and Will Scarlet gone. The green light died away gently. Beneath her hands, Martin's heart beat strong and even.

"He lives." Sparrow breathed the words and lifted

his hands in disbelief. His eyes met Rennie's. "He lives."

Rennie began to weep again, this time with joy. "Aye, by all that is holy, he is with us still."

Chapter Forty-One

"A number of our people intend to go to ground, deeper into Sherwood," Sparrow told Rennie in an even voice which revealed none of his true emotion. He stood before her in the dawn light, seeming calm and quiet. But Rennie could feel that something within him had focused, intensified. Simply, he added, "I would make one of them. Will you come?"

Rennie raised her eyes, considering him. All around her, Sherwood hummed with energy that sounded like music. She could feel it now without effort, just as she could feel her connection to Martin and to this man before her in near-visible trails of magic.

Gently she asked, "Would you have me abandon the rest of my people?" Abandonment, as she knew, was the hardest of things.

Sparrow shook his head. "Nay. But I believe everyone will scatter for a time, until we see how matters stand in Nottingham. 'Tis a good enough season for it, with summer coming on. Before autumn, folk will move back to rebuild Oakham and take up their lives."

Rennie nodded. "Under the guidance of their staunch headman, Martin Scarlet."

"And with hope of a better life."

"And, pray," Rennie tipped her head, "who has

decided how all this will be?"

"Martin and I, together, whilst you slept."

"Together?" Rennie's eyebrows twitched. "And does Martin also mean to avail himself of the bosom of Sherwood before taking up his place in Oakham?"

Sparrow shrugged. "He needs healing. That is the place for it—I do not think any among us can deny that, now."

"No." Rennie drew a breath. "Walk with me."

She reached for his hand, and a small shower of sparks erupted between their fingers. This had happened every time she touched him, all the night. She glanced behind as they moved off into the trees: the rough camp looked deceptively peaceful and quiet with the golden light arcing overhead. She could see that most folk had bundled up their few belongings. All spoke in hushed tones.

Martin lay with two women bending over him— Madlyn, with a mother's grace, and Sally, who had not once left his side since he was carried in. Rennie narrowed her eyes. A slight haze of crimson light danced over and about Martin.

Sparrow said, "I can barely get my head around what happened yesterday. Martin, I mean. I do not think I realized, until that moment, how surely the three of us are connected."

"The three of us, and Sherwood," Rennie corrected. "You and I called him back, but 'twas Sherwood did the giving."

"Aye," Sparrow agreed gravely. "And the three of us are now its stewards and guardians, our lives long."

Above and around them, the trees stirred and spoke in their own language; Rennie cocked her head to listen.

"Yet," she said thoughtfully, "we cannot stay all together, can we?" She turned to face Sparrow. "'Tis what I need to tell you. I have made up my mind."

****

Sparrow stared deep into Wren's golden eyes, seeing there the sweet coming of the dawn, the return of radiance after a storm. In Wren's eyes lay the very light of Sherwood. He searched for an answer to the question that burned inside him. For he had been linked with her when they drew Martin back into life, and he knew what she had felt then. Aye, he knew without doubt how Wren loved Martin. And Sparrow had never succeeded in losing his fear that Wren would choose Martin after all.

Now she said she had chosen.

Sparrow trembled. He plundered her eyes and he plundered her emotions, but all that came to him was a sense of strength and resolution.

Aye, his Wren had become strong. No more the half-wild creature who had burst from Lil's scullery but still, and ever, Sherwood's daughter.

"Tell me," he bade. His fingers clenched on hers.

She drew a breath. "We do need time to regain our strength. Martin needs healing, and I agree with you, Sherwood is the place for that. But when we return, it will be to a whole new fight. The King will appoint another sheriff, and we will need to be strong and sure."

She means to choose him, Sparrow thought, pain erupting inside him. She will throw her support behind the man whose strength is his defiance. He said, woodenly, "Martin."

"Surely you see he is the best choice for leading our fight? He has earned the place. He deserves it."

Agonized, Sparrow asked, "And what do I deserve?"

She gazed away from him for an instant, into the trees, as if once more listening to Sherwood. Her eyes returned to Sparrow's, but she did not reply.

He burst, on a sudden rush of bitterness, "So, it is banishment to the hermitage for me, is it? A life alone? Solitary—"

A curious smile touched her lips. "Alone, you say? In Sherwood? How can you call it so, given all we have experienced? You know what—who—dwells within Sherwood. You know the holiness at its heart. How can you say life there would be lived alone?"

"I would be alone anywhere, without you." Sparrow no longer cared what it took to persuade her. He would bare his soul if he had to. He would make her see how he needed her, as the trees needed sunlight, as the roots needed the deep loam. Aye, perhaps Martin had been born for the place of leader of their cause. But Sparrow had been born—he lived and breathed—for the place beside this woman.

He seized both her hands, threaded his fingers through hers, assuring she felt what he felt. "What of our child," he appealed, "that you may well carry? Am I to live apart from her, or him?"

"Ah, the children of Sherwood." She looked back through the trees toward Sally, still bent over Martin. "The next generation of guardians, two already on their way and one no doubt yet to be conceived. You are right. They will need their parents."

"Aye." Sparrow's heart leaped and trembled. "Do you forget what it is like to grow without mother and father?"

Her gaze returned to his. "I forget nothing. But I say to you, Sparrow Little—you of the speeding arrows and the true heart—things in the future need not be as they have been in the past."

Sparrow shook his head. "I am not sure I understand."

"Sherwood once had a lord—Robin Hood. It now has a lady—Wren Wolfshead. Why should the triad not adjust itself accordingly?" She leaned toward him, so close her lips nearly brushed his, and her eyes glowed.

"Go to Sherwood, Sparrow. Make for yourself a place deep in solitude where the rarest and truest magic may be learned, where the trees and waters speak. And I—"

"You?"

She breathed onto his lips, and into his soul, "I will come with you."

He felt it then, the gladness rushing up through her, a mighty force of pure love that filled him where he stood and set all the trees around them to dancing.

"You will come with me?" Sparrow repeated in joy. "Live with me?"

"Why cannot the hermitage shelter two? Two, for a time." A wise smile curved her lips. "Three, before too long. Why cannot Martin return to lead the folks here?" She added decisively, "Martin and Sally. It is time he did what is right."

"And we?"

"We shall harbor, cherish, and grow a deeper magic along with this child. For we know the fight will go on. Yet it has become apparent our greatest weapon is not Martin's sword, or even your arrows, but it is the magic of this place that will save us all. When we come back to fight, it will be as the lord and lady of the forest, and none shall stand against us."

Sparrow believed her. Amazement touched him, love taller than the trees and gratitude deeper than the ancient roots. He drew her closer and gazed into her eyes, into her soul.

"You have chosen me for this?"

"I have chosen you." Each word came punctuated by a small kiss, each burning brighter than the last. "My heart chooses. Sparrow Little, will you plight yourself to me?"

He drew a breath that contained her essence and felt magic swirl around them: blue and gold twining together into eternal green.

Ah, but that pledge had been made the first time he saw her in Lil's kitchen. "My heart is already yours," he told her. "I pledge my life also—pledge it new every day, every hour, so long as any part of me remains in Sherwood."

Wren smiled. "Then come, my Sparrow, and fly with me."

A word about the author...

Born and raised in Western New York, Laura Strickland has been an avid reader and writer since childhood. Embracing her mother's heritage, she pursues a lifelong interest in Celtic lore, legend, and music, all reflected in her writing.

She has made pilgrimages to both Newfoundland and Scotland in the company of her daughter, but is usually happiest at home not far from Lake Ontario, with her husband and her "fur" child, a rescue dog. She practices gratitude every day.